HOLLYWOOD
HUSTLE

HOLLYWOOD HUSTLE

A THRILLER

JON LINDSTROM

CROOKED
LANE

NEW YORK

Published in the United States by Crooked Lane Books, an imprint of The Quick Brown Fox & Company LLC.

Crooked Lane Books and its logo are trademarks of The Quick Brown Fox & Company LLC.

Library of Congress Catalog-in-Publication data available upon request.

ISBN (hardcover): 978-1-63910-629-5
ISBN (ebook): 978-1-63910-630-1

Cover design by Gregg Kulick

Printed in the United States.

www.crookedlanebooks.com

Crooked Lane Books
34 West 27th St., 10th Floor
New York, NY 10001

First Edition: February 2024

10 9 8 7 6 5 4 3 2 1

For anyone who gives it their best shot

PART 1

"Crime is just one more way to get something done."
—Winston Greene in *Key to the Garden* (1989)

CHAPTER

1

WRIGHTWOOD, CALIFORNIA—81 MILES NORTHEAST
OF HOLLYWOOD

WINSTON'S LEFT EYE peeled open to see a six-year-old girl
who shouldn't have been there. When her tiny finger
had begun poking his face, he'd been sound asleep, dreaming of
bourbon—Maker's Mark, served neat—wondering how long it
had been since he'd had a drink. *Too long, but not long enough,* the
dream had answered.

Through his one open eye (his right being buried in the pillow), he recognized the sharp blue eyes and dirty-blond hair he
and the girl shared, owing to Win's Scottish–Scandinavian background. She was clutching a stuffed puppy with black plastic eyes
and a pink felt tongue that dangled to her shoulder.

"Amy?" His voice was a dry croak. Her name was Amelia, but
everyone called her Amy. She stared at him, her blank gaze competing with the puppy's. He raised his head, which today felt more
like the dead weight of a bowling ball between his ears. "Amy,
what are you doing here?"

Winston lived outside the village of Wrightwood, more than
a mile up in the mountains and a good half hour north of the Los
Angeles suburb where Amy lived with her parents. Win hadn't
seen any of them for close to six months, partly because his last

two gigs had been location shoots out of town, but mostly owing to a falling out with Amy's mother.

"He told me to get you," Amy replied, so matter-of-factly that Win raised his head further.

His connection with his only grandchild was deep, so despite their recent time apart, and the early morning brain fog, he could tell something was wrong. He squinted against the bright glare coming through the skylight. *What fucking time is it?* He worried for a second that he'd just cussed in front of her—if he had, he'd owe her a dollar, and she'd make sure he knew it. So, when she said nothing, he figured he'd safely kept the thought to himself.

"Who brought you here?" he asked, trying to wrap his bleary brain around the fact that his granddaughter was here. By herself.

"You're not listening," she insisted.

"I'm listening, honey. I just woke up, is all."

He reached out and poked her gently in the ribs, which usually elicited a delighted yelp, but not this time. She just stared at him.

Confused, he swung his legs over and pushed his lean six-foot frame up to a sitting position. He glanced at the digital clock he kept across the room on the antique six-drawer dresser—6:33 am. *What the hell?* He winced when he caught sight of his fifty-nine-year-old self in the beveled mirror above it: his unshaven face, lined with deep creases, and circles under his eyes darker than they should be. He wasn't pretty anymore, but it was still a good face for the movies. He scraped his hand across his graying buzz cut left over from the job he'd just wrapped, a formulaic Asia-based action flick that on this side of the Pacific would only be seen on a Torrent site.

His T-shirt and boxers had the faint aroma of fried food. The night before came back to him: an industry screening at the Directors Guild building. Situated hard on Sunset Boulevard in Hollywood, the modernist structure was shaped like a stack of film spools, a monument to the industry's dominance of film and TV directors (and their extensive, expensive support crews). All mauve and burgundy polished granite with smoothly curved, rose glass panels, it spiraled up from its foundation in concentric circles. There had been a Chinese buffet afterward in the lobby. He thought the movie, an independent drama, was pretty good. He couldn't remember what time he'd gotten home, but it had been late.

"Did Mommy bring you here?"

Amy shook her head.

"*Who* brought you over, exactly?" he asked again.

"The man out *there*," she said, pointing in the direction of his front door.

Win climbed out of bed and pulled on jeans and a T-shirt. Amy followed him as far as the front entrance but then hung back, peering through the screen door as Winston stepped outside onto his porch. Despite the early hour, the sun was intense in that southern California way, and he squinted into it. It felt like a heat lamp aimed directly at his forehead.

In his driveway was a car he didn't recognize—definitely from the '70s, maybe a Pontiac. The muscle car rode so low on its shocks, it almost looked like a lowrider, but not cherried out like one you'd see in East LA. It sported factory-stock rims and cracked tires, and there were rust spots and dings everywhere. And it was filthy, coated from bumper to bumper in dust. He normally would have credited that to his unpaved drive, but this thing looked like it hadn't been washed in a decade.

Leaning against the hood near the driver's side headlight was a young man. He had light brown skin, a wispy mustache, and a matching attempt at sideburns. Even from where he stood, Win could see the acne scars on his cheeks. He was skinny, dressed in dark brown khakis, black ankle boots, and a black T-shirt under a matching lightweight baseball jacket. His arms were folded across his chest, and he was smirking at Winston below mirrored aviator sunglasses.

Despite his passive stance, the man's demeanor felt like a challenge. Win considered walking down the five steps from his front porch to confront him but thought better of it. A couple of the boards were loose, and he didn't think gingerly navigating over them would send the right message. And if he was being completely honest, he wanted to be able to jump inside and lock the door if it came to it. Then again, Amy had gotten into the house, maybe with her mother's key. Or had he forgotten to lock it when he came in last night?

"Tienes una casa bonita, señor," the man said.

"Who are you?"

"I just complimented your home, you don't say 'thank you'?" The man had a smooth voice with a trace of a whine in the delivery. Despite his use of español, this guy was definitely American.

"I don't speak Spanish," said Winston.

"Then how do you know I was speaking Spanish, cabrón?"

Like anyone who'd spent any length of time in and around Los Angeles, Win knew what "cabrón" meant. "What do you want?"

The man shrugged. "An autograph." The sides of his lips turned slightly upward, and he seemed to chuckle. Winston's spine tingled. The man cocked his head toward Amy, her face visible as she peered through the screen. "She's a beautiful little girl. Looks like her puta mother."

Winston's stomach roiled. His daughter Clarissa—Clare—had grown up full of rage, most of it directed at him. As an adult she was impulsive, reckless. He had hoped that Amy's arrival would settle her down. But she and the man she'd married, Zeke, had even worse substance-abuse issues than Win did. Win had the remains of a career to keep him going, but Clare and Zeke never seemed to stick with anything long enough to find out if it might be more interesting than their next high. It was unfortunate that that often extended to parenthood.

Winston cocked his head in Amy's direction. "Where *is* her mother?"

"The puta?" That smirk again. "Let's just say she's . . . indisposed."

"Look, if my daughter—"

"The *puta*."

Win had to shove down a sudden desire to beat the shit out of this guy. Without alcohol dulling his senses, his temper had become something he monitored, like he would his urge to drink. He could've easily given in to the impulse, and he had the advantage of twenty pounds and more than a few inches on the guy. "Why don't you just tell me what you want," said Win. "I'll tell you if I have it, and then you can leave."

"Oh, I know you don't have it here," the man said. "It'll take some footwork. How that goes depends on you, cabrón." The sarcasm he laid on that last word was unmistakable.

There was that impulse again: to pound this skinny little prick into the dirt like a spike. But he couldn't overreact. The guy could have a gun or a knife on him, and right now, Win had to think about Amy. And Clare. "If she's done something to you, I'm sorry. Maybe there's some way I can make up for it."

"Oh, there is. We'll let you know, but for now, you just sit tight." The man uncrossed his arms to reveal he'd been holding a cell phone in his hand, an older flip kind. He touched a couple of buttons on the keypad, slid it into his jacket pocket, and crossed his arms again.

A hint of movement behind the man caught Winston's eye, a car coming down his driveway. He had let the property overgrow for years, a chaotic mix of trees filling in the gaps so the house couldn't be seen from the road: oaks, pines, sycamores, elms, spruce, and even jacaranda. The tangled landscape did a good job of hiding the house, and the relatively remote location discouraged all but the most ardent fans from dropping by uninvited; the downside was that he couldn't see who was coming until they were almost to the front door.

A sleek, black SUV with dark-tinted windows slowly crept into view and made its way up the drive. The high-efficiency engine under the hood of the massive vehicle was so quiet that without the faint sound of the gravel under its tires, it would have been nearly silent. The effect was chilling, especially since it was big enough to contain five or six more of these pricks. It pulled up directly behind the filthy muscle car and stopped, barely raising any dust.

In the bright morning light Win could make out the frame of a large man behind the wheel. Longish white hair, possibly blond. Large, but not fat. Like an athlete a few years past his prime. Win found himself wishing for a whole truckload of fans to show up right now. *Where are they when you need 'em?*

The skinny man pushed off from the lowrider and moved to the SUV. His gait was relaxed, as if there would never be any reason to rush. The driver was staring right at Win, motionless. When the skinny man reached the passenger door, he turned back to Win.

"Hey, we'll even cut you a deal. Something to honor all the joy you've brought to the world with your movies." He dropped his chin and fixed his gaze over his sunglasses. To Win his eyes appeared so dark they looked . . . soulless, like a shark's. "I don't think I need to tell you not to call the cops. Not if you ever want to see that puta madre again. Now, go see your granddaughter." His voice became an overdone, clichéd, singsong tease: "Chee's got sumteen for joo . . . cabrón."

The skinny man climbed into the SUV, and the driver reversed the rig down the drive. There was no license plate on the front bumper. It backed out as quietly as it had come and then disappeared, leaving only the sound of the soft breeze and the beat-up roadster in the driveway.

Win looked around at his overgrown property. If it had never felt claustrophobic before, it sure did now.

2

WINSTON CLOSED THE heavy front door behind him and made sure he locked it. Eighty years old, the house had a thick, wide entranceway secured by an oak door that must have been trucked in from up north, someplace where old-growth lumber was milled. It had hung there since the place was built (by hand), and was set dead center with a two-foot-by-one-foot, diamond-shaped, beveled window. Plenty large to see anyone outside waiting to get in.

"Is he gone?" Amy asked.

"Yes, honey, he's gone. It's okay now." She looked up at him, her little eyes filled with worry. Win kneeled to her height. "That man brought you here?"

She nodded.

"From where?"

Amy remained quiet.

"Amy, honey, you can tell me."

She clutched the stuffed puppy tighter and looked away from him.

"Amy?"

"From my house!" she said. "He gave me the heejees."

"Heejees" was their code for "heebie-jeebies." They'd use it if they happened across a slime trail of a big slug in the woods or a rotting animal carcass. It also meant a feeling that was just about as bad as could be, something Amy had already experienced too many times in her short life—Clare and Zeke had made life harder than it ever should have been for this little girl. And now this.

Winston set his hands gently on her shoulders and nodded in agreement. "Me too, honey. But he's gone now."

Win saw a hint of relief in her eyes. He knew she felt safe with him, more than with anyone. Perhaps because she'd never once seen him drunk or high, the way her parents usually were. Clare had grown up around him when he was at his most alcoholic, something he regretted deeply, and now she seemed determined to follow in his footsteps. Win didn't want the pattern to be repeated with Amy.

"Did he hurt you?"

She shook her head, then looked at her feet. "He made me lie down in the car. On the floor. It smelled bad."

Anger rose in Win's chest, but he was careful not to show it. Thus far, this kid had not gotten a fair shake in life, and he felt responsible for that. After all, it had been his demons that had caused him to lose the plot when it came to raising her mother. But what was done was done as far as Clare went. He would do everything he could to get her back from God knows what she'd gotten herself into this time, but Amy was his focus right now.

He envisioned wrapping his hands around that skinny prick's neck, watching his stunned, agonized face turn crimson as his eyes swelled beyond the sockets and burst in bloody twin explosions like special effects squibs. Just like in the movies.

Win knocked out that grim fantasy with a shake of his head. "Did he tell you to give me something?"

Amy nodded and dug deep into her jeans pocket. She held up a small lime-green rectangle of plastic that he first took for a miniature cigarette lighter. It was a thumb drive.

Win snatched the Trimline phone from its wall mount in the narrow kitchen and dialed his daughter's cell number with his thumb. Since he paid her wireless bill (and a few others), it was the only number of hers he could count on to be connected.

As the phone rang, he retrieved two boxes of cereal from a cabinet with his free hand. Amy liked the way he would mix a couple of different kinds together, a trick he'd learned by accident when he didn't have enough of one to fill a bowl. Today would be Grape Nuts over a bed of Raisin Bran. He fetched oat milk from the refrigerator just as the call went to Clare's voicemail.

"It's me," he said as he turned his back to Amy and lowered his voice. "Amy's here. She's all right, but I'd like to know what's going on. Like who that guy is, the skinny one with the mustache. I know we haven't talked for a while, but call me as soon as you get this." As he hung up, he realized he may have sounded more "fatherly" than Clare would appreciate.

Their last meeting had been a regrettable encounter at the upscale restaurant his younger brother managed. Clare had lost her temper at Win's suggestion that she and Amy move in with him, but without her husband. She'd stormed out in the middle of the lunch rush, bumping into tables and customers as she went. Winston could only cringe as he watched her inelegant exit in the wall mirror, with her shouting profanities all the way out the door. He was sure her outburst had more to do with her own guilt over her shortcomings raising Amy—and decided that when Shakespeare wrote, *"The lady doth protest too much, methinks,"* he must've been dealing with an addict. They hadn't spoken since.

He dressed the cereal with blueberries and sliced banana and poured in the milk, then picked up the bowl and a spoon. "Let's go upstairs."

Win led Amy up to his office, where he kept a folded futon for her overnight visits. He pointed for her to sit, handed her the cereal and spoon, and took a seat at his desk. He opened the center drawer, retrieved a set of tangled earbuds, and leaned back in his big wooden desk chair—a leather-padded gem from the 1930s that he'd found along with a matching pedestal-style oak desk at a local garage sale and then refinished himself.

As he unraveled the buds' cord, he swiveled the chair to look out the window. He had put the office upstairs on the northwest corner, an ample room with windows on two sides. Built-in bookshelves he'd installed himself covered one entire wall, lined with hundreds of titles. This room was a place he could be alone with his thoughts, read scripts, plot his next move, and embrace his remorse. It had been in this very chair that he'd realized if C-grade genre flicks were what life had in store for him, then he'd rather do them sober.

He plugged the earbuds into the black computer tower, which shared the space with a monitor and keyboard on the expansive leather writing surface. He'd gotten the pro model Mac a few years earlier so he could keep up with the latest film editing software that seemed to drop into the market every ten minutes. Win didn't direct often, but when he did, he loved the process of stitching his first cut into a cohesive whole, right here in this room. It was a thousand times better than getting stuck in an editing bay with some guy who'd felt the business had passed him over and wasn't shy about expressing the idea that *he* should've directed this piece of shit, having just seen proof that Winston Greene, that over-the-hill excuse of a washed-up movie star, couldn't direct traffic through a crosswalk. This business could make some people bitter.

He typed in his password (Amy's birthday with an exclamation point, October13!) and twisted the earbuds into place. As he did, he glanced at his granddaughter, who was munching her cereal slowly, clearly distracted. He rotated the monitor so she couldn't see the screen, but kept an eye on her in case she stood up and tried to see something she shouldn't.

Win inserted the thumb drive into a USB slot on the tower. A small folder icon appeared on the screen. It could be porn—Clare might have finally found a "career" but then gotten cold feet, and now they could be trying to blackmail him. Then again, how many famous fathers did he know of whose daughters had posted their homemade sex tapes online? He could name two without even thinking about it. Then Win considered the horrific possibility of his daughter being tortured on camera. Or maybe it would just be audio, someone giving him instructions with one of those voice-altering filters. Or it could be a virus, something to hack his information and empty his life savings. *All right, just rip the bandage off.*

With another quick glance at Amy, Win double-clicked the folder. A window opened, inside of which was an .mpeg file. It *was* a video. He took a breath and opened it.

The video rectangle filled the screen. He hit "Play" and the rectangle went black. It rolled on in inky silence for a few beats before music kicked in, a saxophone playing a rising arpeggio, joined by a small band playing an upbeat, bouncy tune. He recognized it from somewhere, from way back in his youth. *What is that?* Then a memory came into focus: childhood, possibly early teens. The family room of his parents' modest house, a Saturday evening, the magic hour when the rosy light of dusk streamed in through the westerly window, his father in his easy chair laughing at the TV, a cold beer in his hand. *That's it!* The opening theme of *The Benny Hill Show*, an import from England starring a pudgy, impish, round-faced comedian who wrote and performed weekly sketches of sexist double entendres and innuendo. His father had looked forward to it every weekend.

Then a pale blue title card with blood red letters blasted onto the screen:

HI WINSTON HOPE YOU'RE HAVING A NICE DAY!

Black again for a few beats, then another card:

SOMEONE WANTS TO SAY HI.

Black.

THAT IS, IF YOU CAN MAKE ROOM IN YOUR BUSY SCHEDULE!

Black.

Then a still image, sharp, the colors rich. It was Clare, her blue eyes clearly terrified over the stranger's hand covering her mouth. She was looking straight into the camera, and Win felt a father's kneejerk protectiveness for his child—a torment that becomes magnified in moments like these, when he's unable to do a damn thing about it. He glanced over at Amy. She was still on the futon, now playing with a small tablet, one he got for her to keep here at the house, the empty cereal bowl abandoned next to her.

Black.

SHE SAYS HI!

Black.

WHAT'S THAT? CAN'T HEAR?

Black.

The music abruptly stopped. Then a video started, taken by a static camera, perhaps mounted on a tripod. It looked like a basement. No, a cellar. The wall facing the camera was dirt, and the only light was harsh, artificial, coming from somewhere above camera, perhaps from a bulb in the ceiling. There was no fade-up to a picture or a swell of music to intro this section. Just the sound of scuffling feet and whispering voices that sounded male. He couldn't make out what they were saying except for when an insistent muffled voice said, "Go!"

Win straightened up when Clarissa stepped apprehensively into the frame. At twenty-six, she often seemed weary beyond her years, but whatever had transpired during these last few months had added a new layer of fatigue. She wore a dark green hooded sweatshirt, the zipper all the way open, over a white V-neck T-shirt and blue jeans. The right sleeve of the hoodie was pushed up to her elbow, the left hung at her wrist. She stopped about six or seven feet in front of the camera, and when she turned, he could make out a set of small bruises on her right forearm. Her hair, long loose curls like her mother's, hung to her shoulders, the way she normally wore it, but a thick strand dangled in front, blocking one eye. She looked back behind the camera, to where she'd entered from.

"C'mon!" a disembodied voice hissed impatiently. It sounded like someone was speaking through cloth. Clare looked straight into the lens.

"Dad? It's me," she said, then drew in a breath. "I guess I really screwed up this time."

Her voice was trembling, and Win could see fear every time her eyes darted over to whoever was behind the camera. Her voice started to crack. "They said they were taking Amy to you. You should have her by now. Please take care of her—"

The muffled voice cut in again. "Tell him!"

Clare jerked when the man spoke, and she turned toward the voice, her blue eyes wide. She looked back to the camera.

"They want money. They said if they don't get it they'll kill me . . . and Zeke . . . and then they'll come for you and . . . and Amy!" She seemed to force that last bit out, as if the threat of her baby girl being murdered hadn't seemed real until she heard herself say it.

She shook her head to pull herself together and took a breath. "They'll tell you what to do soon."

BOOM! Win jumped at the sound of the gunshot coming through the earbuds and knocked over his wooden pen holder, scattering writing utensils and paper clips across his desktop. The sudden movement startled Amy, and she looked up at him.

"It's okay," he said, forcing a smile.

He'd seen the bullet plow into the dry earthen wall behind Clare, missing her head by inches and spraying chunks of dirt behind her. Clare, visibly shaking, clenched her fists tightly under her chin. Her eyes were closed, and her mouth was frozen in a pursed grimace, as if she expected someone to hit her.

The screen went black again for a few more seconds, and the video ended. Win had to control his breathing, which verged on hyperventilating. He removed the earbuds and unplugged the thumb drive, slipping it into the center drawer of the desk, under a notepad. Amy was again fully engrossed by something on her tablet.

Win cleared his throat. "Whatcha got over there?" he asked, making an effort to keep his voice even. Amy had long ago learned to read the moods of the adults in her life.

"Angry Birds," she replied, her face angled into the screen. He was grateful she had something to keep her occupied while he calmed himself down. His heart pounded inside his ribcage, and the veins in his neck pulsed.

"C'mon, you can play your game downstairs."

Win moved Amy into the den he'd converted into a movie-viewing room. It was the only place he displayed visual reminders of his career, having hung a handful of memorabilia from his films among many more vintage posters from his all-time favorites: *Breathless, The Wild Bunch, Le Cercle Rouge, Yojimbo, A Clockwork Orange, Bullitt.* One wall was dominated by the oversized flatscreen he'd splurged on. He picked up the remote, but she took it from him, punched and swiped the center button a few times until she landed on a streaming app, punched and swiped again, and the room filled with the sounds of animated mayhem.

Winston went to the living room window and stared out at the filthy car in his driveway. Should he call the police, even though he'd been warned not to? In the movies, it rarely worked out well. But would it be the right thing to do? Maybe not—it wasn't like he was on the A-list anymore, but he was famous enough that someone at the police station could leak it to the press. And that would just make things *more* dangerous for Clare.

He needed help.

As a young man, Winston had modeled himself after his screen hero, Steve McQueen. His first (and forever) manager had even pitched him as "the new McQueen." Like his idol, Win had piercing blue eyes that popped off the screen, had developed an economy of graceful movements, and could hold a gun like he knew what he was doing. But Winston also had the quality you can't teach but every actor blessed with a Hollywood career has: you could see him *think* on camera. He'd been playing variations on the same role ever since: strong, silent types with a hint of menace, always threatening to snap but never quite giving in to the impulse. One director described Winston as "a land mine that's been stepped on, just waiting for you to step off."

Nearly twenty years earlier, one of those roles was in a movie set in New Orleans, about a modern hardboiled detective who gets framed for murder and must prove his innocence. Win's detective winds up killing all the conspirators except for the beautiful woman who betrays the villains she was once in league with, because of the hero's bravery, natural charisma, and rugged good looks. He'd played it as a rumpled, Big Easy Philip Marlowe, but taller than Bogart.

A decorated local cop named Theodore (Teddy) Beauregard had been assigned by the NOPD as official consultant to the production. He and Win became tight right away and had been friends ever since. Whenever Win needed insight into how the police thought or how to handle various firearms for a role, Teddy was the first person he'd turn to.

Win pulled his cell out and dialed Teddy's number.

AN HOUR LATER, Win eyed Teddy, who lay on his back on the floor of the mystery car in his sport jacket, peering under the dashboard, his broad shoulders filling the driver's side footwell.

"Well, it wasn't hot-wired," he said in his New Orleans drawl. He grunted as he pulled up his sturdy forty-seven-year-old frame with help from the steering wheel. "Key's not here. Don't know why they would bother to take that. I'll run the VIN, see if this car has any stories to tell."

"You can do that?" Win asked, his hands shoved into his jeans pockets.

"I still have *some* friends in law enforcement, Winston."

The late morning sun highlighted Teddy's features. His stocky physique and dark eyes and hair had been inherited from his Choctaw father, but his lithe fluidity came from his French-Cajun mother's side of the family. He was a calm, formidable man who could move quickly, if needed.

During his time on the movie set, Teddy had become smitten with the idea of getting closer to Hollywood. Shortly after that, he landed a job with the LAPD and made the move west. He'd done well in Los Angeles, solved a few cases right from the start and gained a reputation for being good on the stand—with that drawl and deep-fried-catfish sense of humor, juries ate him up. He became popular among the other officers, and the DA's office loved him.

Unfortunately, Teddy also brought with him a bit too much of the darker side of the Crescent City. In New Orleans he'd gotten used to augmenting his investigative techniques just enough to make cases stick. The LAPD was hardly innocent of that kind of thing, but ever since the O. J. case they'd worked much harder to make sure no one got caught. Teddy got caught. An otherwise forgettable case went embarrassingly public thanks to an inexplicable transgression on his part. So, instead of starting a new chapter in the City of Angels, Teddy wound up having to hang up his badge and put his well-honed investigative skills to use working for himself as a PI.

Teddy stooped over the windshield to read the VIN stamped into the dashboard. He produced a small notepad from inside his jacket and a golf pencil from his shirt pocket, where he also kept his business card case. That was originally an antique brass cigarette case that he'd found at a vintage shop in the French Quarter and repurposed not long before he left New Orleans for LA. It fit perfectly into his dress shirt pockets, and even though solid brass was a bit hefty, he got used to the weight. The elaborate fleur-de-lis engraving was always a good conversation starter.

A notepad and pencil, just like he'd used all those years ago when he and Win first met. *"If you write it down, it commits better to memory,"* he'd said at the time. He made a note and wrote down the VIN. Then he pulled out his cell phone, tapped it a couple times, and stepped away for privacy.

Win looked down at the dirt, feeling helpless. He shifted back and forth on his feet, then checked to see if Amy had come to the window to watch him, but no. She must be on a new cartoon.

"Well, this is interesting," Teddy drawled as he came back. "Let's go to your office. I need a computer."

4

SOMEWHERE IN LA

For once, Clare was really thinking about things. There wasn't much to do here, wherever this was, *but* think. Mostly she thought about waste: wasted actions, wasted words. And above all, wasted time.

She lay on the wool blanket thrown over the thin mattress on the floor of the basement, which must have been converted to a bomb shelter during the nuclear hysteria of the 1950s. Her father had once told her that the government had feared that LA was a prime target for a nuclear attack, along with Seattle and San Francisco. A thick round glass pane secured over a single bulb recessed into the ceiling magnified the light, emitting a harsh glare. The switch was up the stairs beyond the locked door, so she had no way to turn it off. Aside from the mattress, there was no furniture in the room, not even a chair. Three of the walls were lined with the gray cinder blocks, the kind mistakenly believed to keep out the radioactive waves of an atomic blast. The fourth wall, across from the door, the one they had recorded her in front of, was naked dirt. It filled the air with the dank scent of damp earth.

But none of that mattered now. Her jumbled mind kept coming back to all the wasted time she'd spent hating her father and missing her mother, and being angry at Zeke, and wondering why she'd had Amy. All the endless days and nights she'd spent getting high instead of enjoying time with her daughter. And with her father, after her mother died. She thought about all the time she and Zeke had wasted in each other's company. Was it even love? Or just a sick kind of codependence? *I should have kicked him out years ago and gotten a damn job.* But she hadn't. She hadn't done any of those things. All that time . . . wasted.

And now she was on this mattress on the floor. Alone. With her thoughts.

5

TEDDY TAPPED THE keyboard while Win perched on the futon where he had served Amy her cereal, elbows on his knees. His fingers tingled and the back of his neck was sticky with sweat. Finally, Teddy broke the silence.

"This car's been missin' for over a year," he said. "Reported stolen. Tied to a kidnapping. Belonged to the victim."

"Victim?" said Win, crossing the room to look over Teddy's shoulder.

"Kidnap," Teddy said. The search engine had aggregated a list of related news stories from the *Los Angeles Times, Los Angeles Daily News, Pasadena Star, Inyo Register.* "The vic was a car nut. Name of Alberto Velez. Lived with his family down in Santa Fe Springs. Floor manager of a factory over in Bell. Now here's the kicker: Alberto was a distant cousin to one of the scumbags involved in that big scandal down there."

The city of Bell had been at the center of one of the most flagrant political graft cases in recent memory. A small group of elected officials and their families had, between voter fraud to ensure reelection, looting the city's coffers via overinflated salaries, steering city services contracts to their own companies, and encouraging good old-fashioned bribes from industries that wanted environmental exemptions, diverted tens of millions of ill-gotten dollars to themselves, most of which had never been recovered.

"Alberto's hobby was buying and restoring old cars, then sellin' 'em off. Some of the *really* valuable ones, he kept. The police discovered he'd been grabbed shortly after taking possession of the car sittin' in your driveway. Family paid what they could, sold his car collection at a loss to do it, but never got him back. His decomposed body was found up near Independence about six months ago."

Win looked at him. "You mean, murdered?"

"Yeah, bullet in the head. What we in the profession call 'execution style.' They must've taken him with the car, which hasn't been seen since then. Till now, of course."

Winston stood up straight, rubbing his scalp through his short hair as Teddy continued.

"The smart money would say the kidnappers believed Alberto was collectin' from the same grifters who were funnelin' cash to some of their other relatives. But accordin' to these"—Teddy pointed again at the articles on the monitor—"Alberto didn't have any part of it. Just wanted to work his job, feed his family, pay his taxes, and fix his cars. In the end, the kidnappers didn't get the ransom they wanted so they . . . cut their losses."

"So," Win said, scanning the screen, "these guys thought Velez had a shitload of cash that he didn't have."

"Looks like. Kidnappers always target someone they figure has money, so no surprise there." Teddy rubbed his chin. "I'd say that wreck in your driveway is a message."

"You mean, if they don't get what they want, Clare ends up like this guy from Bell?"

"Santa Fe Springs," Teddy corrected. "He just worked in Bell."

Win looked down and interlaced his fingers. He rubbed his thumb into the opposing palm, something he would sometimes do to alleviate stress. "Should I call the police?"

Teddy took in a long breath and let it out. "This is a crew, Win. They've done it before. Maybe that's all they do, and they're usin' this car to let you know how far they'll take it. On a regular ol' sunny day, I'd recommend callin' in the cavalry, but this time . . . I don't know." Faint sounds from the TV wafted through the floorboards. "What puzzles me is why they didn't just take *her,*" he said, cocking his head downstairs toward Amy. "They name a number? A specific amount?"

Win shook his head. "No, nothing. Just said they'd be in touch."

Teddy thought for a beat. "I think we need to have a talk with your favorite son-in-law."

CHAPTER

6

OSVALDO LÓPEZ-FAMOSA Y Fernández-García, known to his friends and colleagues as Ozzie, looked out the window as the SUV wheeled past Palmdale. He watched the unfurling of Pearblossom Highway, nicknamed "Blood Alley" because it averaged ten fatal crashes per year. The landscape passed like one of those phony-looking repeating backgrounds they used to use in the movies. Roadside motels past their prime, dusty country marts, and mobile home parks flashed by in a repeating pattern. The two-lane ribbon separated the northern edge of the Angeles National Forest from a sprawling expanse of monochromatic brown that bled into the Mojave Desert. It was the opposite of picture-postcard.

The ride in the big SUV was real comfortable, though. Smooth and, except for the quiet whoosh of its wheels on the smooth asphalt below, silent. Ozzie didn't know the make or model, and he didn't give a shit. After remounting the license plates when he'd driven away from the actor's home, the driver, Jordy, had tuned in his favorite oldies station. His long blond hair swept across his face whenever he reached over to crank the volume up (something he did *every time* a Beach Boys tune came on, which was often), blocking his view of the road. Ozzie worried the guy would kill them both, so he finally told him to turn it off.

Ozzie needed the quiet anyway, so he could think. There was something wrong: *Why would somebody who's supposed to be loaded live all way out here? Its biggest claim to fame has to be the world's puniest ski resort. Why not Beverly Hills? Or Malibu? And that house was nice and all, but nothing special.* The more he thought about it, the angrier he got.

Ozzie was descended from two formerly illustrious and powerful families in Cuba, both of whom Castro had dethroned after the revolution. His father, Ramón, had been only a teenager when he was jailed for decades before finally being released and escaping to the US, settling in Miami. Ramón soon met a local girl at his job selling cafecitos in South Beach, with whom he quickly welcomed a son. He insisted they name him Osvaldo, meaning "God's power." As Osvaldo grew, Ramón would regale him with stories of his rarefied lineage.

Money was always tight, so Ramón began moonlighting for the smugglers operating in south Florida by retrieving bales of cocaine they dropped into the Gulf. One day in sixth grade, the Miami sky dark from a warm spring rain, Osvaldo found the front door of the house kicked in and his parents riddled with bullets. A fútbol match was playing on the TV, the light flickering across their bodies, and the odor of cordite hung in the air. The Miami PD determined that Ramón's bosses believed he'd been stealing from them. Osvaldo would often be haunted by this over the coming years—he had stopped for a soda on the way home, missing the asesinos by minutes.

Osvaldo had gone to live with his aunt and her husband in Tucson and was put to work as his uncle's new assistant landscaper. He detested the long hours in the desert sun, carving the dirt with a pickax while his uncle sat in his pickup, sipping cheap beer. With no desire to remain in Arizona for a day longer than necessary, Ozzie, as he came to be known there, dropped out of high school and left for Los Angeles.

He found some day labor work in Sylmar and began to hover on the perimeter of local gangs, where he could make some extra cash, usually selling dime bags for them. When he was twenty-three, he started boosting cars and selling the parts at chop shops around the Valley, eventually getting popped for grand theft. He did fifteen months in Soledad. That toughened him up—doing a stretch in a prison operating at one hundred and forty-five percent capacity is bound to harden a guy.

A month out from Ozzie's release, a gang member from neighboring Panorama City, who was in the first year of a twenty-five-to-life bid, approached Ozzie with a proposition: if Ozzie murdered the guy's wife when he got out the next month, he could become one of the gang's well-paid operators on the street. The wife wasn't about to testify or anything—he was just convinced she was cheating on him and felt that she should be able to wait. Maybe not twenty-five years, but at least a while.

Ozzie agreed. When he got out, he tracked the wife down, walked right up and knocked on her door. But then Mrs. Gangbanger surprised Ozzie with a proposal: "Which would you rather do, kill me or fuck me?" The lady had obviously expected this. She knew exactly who she was married to, after all. And who was Ozzie to argue? A couple months later, the news got back to the husband, who was now looking for someone who would take out the wife *and* Ozzie.

So, Ozzie *really* needed this movie star score to pan out—he could hit the road, go back to Miami. Start fresh. He figured he'd change his name, wait for the gang to forget about him. But this job was starting to feel like that other one, the guy with the old cars. When that job went south, Ozzie had demanded that Rocket (always the wannabe jefe in charge) pull the trigger. It had been his plan, after all. And he did. *Pow!* One shot in the back of the head. Ozzie thought he saw Rocket crack a little smile after, as if he liked the power the gun gave him. Made him wonder if this was his first kill.

It's not like Ozzie had a problem with murder. Plenty of stiffs out there had it coming. But it had to be *justified*—you had to *earn* getting your head blown off. This guy had earned it, for sure, us coming up short like this. And with all that egg dripping off Rocket's face, he *should* be the one to do it. Ozzie thought Rocket did good. Didn't plan so hot, but he did the killing right.

But now, Ozzie could feel in his gut there was something wrong with *this* picture, too, but he couldn't put his finger on what it was. Everybody knew actors were a bunch of lazy, underworked, overpaid pendejos, and this Winston Greene was famous all right, and had a nice, big house (even if it was in a crappy town). You couldn't turn on the TV without seeing him in some old movie from the 1980s or a new one on cable or Amazon. Even if the films looked kind of cheap, this Winston guy seemed to have two or three of them coming out every year, and that had to count for something.

So, what the hell was it?

7

SYLMAR, 18 MILES NORTHWEST OF HOLLYWOOD

WIN WISHED HE didn't have to drag Amy along, but at this moment he didn't dare leave her with anyone. He invited Teddy to ride with them, but he declined; he was so far from home it made sense to take his own car. So Win strapped Amy into the backseat booster he kept in his Bronco, and with Teddy's sedan close behind, they made the half-hour drive to the San Fernando Valley.

He tuned the car radio to a station playing soft rock, thinking it might help to soothe Amy. To him, it sounded so saccharine he thought it might give them both diabetes. He knew his friends thought of him as a purist when it came to music; give him some kids with guitars and drums and a mission to change the world any day. Or post-bop jazz: Thelonious, Miles. Or straight classical, even, played by an orchestra that knew what it was doing. Truth was, Win loved all kinds of music, as long as it was done well. But *this* shit . . .?

"Honey? Do you mind if we turn off the music for a bit?"

"No. This stuff sucks," Amy stated simply as she looked out her window, clutching her stuffed dog, its tongue flopped onto her shoulder.

Win stifled a chuckle. She was smart and he loved her for that. But she seemed a bit older today, like she'd been forced to grow up this morning faster than she should (as if that wasn't already the case), and it broke his heart a little.

Win felt sympathy for his daughter, and more than a little responsibility for how things had turned out for her—she had made her choices in life, but he knew he was the source of a lot of her troubles. But he had a hard time feeling anything positive toward his son-in-law. Not just because the guy wasn't good enough for his daughter, but because if there was any truth to the idea that daughters marry their fathers, Clare had managed to land the absolute worst version of Win.

Like most with the affliction, Win's alcoholism had taken hold of him young. When he'd hit his preteens, his heavy-drinking father had encouraged Win and his younger brother, Wally, to be more like him. "A real man can hold his liquor," he'd told them. Wally never took to it, but Win seemed born to the booze. He rarely slurred his speech or swayed when he walked, even when he was pretty damn wasted. He maintained more or less complete control over his body. And as long as he showed up and worked his groove, he could party all he wanted, right?

Even at the nadir of his addiction, Win always managed to make his call time. He didn't always deliver his best work, but he never caused a production to go into overtime, always made sure his directors made their day. It was said Montgomery Clift could be brilliant even under the influence of a rainbow of different pills. The acting coach who'd told Win this story had said, "Like a rock star, you get so good at your instrument you can play it no matter the condition you're in." As a committed alcoholic, Win had taken that as a license.

When he started making some money and gaining some notoriety, his addiction deepened, competing for his attention with his family and career.

Winston had met Joanie one random weeknight in an acting class. As Win and the other students were watching a pair of actors workshop a scene, he had felt eyes on him. He looked across the darkened rehearsal space, and there was Joan, staring at him. He liked to say that her dark brown eyes had somehow glowed in the low light, like a beacon. When class broke up for the night and the students reconvened at the dive bar down the block for their weekly showbiz bitch fest, Win and Joan drifted toward each other. The bar closed and they all decamped to a classmate's apartment. And when the sun rose the next morning, with everyone else passed out, Win and Joanie were still talking. And they never stopped, not once in their twenty-two years together.

Their marriage was mostly a blissful one, thanks in part to the fact that Joanie had made many sacrifices for the sake of their partnership. She had done the bulk of the work raising their daughter, walking away from her own promising career to do it, and then stuck by him through the darkest periods of his battles with alcohol.

No doubt it was fame that had pushed him into the depths of his addiction. Joanie had said the pressure would ease once Win adjusted to life in the spotlight, but he never did get used to it, not really. In fact, he came to resent it. Resented that he could no longer do the simple things that had once brought him pleasure—shopping at the supermarket, pumping his own gas, taking in a game at Dodger Stadium—without a crowd of people asking for his autograph or for a selfie with him. Inebriation became the perfect veil to disappear behind, enabled him to feel less judged. Less like a specimen in a fishbowl. But the loss of his anonymity wasn't the source of his resentment. It was because fame had also stolen his most beloved involvement with his art: the ability to observe, and then mimic, his fellow man.

After more than two decades together filled with their never-ending conversation, Joanie knew him well enough to know he was doing his best to cope, even if he wasn't doing a very good job of it. He loved her even more for that, just as he was grateful to her for making sure he got to the set on time, always knew his lines, went to the gym—in other words, that he behaved like a professional. Without Joanie, everything would have fallen apart.

And when she died, everything did.

Then Win's drinking really went out of control. He started keeping a box of black leaf bags at his bedside so he could drop them into his bedroom wastebasket and tie off the stink of his vomit before going back to sleep. Teenaged Clare would wait until he'd passed out again, then come in and drag the barf-laden bag to the trash cans outside—but not before cracking the window. Because no matter what Win had believed, his method of deodorizing his puke had done almost nothing to cut the stench.

Win had hoped that by getting sober and reclaiming his paren-
tal duties—as he'd done, eventually, in his forties—that Clare
would be inspired to choose a new path in life, too. But by then
she'd become an adult herself and carried on the family tradition,
slowly dissolving her personality in a stew of alcohol and drugs,
just like he had. He'd at least hoped she'd find a partner who
reflected the better parts of Win's nature, the caring, responsible
parts. Instead she'd settled on Zeke. It was as if Clare had chosen
the man as a form of revenge on her father. Yes, Win would do
everything he could to save Clarissa—he loved her and he owed it
to her. But if he was honest with himself, his hopes for the future
hung on Amy.

Sandwiched between the junction of the I-5 and 210 freeways
on the north, and the equally unremarkable community of San
Fernando to the south, lay Sylmar. In the flats below the more
upscale developments in the nearby San Gabriel foothills, it was in
municipal patches like this where working people built their lives.
These spreads of flatland were ribboned by four-lane boulevards,
lined with one- and two-story buildings, dissected with two-lane
streets leading to residential plots filled with single-family homes,
orbiting a cluster of glittery office buildings marking the financial "civic center," where the banks and insurance companies sold
peace of mind and the promise of a brighter future.

Win had taken the fastest route, west across the Pearblossom and the 14, onto the I-5 south, and only a short strip east on
the 210. Shaped like an irregular oval, the unremarkable munici-
pality of Sylmar was a "bedroom community," one of countless
neighborhoods that exploded the city outward as every desirable
destination at its center, where the rooftop, pool-party celebrity
selfies were taken, became too expensive for regular folk. Places
like Hollywood, Beverly Hills, Silver Lake, Santa Monica, Venice
Beach, and more recently Downtown, were mostly out of reach
to the lower and middle classes. Los Angeles, for all the urban
legends that made it loom large in the popular imagination and
its considerable cultural and creative sophistication, was still a vast
collection of small towns that spilled into each other at carelessly
drawn borders.

Clare and Zeke Montgomery's house was a two-bedroom
bungalow in a cul-de-sac that had been rented with Win's help.

The powder blue exterior was now sun-bleached nearly white, and the flat roof was covered with a hodgepodge of insulated pipes, the result of the landlord's attempt to upgrade to air conditioning at the least possible expense.

The windows were blocked by curtains that were almost always drawn, since Clare and Zeke rarely bothered to make nice with the neighbors and always had plenty to hide. Plus, like all kids of the Hollywood pantheon, Clare had long ago learned that if a neighbor discovered her lineage, any outreach was likely as not an attempt to be introduced to her famous dad. Curse of the Hollywood Baby.

Win followed the curve at the end of the key-shaped cul-de-sac and parked on the street in front of the house. He turned around to look at his granddaughter, who was staring at the house, her home, fear etched into her features.

"Amy?" he asked softly. "You okay?" She nodded, focused on the front door. "Wait here. I'll be right back." Win got out and walked back to where Teddy had parked behind him.

Teddy, already out of his own car, said, "Call him. Have him come out here."

Win raised his phone, then stopped. "Maybe I should see him alone . . ."

"You could," Teddy answered. "But then, they could be in there, keeping him company. What are you going to do if they are?"

Good question. What would *I do?*

Winston sighed and opened his phone, tapped the screen, and held it to his ear. A thin, nervous voice answered on the other end.

"Yeah?"

"Zeke," Win said. "I'm out front with Amy and a friend of mine. You alone in there?" From the sidewalk he and Teddy saw the curtains covering the front window part. The indoors looked black but he could see Zeke behind the glass. He peered out, his eyes darting back and forth.

"Maybe."

Win felt of jolt of frustration. Zeke always had that effect on him. "Answer the question."

"I'm alone."

"Then come out here."

"You come in here," Zeke said, an unfamiliar firmness in his voice. "They might be watching."

Win looked at Teddy. "He wants us to come in."

Teddy nodded. "I'll go."

"Who's that?" said Zeke.

"I told you, a friend of mine. He knows what to do. Just let him in."

Zeke was silent for a moment. "Okay." Then he disappeared as the curtains fell back together.

"Go ahead," said Win.

Teddy strode up the short walk to the front door. Zeke opened it just enough to let Teddy in, glanced around again, and shut it. Win noted that Zeke didn't acknowledge his daughter. He walked back to the car and got in. "You want to see your daddy?" he asked Amy.

She answered with a question. "Are you coming?"

"Yes, honey, I am."

She looked from Win to the house. "Okay."

They waited a few interminable minutes more as the heat of the sun filled the car. Win could feel sweat beading on his forehead.

Finally, the front door swung open. Teddy waved them inside.

CHAPTER

8

THE MUSTY ODOR hit Win like a wall when he entered his daughter's house. Even in spring the heat and smog in this part of the Valley could be so oppressive that opening a window was abhorrent, so the residue of the AC condensation permeated every carpet, rug, and swath of upholstery. Just airing it out for a day or two would dry it up, but Win figured they must not even notice anymore. He worried how mold might affect Amy's health.

Amy held his hand as they entered, keeping herself slightly behind him as he led her into this latest of several abodes she'd called home in her short life. The closed curtains darkened the living room to a murky gray, aided by the off-white wall paint that even in this dim light showed scuffs and stains.

A few pictures were hung in a spotty, uneven manner around the room in an attempt to make the place seem homey. Secondhand furniture completed the ambience: a ratty sofa, two mismatched chairs across from it, and a low, beer-bottle-ringed coffee table plopped in the middle. Sunlight glowed from the two doorways on either end of the living room that led to the kitchen. A 1960s-style Vu Thru fireplace was set in the center of the wall between the doors, the narrow, flat bricks blackened. A hallway perpendicular to the front door led to the rest of the house. With those generous windows and a fireplace that opened to both the living and kitchen areas, this house had once been a decent example of cheerful, mid-century modern architecture. Now it was just depressing.

"He won't put it down," Teddy said.

Win looked closer at Zeke in the gloom to see that he was holding a handgun, a revolver of the small caliber, snub-nosed variety—a .38 Special, maybe. He held it slightly behind him, either to hide it or make it known, Win couldn't say. But just seeing that thing at the end of his son-in-law's arm with his granddaughter in the room made Win want to smack the shit out of him right there.

Zeke's eyes shifted from Win to Teddy. His shoulder-length hair was greasy, with wide rows from using his fingers to sweep it back off his face. His beard was five or six days old and his hazel eyes were tense. In a strange way, he resembled Winston at that age.

But Win would never have let himself go to pieces like this. Zeke's T-shirt hung loose over his chinos, both garments looking like they hadn't been washed in weeks. He was slouching near the far doorway to the kitchen, as if he might make a run for it at the slightest sign of trouble. Whether because of the substance abuse or because he was made that way, Zeke didn't have good sense about people, who he should stay away from and who he should keep close. His father-in-law—the man who paid for the home he and his family lived in—was standing right in front of him, but you'd think Al Capone had just walked in with a chain saw.

Win felt a little pull on his jeans. He looked down and saw that Amy had closed her tiny fist on the back of his pant leg, like she was trying to attach herself to him.

"It's okay, honey," he said to her. "Your daddy's just shaken up. He's not going to hurt anybody." She took her eyes off Zeke just long enough to make eye contact with Win, but then moved a little farther behind him.

Maybe Zeke hadn't seen Amy enter, but he brightened as if his daughter had just magically appeared.

"Hey, Green Pea," he said, forcing a smile, his voice scraping like sandpaper. "You having fun with Grandpa?" Amy stared at him in silence.

"You checked the whole place?" Win asked Teddy.

"Yep."

Win unhooked Amy's fingers from his pants and kneeled, holding her gently by the shoulders. "Honey, go to your room and get some clothes and anything else you want. You're gonna stay with me for a little while."

Seeing Amy looking at him for approval—he was still her father—Zeke took a breath, filling his narrow chest with air, and let it out in a way that revealed the softness of his belly. To Win it sounded like a sigh of relief. "Grandpa's right, Green Pea. You should go with him for a bit."

"Go ahead, honey," Win said, and she shuffled down the hallway toward the back of the house. Once he heard her bedroom door softly close, he turned to Teddy. "Why'd you let me bring her in here when he's waving that thing around?"

"Aw, he ain't gonna hurt anybody with that but hisself." He looked at Zeke. "Are ya, kid?" Zeke's eyes widened and darted again back to Win, the hand holding the gun moving a little farther behind him.

"Zeke," said Win, "get rid of that gun or Teddy here is going to take it away from you. Trust me, you don't want that."

Zeke's eyes flashed with rage as Win looked on. With Clare, his son-in-law might have lashed out, if for no other reason than to convince himself he was a man who couldn't be pushed around. Win knew that the only real lesson Zeke had learned from his own drunk excuse of a father, back on the dirt floor of his Oklahoma panhandle home, was that you have to *act* like you're tougher than you really are. Zeke controlled himself and he stood up a little straighter, his eyes moving once again from Win to Teddy, who radiated perfect confidence in his ability to disarm Zeke and bring him to the floor.

Teddy held out his palm and Zeke handed him the gun.

In the months since Win had last been at Clare's bungalow, before their latest spat, the kitchen, too, had taken on a tragic air of neglect. It would be funny, perhaps, if it didn't stink of rancid grease and rotting vegetables. The room had once had a sunny-side-up cheerfulness to it; he remembered when Clare and Zeke first moved in how the yellow walls and tiles seemed to encourage starting every day on the right foot. But now, with the color washed out and many of the tiles either cracked or missing, and plates and pans filling the sink and littering the countertop, it was downright sad. The only silver lining to the house being sealed up tight all the time was that it prevented the otherwise unavoidable invasion of flies. At the moment, Win noticed only two circling over the sink.

Win couldn't believe they'd come to allow their child to live like this, and he swore to himself that, once this was all over and Clare was home safe, he would try once again to convince her to bring Amy and move in with him. But on the condition it would be without Zeke.

Zeke sat on one of the four chrome-and-vinyl chairs that matched the square chrome and Formica kitchen table, a score from a garage sale. Teddy had foraged and brewed a pot of coffee and set a mug of the hot stuff down in front of Zeke. Win sat across from him, his elbows on the table, his fingers interlaced. Teddy leaned against one of the doorjambs where, having opened the living room curtains, he could keep an eye on both the front lawn and, through the kitchen's sliding glass door, the back yard.

"They came about three o'clock this morning. They just took Clare and left." Zeke pushed the words out, his voice cracking.

"How'd they get in?" asked Teddy. "I don't see any broken windows or anything."

Zeke gazed down into his mug.

Win straightened up. "You didn't lock the doors."

"Guess I forgot. I think they came in through there," he said, cocking his head toward the glass slider. "But they went out the front."

Win was accustomed to Zeke and Clare telling half the story, or more to the point, half the truth. He glanced up at Teddy. Teddy shrugged.

"And they took Amy with them?"

"Not right then. One of them stayed here, about an hour, then he took her a little before sunup. Said he was bringing her to you," he croaked.

"What did he look like?" Teddy asked.

"Uh, what do . . . what do you mean?"

"He means, what did he *look* like?" There was that frustration again. "The guy who took Amy."

"Uh . . . he," he stammered, "he was Mexican, I think. Not from Mexico, he spoke English, but like, Latino. Had a mustache."

"Tall? Short? Skinny?" asked Teddy.

"Just regular, I guess." He thought a moment. "Kind of skinny."

"Clothes?"

"It was all dark. What he had on, I mean . . . a jacket. Boots! He was wearing boots. I remember 'cause of the sound they made."

Teddy looked at Winston. "Sound familiar?"

Win took a deep breath and let it out. "About your age? Late twenties?"

Zeke nodded. "That sounds right."

"It *sounds* right, or it *is* right?" Win said.

"Yeah," Zeke nodded. "I'd say so."

"What about the others?" said Teddy. "And how many?"

"Uh . . . two. White guys. The one that took Clare was real big. Blonde. The other guy was kinda pudgy. Had on a baseball cap."

"What did they tell you to do?" asked Teddy. "And what did they say *they* were gonna do?"

Zeke searched his coffee mug for guidance again. "Said if I called the cops, they'd know it. And they'd kill Clare." He sent his gaze to Teddy, avoiding Win's eyes.

"Then what?" Teddy asked, keeping a lid on his impatience.

"That's really all. 'Cept that the guy that stayed behind . . . the one that took Amy? He just sat here, watchin' us. And then he took her. He had a gun!" he blurted, as if pleading for understanding. But then he saw the fury rising in Win's eyes and looked back at Teddy. "Said they'd call. Just to wait."

Winston's ears and neck burned, and heat began building behind his eyes. Even at his worst, there was no way he would've let anyone touch his daughter or his wife, let alone take them without a fight.

"How do you know 'em?" Teddy asked.

Zeke looked surprised and needed a beat before he responded, his voice weaker. "Huh?"

"You weren't picked at random," said Teddy. "They didn't happen by and say, 'Hey, I bet somebody livin' in that little place has a famous daddy who can get us some money real easy.'" Zeke's stunned look suggested he hadn't expected that question. "Now, how do you *know* 'em?"

Zeke looked at Win, perhaps hoping he would help him out of this jam, the way he had so many times in the past.

Instead, Winston said, "You better answer him."

Zeke ran his fingers through his oily hair, then scratched his stubbled face with both hands. Finally, he said, "One was a connection. Met him at a bar, scored a powerball off him."

"A lottery ticket?" asked Win, confused.

"No, a *power*ball." His eyes went from Win to Teddy and back again. "I think they used to call it a speedball."

A speedball was a mixture of heroin and cocaine, meant to give you the opiate euphoria and the kick of the coke so you didn't nod off and miss out on any of the high. A greedy user's drug if there ever was one. And flexible. You could snort it or shoot it, depending on how far you were willing to go, how high you wanted to get, and how fast you wanted to get there. Speedballs, thankfully, had never been Winston's thing. He hadn't heard the word in at least twenty years. Didn't they have other, better drugs now? Or maybe it was just that he was too old for that shit these days.

Thirty years ago, back when Winston was just beginning his career, after hours clubs were all the rage. After the bars had closed at two AM, you could pay an entry fee at the door of one of these under-the-radar clubs and drink "free" all night long in a warehouse or office building. And because any such gathering was a "private party," all sorts of illicit pursuits—from sex to drugs—were part of the fun.

One night he went to an old Sunset Strip restaurant that had gone out of business, a Rat Pack–era spot called Sneaky Pete's. It was a perfect setup for a late-night happening. The club's organizers used the restaurant bar to hand out the cheap beer and well liquor that the cover charges more than paid for, guaranteeing a nice profit for the night, and the "guests" would use the cracked and decaying red leather booths and dance floor to schmooze and party.

Win paid his twenty bucks, got a beer, mingled a bit, and then wandered back through the abandoned kitchen. People were hanging around, smoking, drinking, making out. Then he reached the walk-in freezer. On the big metal door someone had scrawled the words *The Belushi Room* in red paint. Curious, he pulled the handle to peek inside and found himself staring at a group of attractive, sweaty young men and women, maybe ten, fifteen in all, crammed into the unused cooler, leaning on the empty metal shelves or crouching on the concrete. Half of them had their arms tied off with rubber strips and hypodermic needles stuck into their veins. They barely noticed him. One guy, though, was mid-plunge, and he'd looked up, his eyes wild with craving, then looked right back down to watch the needle deliver the drugs to his bloodstream. Win closed the door, finished his beer, and called it a night.

That was as close as he ever wanted to get to heroin or anything like it. Win was never one to cast stones—how could he?—but he recognized that look of wild craving. He'd seen it in his own eyes, and he knew what it could lead someone to do.

The fact that Clare and Zeke were in the grip of heroin flooded him with despair. He had always figured they were drinking too much and smoking weed, maybe even a line of coke every now and then, but the idea of his daughter snorting, smoking, or injecting smack made him feel like throwing up. He wanted a drink of water, but the thought of rummaging for a clean glass only made his guts roil even more.

"What bar?" asked Teddy.

"The one we always go to, at a bowling alley on San Fernando. It's called The Hideaway." Then Zeke added with a sly smile, "Good happy hour."

The anger Win felt for Zeke had been simmering for years, but to hear him attempt a joke after his litany of shortcomings to his family; allowing their home to fall into squalor, not even a mild protest as his child was packing to leave not fifty feet from him, and utterly failing to protect his wife . . . molten rage rose through his body. Before he even sensed his arm was in motion, Win had risen from his seat, wound up, and slapped Zeke across the face. Zeke's mug was swept off the table, splattering milky coffee and bouncing across the floor, miraculously without breaking.

Zeke managed to grab the table's edge and right himself before tumbling ass over teakettle. He might have impulsively struck back, but outnumbered by two larger men, he surely knew that any comeback would likely be met with more violence. So, he just glared at Win, his lips shaking, his quickened breath vainly trying to stem the tide of the humiliating tears forming in his eyes. He raised a palm to his stinging cheek, where a red splotch the shape of Win's hand was already visible.

"Now," said Teddy, leaning into Zeke, his hands resting on the table. "Which one of these assholes likes to hang out at your beloved bowlin' alley?"

As Win and Teddy watched, Zeke's face began to quiver, and then he burst out in tears, sobbing like a child. It's said that an addict's emotional maturation process stops the minute they first give themself over to their substance of choice. These were the tears of a teenager feeling unfairly chastised, flowing unabated.

"He calls himself Rocket," Zeke blubbered. "White guy, kind of heavyset, maybe thirty. Dresses like a rapper, always wears a baseball cap."

"Now that's more like it," Teddy said, pushing himself to a full standing position.

"Pull yourself together," said Win. Zeke's sobs slowed a bit. Win's guilt caught up to him. He pictured Zeke the night before, helpless as much more powerful adversaries yanked his wife out of their home. "I'm sorry I lost my temper." Zeke nodded as the tears subsided. Win continued, "You should go say goodbye to your daughter."

Win and Teddy squinted against the sun as they stepped outside. Amy hopped into Win's vehicle, and he fastened her into her booster seat. As he closed the car door, he saw she had opened her tablet, perhaps to distract herself from the fact that she was leaving home again.

Win came around the Bronco to the driver's side, where Teddy was standing. In a low voice, Teddy said, "Notice how he didn't even look relieved when he saw his daughter, knowin' she was okay?"

"Didn't mention being worried about Clare either," replied Win.

Zeke's face reappeared in the front window. He stared at them for a moment, then closed the curtains again.

"No, he did not," said Teddy.

"I can't believe I hit him," Win said, his voice laden with self-recrimination.

"I can't believe it took you so long." Win looked at him. "That boy was dancin' like a circus bear. People only do that when they got somethin' to hide."

Win thought for a moment. "What do you think it is?"

"Hell if I know. I'll go check out that bowling alley, but I doubt it'll lead anywhere. If it were me, I wouldn't go back." He tipped his head toward Amy in the car, deep into her tablet. "Win, we can't be haulin' luggage when we're out and about asking questions."

"Yeah." Win thought for a moment, then opened his phone's address book until he found a name and tapped the number. A familiar voice answered.

"Hey," he said. "I need a big favor."

9

CLARE HAD THE shakes for real. This time she couldn't deny it. Like so many addicts, she had convinced herself she could walk away from it anytime. All she needed was a good enough reason.

Of course, the reason to quit never materialized. Instead, there was always a reason to draw the curtains and fire up a pipe or pour another drink. Fighting with Zeke all the time might be a good enough reason to look for the exit, but then they'd never get to make up over cheap vodka and blow. And Amy? Well, before Clare had made the mistake of having a public meltdown the last time she saw him, they could always send her over to Grandpa's house for a few days and have a *really* good time. Maybe go to the bowling alley early and see Rocket.

Rocket had appeared one evening like a wizard. Every night at the same table, his minions swirling about him, topping off his beer, seeing that his French fries were done right (well done and crunchy). The magic with which he would produce his wares from one of his many pockets. "A little coke? Codeine? Smoke? Rocket's got you." Always with the big grin, his perfect white teeth gleaming. And those eyes. Big and round and soulful, behind which she could sense the mixture of yearning and sadness and fury—all things she could empathize with. She felt that was their bond, their real connection, what they held in common. Not the high thrills of the low outlaws, but their tragic Hollywood histories.

And now Clare was lying in this basement, shaking from withdrawal. From the drugs. From the alcohol. From her daughter. From her life. She looked over at the bucket they'd left for her to use in case she needed to pee or throw up. Her mouth and throat were dry, and she was beginning to feel the desperate pull of dehydration. She held the thin blanket tighter against her chin, wondering how long it might be before she could get these shakes under control. If she would even live to see it. Her mind drifted to the night before.

She had been lost in a dreamless sleep, then yanked from her bed, lifted into the air, and restrained like chattel. She had kicked her legs, desperately trying to free herself. She could sense that she was being carried to the living room. She saw her husband, standing frozen, eyes wide, mouth agape, hair hanging wildly in his face. A gun was pressed to his head.

Someone said, "Just be chill," and she saw Zeke look toward the voice, his eyes wide in shock. She recognized that voice, but the sound of Amy loudly calling for her mother distracted her before she could put it with a face. Her daughter's voice was muffled, coming from the next room: *Mommy! Mommy!*

She'd struggled hard against the large hand pressed to her face, covering her nose and mouth, making it difficult to breathe. The man's other arm was wrapped around her torso, locking her arms against her body. She was starting to lose consciousness when the man held her still, just long enough to face the flash of a camera that left her temporarily blind.

Then she noticed a strange odor, a sweet chemical smell, like caramelizing sugar. She became aware of the fabric of a cloth pressed over her nose and mouth. Her vision clouded, then everything went black.

10

I N THE LIVING room directly above Clare, Rocket had settled into *Rock Band 4*. His headphones snug over his ears, music pounding, his eyes glued to the screen, he worked the plastic guitar, his fingers deftly tapping and flicking. He was shredding Linkin Park's "Rebellion."

Rocket had been taking refuge in some version of this game ever since his wannabe stage father had had the idea to dump him into the orphanage known as Camp Hollygrove when he was eleven years old. Turned out video games were a good way to tune out all the screaming kids. Rocket's father had convinced the state that his treasured son, who back then went by his given name of Terrence, needed to be housed there because the family had rup-tured and there was nobody to care for him. Now shuttered, at that time Hollygrove happened to have a well-known reputation for preparing youngsters for entertainment careers. What Daddy had *really* wanted was a shortcut to fame for the boy and, in turn, his own fortune. And it worked. Sort of.

At fourteen, Terrence auditioned for a role on a cheesy super-hero TV show, featuring teenage leads who would morph into high-tech, armored crusaders, and landed the part. The role was what was known in the business as an "under five," meaning he spoke no more than five lines of dialogue per episode, and some-times none. During fight scenes he was often directed to hide behind a tree or building and shout encouragement to the lead actors, like "Wow! You guys are awesome! Get 'em!" With no future for the character, the show dropped him.

Once his father realized the fame and fortune thing wasn't going to happen fast enough, he disappeared, and the kids at the orphanage became Terrence's entire clan. Soon, he was just another forgotten child actor whose star had barely burned even briefly bright. The whole experience left him wishing he could morph into something, anything, other than what he was: a ward of the state.

His next home brought with it some culture shock. When it became clear his father was gone for good, the orphanage entered Terrence into their foster program. After two years (and two unfortunate early pairings) he was placed with a well-meaning but self-satisfied family in the elegant, uber-exclusive neighborhood of Pacific Palisades (where film and sports luminaries like Bradley Cooper, Kahwi Leonard, Anthony Hopkins, and Hilary Swank had found refuge).

It was in Palisades where he got his first real taste of opulence. Mansions full of beautiful people. Sunny champagne barbecues around what seemed like Olympic-sized swimming pools set into backyards that had a one-hundred-and-eighty-degree view of the Pacific. Or at their kids' basketball games at their shiny private schools, every kid's desk outfitted with a new computer. Rare, exotic cars and sleek, super-expensive restaurants. Captains of industry mingling with famous movie actors and rockstars. Every woman had an athlete's body (and not a strand of gray hair) while their well-fed husbands struggled to hold their stomachs flat. Everything there seemed . . . brighter. Even the sunsets contained colors he'd never seen before.

A music mogul from the Bronx, who'd spent time in the foster system himself, lived in a massive house down the block from the family where Terrence was fostered, and took a shine to the boy. Music Man, as he called himself, was rumored to have financed the start of his career by selling crack back in the 1990s. That impressed Terrence. They'd met on the Fourth of July, the day residents of their private street would open their front doors, and neighbors would wander in and out of the mansions, party-ing until sunset. Then they'd all gather in the yard with the best ocean view to watch the fireworks. Terrence couldn't remember whose yard it was—some tech guy—but he didn't really care. The rumor that year was that Steven Spielberg and David Geffen had arranged for the US Navy to send in the Cruiser that had provided over an hour of dazzling, explosive entertainment. *That* he remembered.

Music Man gave Terrence some advice: "I know it's all pretty and shit around here, but these kids . . . they can't even drive yet, and their daddies already *gave* 'em a career. And *their* daddies mostly did too. They're not like you and me. Nobody gives us anything. *We* do what we *got* to do."

Terrence had found someone he could look up to, and started hanging around Music Man as often he could. He even began to wear merch from Music Man's company. Ever-present on his head was a black, flat-billed cap, skewed to one side, with the logo of a musical note being pierced by a bullet. He even did his best to mimic Music Man's Bronx dialect, though he soon gave up on that.

When Terrence was seventeen, Music Man was sentenced to ten years for ordering the unsuccessful murder of an East Coast rival. Terrence felt bad for him, but he saw it as bad luck, just like Music Man did. The moral was clear: Don't get caught.

Though his foster parents made a big deal about how Terrence was "part of the family," he couldn't shake the feeling that they thought of him as a different *class* of family member (in other words, "the help"). "You have work to do here," the mother would say, pointing to the kitchen trash can that any one of her three *actual* children could have emptied, except they were usually in the game room, beating their father at VR golf. When Terrence turned eighteen, he took his last bag of kitchen trash out to the garbage can in front of the house, dumped it out *next* to the can, and kept walking. He caught a bus to the Army recruitment office in Santa Monica and enlisted. After a month of the heat and sweat and verbal abuse of basic training at Fort Benning, Georgia, he went AWOL and headed back to LA.

Some friends in Sylmar, ex-foster kids like him, let him crash on couches while he lay low. One gave him a little work selling hundred-dollar packets of blow along San Fernando Road to the workers pulling night shifts at the local warehouses. Within weeks he was fluent in the language of street life. Everyone started to call him "Rocket" because he could outsprint everyone, from cops to rival drug dealers. Terrence was reborn. In a few months he'd soon saved enough to put down first and last on a studio apartment.

Music Man had told him once that the road to success is never a straight line, and Rocket found this to be true. Hollygrove had taught him to resent the advantaged, then Palisades filled him with the desire to conquer that glamorous world. Finally, Music Man had shown him that anything was possible, and the mistakes to be avoided, and Rocket paid attention. Most importantly, he'd found a goal. He'd see the same names at the top of every big-time movie or TV show, and he wanted to see his name up there too.

Terrence had no desire for fame, and he definitely didn't want his image on the screen. He'd had his fill of that with the shitty TV show (plus, he wasn't sure when the Army might get tired of looking for him). No, his goal was to be a big man behind the scenes. He wanted to be a producer. (Oh, he liked the sound of that.) Better still, a rich and powerful producer. After all, producers give the orders and make all the money. He even had a name for his future company: RocketTerre Productions.

Until that happy day arrived, he held court at his unofficial office: table three in a Tiki-themed restaurant and bar that overlooked the bowling lanes. His lookout at The Hideaway: the bartender, Ozzie. The guy had a giant chip on his shoulder about his family's stolen fortune or something, but they had a good thing going. The manager got a kickback too, for looking the other way (Rocket hated to pay it, but it was a necessary expense).

But dealing dime bags out of a fried food factory was taking too goddamn long. That's why they went after the damn muscle car guy in the first place. Rocket'd never admit it, but Ozzie was right—the planning for that had been for shit. Should've known the guy wasn't on the take. He hadn't done his homework, what Music Man called the "due diligence," and the whole thing had gone to hell. This new thing, though, this was going to be his ticket. He could feel it.

Normally Rocket didn't like to make friends with his customers—too often they'd get behind and he'd have to pay them an unwanted visit—but when Clare, Zeke, and Rocket all met at the bar that first time, there had been this instant recognition that each had something the other wanted. For a customer,

that was a given. But after a while, the couple would get comfortable around him, get as high as they could afford, and their lips
would start to flap. Rocket discerned that Clare's daddy was a
famous actor. It didn't take long for him to figure out who the
guy was and that the universe had dropped a once-in-a-lifetime
opportunity right in his lap.

It had been Rocket's idea to send Ozzie out to the guy's house
in the muscle car. The big surfer Jordy—*my very own personal, private enforcer*—and that monster SUV sent the right message too.
Appearances were everything to these Hollywood people.

"Why take off the license plates?" Jordy had asked. "Won't the
dude see the car, anyway?"

"Yeah," Rocket said. *I swear to God, sometimes I think this guy
has brain damage,* he thought to himself. "But there's a million
black SUVs, and they all look the same. If there's no license plate,
you can't be identified. Just don't forget to put the plates back on
before you get on the freeway. Getting a ticket is the worst thing
that could happen."

"I know," Ozzie said. "We'll do a doughnut in his front yard.
That'll put the fear in him."

"No," said Rocket. He turned to Jordy. "You go slow. It's like
a show. Make him think you're not in a hurry for anything, ever."

Ozzie wasn't thrilled that it was his face the actor would see,
but Rocket pointed out that big bad Jordy was too easy to recognize. But if Ozzie hid behind his aviators, shaved off that sorry
excuse for facial hair afterward, and never wore those clothes
again, he should be fine.

But what really bothered Ozzie was the little girl. "Why don't
we just take the kid? Nobody fucks with you if you take a kid."

Jordy chimed in. "Yeah, why all the mind games? Just cut to
the chase, man."

But Rocket wouldn't budge. "I said it a thousand times—no
kids. And don't leave her with Zeke. We want him scared shitless
so he does exactly what we want. The old man'll see the video and
do whatever we say. *That's* how it's gonna be."

The rest had been easy. Rocket went to Clare and Zeke's place
with Jordy and Ozzie and walked right in through the back door.
Clare put up a little bit of a fight, but Jordy had no trouble con-
trolling her. Ozzie stayed behind to make sure Zeke didn't do

anything stupid, then delivered the little girl to the actor just after dawn.

Rocket smiled to himself. This was a good plan. Good business. Way better than slinging product out of a shitty restaurant overlooking a sport no one seemed to be good at. Except the Sunday bowling leagues—those people were really good—but Rocket usually took that night off because a lot of the league members were cops.

Best of all, the ransom paid by this aging movie star for the return of his fuck-up of a daughter would launch Rocket's Hollywood career.

Not that the old man would be around long enough to see it.

CHAPTER

11

WHEN THE DOORBELL rang, Zeke was afraid to answer the door.

At first, he thought Win and that Southern bruiser had come back. But when he peeked through the curtains, he saw a slender young man, with mid-length dark hair, holding what looked like a cell phone in his hand. The man jerked his head in time to catch a glimpse of Zeke as he yanked the curtains back into place.

"Zachary? Can I talk to you for a minute?" The man spoke loudly enough to be heard through the door. "Maybe you remember me? I'm Scott Branovich. I work for *LDT*. We talked a couple years ago, and you gave me some good information about a story I was doing. I thought we might be able to help each other out again."

Zeke felt panic rise in his throat. *LDT*—shorthand for *Look, Don't Touch!*—was a hugely popular tabloid TV show and website, infamous for its willingness to pay lavishly, usually in cash, for gossip about celebrity scandals or anything else that could humiliate the rich and famous. Built on a foundation of clickbait, it was the landfill of the entertainment world, where sordid stories went to fester into something worse.

Zeke didn't answer, hoping Branovich would just give up and go away. But this was *LDT*. Once in their crosshairs, most people just gave in and took the money. Zeke could've used the cash, but now was definitely a bad time for this. They'd been tough on Win when his wife had died, the worst of which was when *LDT*'s on-air "pundits" wondered if he was to blame for her violent death.

Years later, Clare and Zeke had accepted cash for feeding Branovich with anecdotes and innuendo around one of the anniversaries of her mother's death: how Joan had fallen into depression after enduring years of Win's alcoholism, how it had contaminated their marriage. But now, ducking under the windowsill like a scared child, he wondered how in the living *fuck* had this guy shown up here *today*?

"Zeke? I happened to see your father-in-law leave here with your daughter and another guy. He didn't look too happy. Want to tell me about that?"

Zeke's pulse pounded in his neck.

"Okay, I'm gonna leave my card here. You come up with anything, give me a call. I'll make it worth your while."

Zeke heard Branovich spin on the concrete porch and take a few steps down the path toward the street, but then the footsteps stopped. Zeke strained his ears. A moment later, he heard someone up against the window, just above where Zeke was sitting with his back against the wall. *Sneaky bastard.*

No longer trying to be heard through a closed door, Branovich's voice was softer. "I know something's going on. Maybe I can help you and Clare get to the other side a lot quicker. And a little bit richer. Looks like you guys could use it."

After a long silence, Zeke heard the footsteps crunch away and fade to nothing.

PART 2

"'Tain't my fault all the wrong people have all the money."
—Winston Greene in *Over Yonder* (1993)

12

The 10 Freeway (West) en route to Venice Beach,
16 miles west of Hollywood

In the rearview, Win could see Amy in the backseat. Teddy,
having phoned the bowling alley, only to learn it wouldn't open
for some hours hence, was trailing them in his car. He'd told Win
he would visit it later.

Win took in the vast urban sprawl as they careened down the
elevated freeway toward the Pacific Ocean. From here, Los Angeles looked to be infinite, its borders constantly spreading to make
room for more people and commerce. A sunbaked former desert, it
was now an expanse of buildings and yards and streets and lawns
that wouldn't have been possible without the miracle of irrigation.
Crystalline light shot down from the sky, heightening the colors
of everything, including the many palm trees that, though not
indigenous, were no less beautiful when the sun sparkled on their
enormous dark green fronds. D. J. Hall was Win's favorite painter
because of her ability to capture that magical, Southern California
light in her portraits.

Win and Joanie had lived in Venice when they first became a
couple, sharing a cottage a few blocks from the beach with two
other young actors hoping to make their way up the Hollywood
food chain. It was there, when they'd take walks on the sand at
dawn, before the rest of the world rose, that they learned they

didn't need much besides each other. It was one of the happiest times of Winston's life.

Despite the immense recent development, many of the original 1960s cottages stubbornly remained, housing some of the families whose forebears had helped build the area.

It was to one of these stalwarts that Win, Amy, and Teddy arrived that afternoon. Fortunately, when he'd called earlier to ask for help, Win had caught his friend Grover at home on a rare day off.

Grover Washington (not the musician nor named after him) lived in the house with his wife, Lauren, and their four children (two girls and two boys), all under the age of fifteen. Though the couple's roots in Venice ran deep, Grover's ancestors hailed from the Cape Verde Islands, and that European–Moorish ancestry was reflected in his powerful frame and patrician features, which he accented with a trim mustache. Lauren, meanwhile, was third-generation Rwandan American, tall, elegant, and dark-skinned.

Grover was one of the most skilled and sought-after stuntmen in Hollywood, which is how he and Win had met. As a young weightlifter on Muscle Beach, Grover had been recruited by network scouts for his size and remarkable physique. It wasn't long before he became the stunt double for an actor on a certain TV show whose star sometimes transformed into a very large and angry green monster.

Over time, what came to distinguish Grover's work was not his size and bulging muscles, but the painstaking planning he put in to computing the real-world physics of the stunts—for instance, the velocity of a stuntperson flying through the air or falling off a building while firing a machine gun back up at the hero on the roof, the cushioned point of impact for someone diving out of a hovering helicopter, the best way to film a cowboy jumping from one sprinting horse to another, or how a fleeing bank robber could straddle two fast-moving vehicles during a getaway.

Due to his combination of fearlessness, concern for others' safety, forethought, and the meticulousness of his work, Grover had entered the pantheon of such stunt legends as Hal Needham, Calvin Brown, Henry Kingi, Terry Leonard, and Yakima Canutt. As modest as he was accomplished, though, he attributed his longevity and success to sticking to the profession's central creed: a real stuntman makes an art out of *not* collecting broken bones.

Win pulled into the driveway behind Lauren's Jaguar. The soft aroma of sea foam was evident before they even exited the car. Grover and Lauren came out to the porch to greet them as Teddy pulled up to the curb.

Amy looked up from her tablet and squealed when she realized where she was. She pushed her door open and ran to Lauren, who bent down to meet her with open arms. In one easy move, Lauren gathered the child up into an embrace, her bright caftan flowing with the ocean breeze. Grover, with a smile just as wide, leaned in, and Amy reached over to hug him with the happy enthusiasm of a child reunited with adults who have always indulged her.

Win felt a twinge of envy for the Pied Piper quality this couple possessed. "Hey, quit making my granddaughter like you better!" he hollered with a smile.

"Want to see the kids?" Lauren asked Amy. The little girl nodded vigorously. Lauren plopped her back on her feet and opened the screen door. "They're in the back. Excited to see you too."

Amy disappeared into the house, her earbuds trailing her. A few moments later, they heard the Washington children greet Amy with shouts of welcome in the backyard.

Teddy came up next to Win in the driveway. He nodded toward the Washingtons. "Sure about this?"

"She's safer here than anywhere," Win said.

"Hello, Win," said Grover in a voice that rumbled like an earthquake from his barrel chest. "How's the hip?"

Grover was referring to an injury Win had suffered performing a stunt some years earlier. In his younger days, Win had been known and quite respected for performing his own stunts—he always rehearsed, and his natural physical gifts gave him an edge over his less athletic costars.

The stunt in question had been deceptively simple: Win would dodge a moving car just before it ran him over. It was an old trick, but it always looked great on film. Win would jump off the road into a ditch, where a camera placed low to the ground would capture his hair's-breadth escape and dramatic roll past the lens. The camera's angle would disguise how the car would actually miss him by a mile. Grover, who was the stunt coordinator for the movie, had insisted on the roll, partly to keep the kinetic energy onscreen but also because the director wanted the camera so low that the ground would be visible in the foreground of the shot, leaving no room to lay a pad to break the fall. Win had incorporated a limp into the performance of every scene that would appear after this one, a limp caused by this very plot point.

To indicate that Win's character had just injured himself, Grover suggested that for the shot of him getting up from the ditch, Win should favor one side as he rose. But Win unilaterally decided it would be far more believable if he landed on his side and thudded to a stop on camera. The audience would *definitely* buy the limp after that. As the car shot past him, Win launched himself into the air, dropped into the ditch (a full three feet below the surface of the road), and cracked his hip in two places.

Rather than pause filming (which is near sacrilege in the movie business) while Win recuperated for a few days, the wardrobe and makeup departments disguised a limp-free Winston Greene double for long shots and walkaways for all the scenes in the movie that came *before* the bad guys had tried to run him down. Humbled, Win returned to set and did the rest of his shots with an *actual* limp. To this day, there were two pins in the head of his femur, and Win had to pop the occasional anti-inflammatory when it started acting up. And Grover never missed an opportunity to bring it up.

"Easy, big boy," said Lauren, her voice dipped in warm honey. "You favor one side in the morning yourself."

Grover's mouth fell open in mock shock.

Win embraced Lauren and said, "I know what he sees in you, but I'll never know what you see in him."

"And you never will."

Win turned to Grover, extending his hand. "Good to see you, big man."

Grover had seen his friend's world fall apart enough times to know when things weren't right. He took Win's hand and pulled him into a one-armed hug, holding him there a moment.

"You too, my friend," Grover said.

Win nodded with gratitude at the sense of compassion and composure this man brought to his life and felt the heat building behind his eyes.

As if to save his friend embarrassment, Grover turned and said, "Teddy, right? I think we met at one of Win's old poker nights."

"That we did," Teddy drawled as he stepped up and shook Grover's hand. "I'm always trying to pick you out in the movies."

"Well, keep trying. If you spot me, I want to know about it." Grover chuckled. "My wife, Lauren."

"Now you, I've heard a *lot* about. Win's always sayin' how he's gonna run away with this 'Lauren' woman. Now I see why."

"A pleasure to meet you too," she replied. "Are all of Win's friends such lying charmers?"

"I understood it was a requirement."

Grover shook his head. "C'mon, let's go in and talk."

13

E VEN WITH THE addition of a second story, the Washington home didn't look like a showstopper from the outside. The Craftsman approach had been tastefully retained in the added level, but the exterior still exhibited the simplicity of the original structure: wide horizontal boards covered with a light yellow-tan paint meant to reflect the sun's heat away from the house. Even the simple asphalt shingles helped it blend into the area.

But the inside could have been the centerfold of any top-flight architectural magazine. Lauren and Grover's love of travel and interest in different cultures were in evidence throughout the home in the form of arts and crafts collected around the world: exotic silks thrown over handmade lampshades, wooden and brass sculptures everywhere, and the walls a world tour of indigenous art.

The dark wood furniture, custom-made for the remodeled contours of the rooms, was hand-polished and upholstered with rich fabrics in earth tones. It was so welcoming and warm that Win felt his shoulders relax just stepping inside the front door— and he noticed Teddy's do the same.

Grover led them to the teakwood dining table, understanding that this visit was a brainstorming event rather than a social visit. The four of them took seats around the table, Grover and Lauren on one side, Win and Teddy across from them.

Lauren passed around an etched crystal pitcher filled with an amber liquid, a tea from Sri Lanka. They all had in front of them an elegant matching highball glass filled with ice. As each poured themselves a glassful, the soft aroma of spice and fruit wafted throughout the room.

Grover leaned forward and nodded to Win. "Let's have it."

Win laid out the entire day and included a quick recap of his troubled history with his daughter. His friends were well aware of his and Clare's estrangement, but he figured it would be better to repeat himself than leave something out.

The Washingtons were excellent parents and close friends, and Win had regularly reached out to them for counsel over the years. Grover and Lauren had tried their best with Clare, even finding reasons to invite her and Amy over for play dates with their kids, but she was rarely receptive.

Win sat up in his chair. "So, can you take Amy for a few days? With any luck this will be over with soon, and Clare'll be back home."

"Why haven't you called the police?" asked Lauren.

"Seems if there was ever a good time, this is it," Grover added.

Win turned to Teddy, who picked up his cue. "I made a quiet inquiry to a trusted friend at the LAPD about the car left in Win's driveway. He was able to confirm these boys mean business." He took a breath. "Now, most any LA cop would lay down his life to retrieve anyone's daughter, let alone a famous actor's, but I do not trust some of the crustier members of the force not to tip off a tabloid for some extra sugar. Publicity like that could make a kidnapper nervous, anxious to get things over with, which could mean a bad outcome for the victim—for Clare. I think it's best if we poke around a bit before bringing them in all the way."

Grover and Lauren looked at each other, then Grover said, "Amy is welcome here as long as you need."

"As one of our own," Lauren added.

Win tried to stem the flood, but sitting at this table with three of the best people he'd ever known, each of them eager to help him out, he began to sob. Out of gratitude, out of worry, out of fear, out of love. People he had met as a direct result of his profession, which was routinely disparaged as being populated by shallow, manipulative, greedy, cruel narcissists. But these people, his friends, put the lie to that stereotype.

"Sorry," Win said. He caught his breath, wiped his cheeks, and looked around at the three faces, all gazing back at him with compassion. He saw that Lauren had a little water pooling in her eyes too. She reached across the table and squeezed his forearm.

In the ensuing silence, they all heard Win's phone buzz in his pocket. It was a text: *Pay phone 10 min 2135552905*

Win swore and showed them the message.

Teddy said, "They're assumin' you haven't called the cops. And ten minutes wouldn't give you time to involve them now, even if you wanted to."

"How would they know that?" asked Lauren. "Are they watching us?"

"Doubtful," Teddy answered. "I think if they were that close, they woulda let us know. They're just confident they've got the upper hand. This is a classic approach: let the mark sweat for a spell, then make the ask. Any phone booths around here?"

"Just one, that I know of," Grover answered. "Lincoln and Venice. I'll drive."

Win pocketed his phone as they all rose from their chairs.

14

THE GAS STATION at the southwest corner of Lincoln and Venice was one of the busiest on the west side. The boulevards were well situated as the simplest way in and out for the crush of tourists flocking to the fabled Venice Beach. Locals had been known to joke that the traffic congestion in this intersection could be seen by satellite.

At the crossroads of two essential thoroughfares, the gas station was a draw because the owner kept prices at market rates, ensuring a continual line of cars at each of its three fuel islands. Behind bulletproof glass, a cashier was on duty twenty-four/ seven. And against a low-lying cinder-block wall separating the lot from the apartments and homes to the east, away from the crowds at the pumps, stood one of Venice Beach's last operating pay phones.

Grover maneuvered his aging blue and tan SUV eastbound through the heavy traffic. He'd taken a straight shot up Venice Boulevard from the west so that he wouldn't have to negotiate a left turn from the intersection at Lincoln, which by itself would take longer than the ten minutes they had to work with. Despite the high cost of filling it with gas, he'd held on to this burly V8 as his on-set vehicular problem-solver. It could conquer any mountainside, and if a stunt car got stuck in a ditch, which happened more often than you'd think, Grover could just pull up, rope it to his trailer hitch, engage the four-wheel drive, and drag it out.

Teddy turned to Win in the back seat, where Grover had suggested he sit to avoid being recognized by passersby. "I want you to keep a few things in mind: One, don't promise what you don't have. No matter what you say, they're gonna figure you for lowballin' 'em and ask for more. Two, get proof of life. You don't talk to her, they get nothin'. But the main thing? Don't argue and don't agree to anything. Just find out what they want for now."

Grover skidded into the lot, past the phone and air/water station, and swiveled the powerful vehicle one hundred and eighty degrees, coming to a stop parallel with the cinder wall. He kept the car running and pointed toward the street in case they had to make a hasty exit. Getting back onto Venice Boulevard in a hurry could be a challenge, but Win was confident that Grover could handle it. Inbound, his route had proven so efficient that they'd beaten the countdown by two minutes.

Win started to open his door, when Grover said, "Hold on," and got out ahead of him, his muscular frame rising with effortless grace from the driver's seat. He stood by the open door and scanned the area to try to pick out anyone who might be observing them.

A man standing on the other side of the lot, by the crosswalk on Lincoln, caught Grover's eye. He seemed to be too still for this corner, and at first thought the man was looking straight at the car, holding a cell phone to his ear. But then he scratched his temple and lowered his hand. No phone. Only when the man boarded the municipal Big Blue Bus that came to a stop next to him, was Grover satisfied they were not being watched.

"Okay," he said, and swung his door shut as Win and Teddy exited the vehicle to join him.

Winston stepped up to the phone, protected from the elements by a narrow hood, and saw that the massive paper directory, once attached by a steel cable, was long gone. Some of the city's phones had been upgraded with a credit card slot, but this was not one of them. He lifted the filthy receiver, pungent with the stink of old cigarettes, and plunged his other hand into his jeans pocket. "I don't have any change."

Teddy dipped into his own pockets, but Grover stepped up, slipping out his wallet.

"I got it." He produced what looked like a credit card and flipped it over, then he took the receiver from Win, held it to his ear, and started punching in numbers from the back of the card. "Puts it on my phone bill. Got 'em for the kids in case they lose their cell."

Win held up his cell for Grover to read the number. "Why would they give us their phone number?" he asked.

Teddy answered. "It's a burner. Someone else will probably have the same number in a coupla hours."

Grover held the phone out to Win. "It's ringing."

"Win," Teddy said, barely audible above the traffic noise. Win covered the mouthpiece. "Remember, don't argue. Just find out what they want."

That thought hovered in Winston's mind like something he couldn't hold but knew was there. He took a breath, then heard the line click open.

"Hola, cabrón." It was the skinny prick. Even through this dilapidated phone, Win recognized the voice. "You're late. Fifteen seconds late."

"I'm not at home," Win said, feeling he should proffer a defense.

"No shit. You think I don't know that?"

Win looked at Grover and widened his eyes, pointing upward and sweeping back and forth. Grover got the message and started scanning the neighboring buildings again.

"Good thing you know how to follow directions," said the guy.

Win blurted out the only thing that really mattered to him. "Is my daughter there?"

"You mean right now? Sure, but she can't talk. Not with my dick in her mouth." The guy cackled loudly at his joke, a sound like sandpaper on rock. "Just kidding, cabrón. You're gonna have to trust she's alive and well."

"What do you want?" Win demanded.

"Well," the guy replied, "it's pretty simple. You have a shitload of money. I want a shitload of money."

Win looked at Teddy and Grover, both of whom were standing close, and held up his free hand and rubbed the ends of his fingers together. Grover nodded. Teddy pulled out his notepad and scribbled furiously.

"So, cabrón," said Ozzie, "what you say to a trade? Everything you got . . . for the puta madre."

Teddy held up his notepad for Win to read what he'd written: *Tell them you DO NOT know what ur doing.*

Win acknowledged it with a nod. Teddy showed Grover the note.

"Listen up, old man. This is how it's gonna go: first thing tomorrow, you're going to the bank. You get it all out, and I mean *all*. You'll hear from us again tomorrow. I suggest you start early. Traffic gets so tough close to the weekend." He cackled again.

Win felt the back of his neck tighten. "I don't know—"

"You don't know *what*?"

Win let a hint of supplication creep into his voice. "I don't know if they'll give it to me that fast. I'm not even sure how much is there."

"You don't know how much you got? Who doesn't know how much they got? I know how much I got."

"I just—I don't know if they'll give all of it to me," Win said, and realized this was true. "How much I can get all at once, I mean."

"Well, you better figure it out real quick, cabrón. Or I might have to put a bullet in the puta." The kidnapper's voice lowered. "By now you know where that car came from, so you know we don't fuck around."

Win felt his mouth go dry. "Okay. I understand. So, tomorrow?"

"Yeah, we'll be in touch. And remember, I did you a favor." He paused. "We coulda taken the kid."

15

WINSTON HUNG UP the phone. He stood stock-still, his palm on the receiver and his shoulders sagging as he gazed down at the base of the phone stand.

"Win?"

That sounds like Grover. Then he heard it again, louder.

"Win!"

Yes. Grover drove me here. He and someone else. Teddy! Teddy's been with me all afternoon.

"You all right?" That drawl was definitely Teddy's. "What'd they ask for?"

Brown spots began to form in his eyes, rising in from the outer edges, shrinking his field of vision. He felt like his skeleton was coming undone and imagined his head hitting the pavement. He forced in several slow, deep breaths, using the influx of oxygen to stay on his feet and drive the circle of spots back to the outer edges. It didn't work.

He turned and felt a familiar tightness in his chest. It was the inside of his rib cage fighting against him. The scar tissue.

"I don't have any money," he said. And then his world went black.

PART 3

"There's never been anyone like him. Psychos like that, the ones with no limits, they come along once every hundred years."

—Winston Greene in *Clear Falls, Minnesota—2 Miles* (2001)

16

SYLMAR

O ZZIE HUNG UP the phone, popped out the SIM card, removed the battery, and dropped the disposable cell phone carcass and components on the table next to him.

Rocket stared from the sofa across the living room. He raised his eyebrows, as if he was expecting a report.

Ozzie ignored him and pushed back in the old La-Z-Boy recliner, raising the footrest. He arched his back and looked over at the cheap roller shades covering the living room windows. He wished he could open them. Even in this part of the Valley, the sunsets reminded him a little of Miami. But they couldn't take any chances until this gig was done. His eyes came to rest on the oxidized wall paint that no longer matched the faded brown 1970s shag carpeting. He interlocked his fingers, tapped his thumbs together, and shook his head.

"I'm telling you," Ozzie said, "something feels off."

"He went along, right?" Rocket asked. "Wasn't looking for a way out or trying to be a 'tough guy'?"

"Nah, he sounded scared. Off his game."

"Then what's the problem?"

"I don't know. No puedo poner mi dedo en eso."

"C'mon, man—*English.*" Jordy, the big surfer, was leaning against the jamb of the kitchen door with a near-empty beer bottle in his hand.

"Sorry, Jordy," Ozzie said. "Forgot you were there. I said, 'I can't put my finger on it.'" Jordy was thick, but Ozzie knew he was no match for the muscular surfer, physically, so he made sure not to tease him too much. Plus, there was something demented behind the guy's cold gray eyes.

"So far, he's doing what we tell him," Rocket said, and then asked Jordy, "He took the kid to Venice? He and that cop?"

"Yeah," replied Jordy, a little miffed he had to repeat himself. "Some friend of his. Big guy and some lady. His wife, I guess."

"No chance they saw you?"

Jordy sighed. "I told you. No. Nice day at the beach, plenty of cars driving by. It was easy."

"You remember where," Rocket said. It wasn't a question.

"I can find it."

Rocket nodded, then turned back to Ozzie. "You met him. You think he'd try to fuck us?"

"No tengo ni puta idea!" Ozzie snapped, then remembered Rocket's little smile when he popped the vintage-car guy. Maybe Rocket wasn't someone he wanted to piss off. "Sorry. It's just . . . maybe there's more there than we think. Something we should know, but don't."

"Yeah. Maybe." Rocket chuckled. "And maybe you're just a fucking downer."

Jordy chuckled, drained the last of his beer, and went back into the kitchen.

17

JORDY WAS HANGRY. Big guy like him needed his meals on the regular, and dinnertime was approaching. He set down the empty beer bottle next to the kitchen sink and stared out the window at the brown yard. He missed the ocean.

He loved to surf. What the hell else was there to do, growing up in Huntington Beach? "HB" to the locals. His old man had worked the oil rigs that still produced crude there today. His mother had worked the night shift at the hospital, where she developed a fondness for amphetamines, then got fired for forging prescriptions. Not long after, Jordy's dad caught her trading favors with a meth dealer on the beach one night. He beat the guy to death right there on the sand and had started in on Jordy's mom by the time the police arrived. He was housed two and a half hours north in Corcoran Prison, same wing as Charles Manson. Jordy never bothered to visit.

Jordy's ambition had been to go pro. Endorsements and travel and clothes and girls. But that dream died with the concussions. Too many big waves, too many hard stops against the bottom. He figured that his size would protect him against the pounding, but he was wrong. One day they pulled him unconscious from Half Moon Bay during an epic swell at Mavericks. When he came to in the hospital a few hours later, the doctors told him that if he continued this punishment, he could end up like Junior Seau. Any sports fan in SoCal knew about the legendary Seau, an NFL great who died by suicide while suffering from something called chronic traumatic encephalopathy—CTE.

"He played football. I'm a surfer!" he'd said.

The doctors just shook their heads and went to check on the next patient.

In the years since, Jordy had certainly experienced some symptoms of CTE. He'd been struggling with mental focus for a while. And his temper was pretty bad these days. Worse than normal. He'd get angry when he couldn't make decisions or his memory blanked out, and sometimes he'd take it out on the people around him. He'd been trying his best to hide it. He couldn't lose his position as muscle for Rocket. It was all he had right now.

But no more big waves for him. Those days were over, along with his dreams of being a professional surfer, even though he could move as well as the guys who'd made it to the pros, and better than some. He still had the look, though. His hair was sun-bleached blond and hung to his shoulders, which were rounded from thousands of paddles past the break. His abs were bricked from countless jumps to his feet on the board.

Jordy's old man may have been a vicious asshole (the words his lawyer used in court to describe him were "misunderstood" and "pushed to the edge," though the DA brought in a guy who said he was an "unhinged psychopath"), but the money he made on the rigs had kept them out of hock. Once he went to prison, a humiliating period of welfare, food stamps, and a stream of HUD apartments began for Jordy and his mom. It was around then that Jordy started spending most of his time out getting trashed with his buds, couch surfing or sleeping on the beach rather than coming home. Good thing he'd gotten used to this lifestyle, because on his sixteenth birthday Jordy's mother tossed him out. By then, the meth had turned what teeth she had left to leopard-spotted stumps. Message received: getting high was what she wanted. Jordy was on his own, and that was just fine with him.

"What do you call a surfer without a girlfriend? Homeless!" Jordy had always hated that joke, even though it was inspired by guys like him. The whole time he'd been working with Rocket and Ozzie, he'd been living with a good-natured young woman named Janette. And before her, there had been a string of "Janettes": Rachel from the Fairfax District, Nevaeh from Inglewood, Ari from Koreatown, Edvina from Beverly Hills. Sweet, usually inse-cure women who were drawn to his size and his dark surfer vibe. They were generous, and most importantly, they had jobs.

Except Edvina, who had an accent he couldn't place and no discernable career. The only two activities she seemed to pur-sue were getting high and buying shit. Clothes and home decor, mostly. She'd buy shit for Jordy too, like the slacks he was wearing right now, the ones with the clean drape. She'd found Jordy at a bonfire party down on Dockweiler Beach, under the constant roar of jumbo jets lifting off from LAX.

She'd invited him back to her condo on the quieter, southern end of Venice, a big open contempo job on Ocean Front Walk, all polished concrete and floor-to-ceiling windows and a stunning view of the water. They'd had enough coke and molly to stay up for a year, fucking and drinking expensive water she must have bought by the case. She hadn't seemed to mind when Jordy stayed on after-ward. From her place he could walk across the sand to the surf break and be the first one out on the morning glass. It was perfect.

But as it turned out, Edvina had not been all that happy with the arrangement. Maybe it was his tendency to drift, whether during conversation or while making love. "I'm bored with you," she'd snapped at him one morning in that mysterious accent as he went out the door with his board. When he came back a few hours later, the locks had been changed and his clothes were in a pile in the open carport. After the confusion (he couldn't remem-ber what had transpired that morning to cause this), all he'd felt was anger. And he'd held onto it for a long time afterward—kept that fire banked even when he drifted in and out of the lives of other women, including Janette. He was grateful to Janette for so many things, but especially for having taken him in. (Her place in Sylmar was nice enough, though he couldn't understand why anyone in LA would live that far from the beach.) She liked Jordy, she'd told him, because he was different. Quiet, deeper, more . . . *introspective* than the boisterous surf-Nazis she was used to. A buddy of his had set them up, asked her if his pal could use her spare room for a little while. She'd agreed, and after two weeks he'd made the move into her bedroom.

A couple months later, early one Wednesday morning, he'd driven Janette to the TV studio in Burbank, where she did makeup

for one of the last remaining soap operas, and beelined to Venice
in her car. He'd parked by the Kinney Plaza roundabout, with
the naked woman sculpture by Robert Graham, next to the now-
shuttered WPA-era post office. As a kid, Jordy had been dragged
inside this post office with his schoolmates, to take in Edward
Biberman's 1940s mural depicting developer Abbott Kinney staring out at the viewer, surrounded by his dreams of the "Venice of
America" to his left and the nightmare of the 1950s oil boom that
polluted the area to his right. This vision of oil slicks on the water
had stuck with him ever since.

Jordy had walked the few blocks to the beach. On the way
he'd pulled on a pair of surgical gloves. He'd woke an old drunk
he found behind a dumpster and bought the man's tattered, greasy
belt for ten bucks and a pint of vodka. Then he'd strolled down to
Edvina's, slipped off his shoes, and hidden in the building's open
carport, near her parking spot.

She'd soon appeared, dressed for her yoga class, and he'd
noticed she'd cut her long hair into a bob. It looked good, he
thought. He'd crept up behind her in his stockinged feet and
looped the belt around her neck, her look of surprise and terror
reflected in the car's window. "Bored with me now?" he'd whispered to her as her flailing arms and legs finally went limp. He'd
lowered her body to the cement floor next to her car, his mother's face floating in his mind's eye. On the way back to Janette's
car, he'd dropped the belt, along with Edvina's purse, next to the
passed-out drunk, the vodka already drained, then ditched the
gloves in a public trash can.

As he'd driven back to Sylmar that day, his mind had felt
clearer.

During the week Janette would be at the studio all day, often
until eight or nine PM. After they'd been together for a month
or so, she'd scored Jordy some work as an extra. It brought some
decent pocket change, but he felt it wasn't worth all the boredom.
All the sitting around, whether in the green room or on set (where
you had to be quiet), drove him nuts.

On one occasion there had been an actress whose stares Jordy
mistook for an invitation. He knocked on her dressing room door,
and not long after, security was escorting him off the lot. When
Jordy told Janette about it later that evening, he made up some

bullshit about how the actress had made the first move and then punished him for rejecting her by having him tossed. He sensed Janette knew he was lying, but in the end she let him stay. That was the end of any TV work, of course, which was fine with him. But that had been six months ago already, and he needed some money of his own.

Hopefully this kidnapping thing would pan out.

Fucking Sylmar, Jordy thought as he looked out the kitchen window. The neighborhood made him nervous. It was where one of the most famous earthquakes ever had struck, back in 1971. Elevated freeways and buildings had come down—almost all sixty-two people who died had been in a VA hospital that collapsed. The death toll would've been in the thousands if the local dam had broken, which it nearly did. The event was legend here. Knowing all this didn't help Jordy's state of mind, not at all.

Jordy wanted to get back to where he could wake up next to the waves, where all he had to do was hop on his board and ride. He knew even a fall off a smaller curl could hurt him, but at least it would be his choice. Not like an earthquake.

His go-to hangout was the bowling alley on San Fernando, where he'd met Rocket and Ozzie. Ozzie was always barking orders like the boss he thought he was (dude never missed a chance to brag about his lost family empire), and Jordy would silently go along, but that was temporary. When he got his cut, he'd give the little Cuban American a brief but meaningful beating and head back to the water.

Ozzie may have been a douche, but Rocket was all right in Jordy's book. He liked how the guy had introduced himself at the bar and asked Jordy if he was interested in being his strongman. Direct, which Jordy liked. And he was impressed Rocket had starred on that hit TV show when he was a kid (though he couldn't remember the name of it). Most of all, though, Rocket was ruthless and smart, qualities Jordy admired.

And he enjoyed being the muscle. Roughing someone up occasionally gave direction for his anger, and it wasn't challenging. The victims were mostly deadbeat meth heads anyway, just like his mom. Rocket would extend them a little credit, and they always fell behind. Once they got in deep enough, Jordy and Ozzie would pay a visit, get the money owed, and take a little something extra. A flat screen, a soundbar, a smartphone, something they could unload quick. It wasn't much—barely enough to bridge one month into another—but it beat the shit outta workin'.

But this new job, the kidnapping, would be his ticket out. That last one, the car guy, hadn't gone as intended, but this time he figured Rocket would get it right. Jordy wasn't well educated, but he knew a good thing when he saw it, and this was the one that would lift him right over the Santa Monica Mountains and put him back on the beach for good.

Jordy stared hard out the kitchen window at the dry, dusty backyard of the decrepit house they were sharing, and imagined himself far away from here. He closed his eyes and saw himself catching a perfect wave, snaking across the surface, one hand skimming the inside of the curl. Maybe he should head south. To Mexico. A guy with a wad could live right on the sand and never even need a warm jacket. Or he could get a house on wheels, a sleeper with satellite TV, and be home wherever he parked.

Jordy opened his eyes, and as soon as he did, he felt weary. He was thirty-one years old and had been living hand to mouth for half of that.

But his time had almost come. He could feel it.

PART 4

"Best laid plans, my ass. Something will fuck your shit up no matter what you do."

—Winston Greene in *Hit and Run* (2008)

18

VENICE BEACH

"WIN?" THE VOICE was gentle, full of concern. Winston's eyes fluttered open. He was lying on his back on something soft, but he didn't recognize the ochre ceiling. With no idea where he was, he felt a jolt of panic and started to lurch to a seated position, when a firm hand pushed him back down.

"Easy now, fella. Get your bearings first," the woman said.

He turned his gaze toward the voice and saw a familiar, welcome face. *Lauren.* She was perched next to him on a sofa in the Washingtons' living room. His eyeline racked to Grover and Teddy standing behind Lauren, who gave him encouraging smiles. He lay back, the plush sofa enveloping him in a momentary feeling of safety.

The last thing he recalled was the din of traffic at the intersection of Venice and Lincoln, a public telephone, and Grover and Teddy, staring at him expectantly. Then . . . nothing until now.

"What happened?" asked Win, his voice as thin as his emerging consciousness.

According to Teddy, Win had started to fall over right after calling the kidnappers, but Grover's quick reflexes had saved him from cracking open his skull on the blacktop. Grover then lifted Win like a child and slid into the back seat of his car, unnoticed

in the bustle and din at the busy gas station. Teddy got behind the
wheel while Grover cradled Win in the back seat, barking directions. By the time they arrived back at the Washington home,
dusk had enveloped the neighborhood. Streetlamps and porch
lights were flickering on as Grover carried Win into the house.

"You gave us bit of a start back there, friend-oh," said Teddy.

Lauren gently pressed a damp towel to Win's forehead, and the
coolness made him breathe easier. Then he tightened up again.

"Amy!" he said, glancing around the room.

"She's fine," Lauren answered, steady. "She's still with the kids,
and they're having a grand time. No need to worry about her.
Right now, I'm worried about you."

"Don't know what hit me," Win said, laying his head back
down. "Just . . . blacked out, I guess."

Actually, Win had a very good idea what had hit him. *That
damn cancer.* He wondered when he'd ever completely recover.

By chance, during his annual wellness CT scan eighteen
months earlier—something Win's doctor had suggested he do
when he'd quit smoking—Winston had learned that he had a
tumor growing in his chest: a thymoma.

Thymomas, tumors of the thymus gland, are rare and tend to
grow slowly, which was lucky for Win since it had been detected
late. The tumor had progressed to the point that it had attached
itself to his outer lung. This was easy enough for his surgeon to
remove, but the bad news was that the tumor had also come into
contact with his aorta. This made the removal of the tumor prob-
lematic: a cut too deep or in the wrong direction could rupture it,
and Win could have bled to death on the operating table.

In the end everything went well with the procedure itself, but
during the operation the surgeon noticed that the cancerous cells
had spread to more of the surrounding tissues than they'd initially
realized.

"You have to have radiation," the surgeon insisted as he stood
over Win's hospital bed. "We can wait to see how your body reacts
before we move ahead with chemo, but that's a distinct possibility
too."

Two days later, Win was released into the care of a private
nurse, who drove him home and stayed in Wrightwood with him
for a week, until he was able to look after himself.

Recovery from the surgery wasn't too bad, but the fatigue he experienced from the six weeks of radiation therapy was overwhelming. The treatment sessions were mercifully short, about thirty minutes each, but kicked his ass so hard he would often only be able to drive as far as his brother's apartment before having to take a break.

Wally had risen to become maître d' at a popular French bistro in Sherman Oaks and had a nice rented two-bedroom in nearby Van Nuys, an easy stop on Win's route home from his treatments. Sometimes he'd nap on Wally's guest bed before getting back on the road, but toward the end of those six grueling weeks, he would often just sleep over.

Luckily, his post-radiation diagnosis was good enough that he didn't need to undergo chemo, news that felt like a hard rain after months of drought.

Eighteen months . . . and he still wasn't a hundred percent. Hell, he'd just passed out. *Why don't they tell you these things?* Everyone here was among the very small circle of friends he'd let in on it.

He cleared his throat. "Anything happen I should know about?"

Grover and Teddy glanced at each other.

Win's eyes bounced between them. "What?" Then he asked again. *"What?"*

"They just said they wanted your money?" Teddy asked. "Not how much?"

"Like Clare said on the video," Win replied, "everything I got."

"Right before you went down," said Grover carefully, "you said you didn't have any money."

"Yeah, that's right." The implications were sinking in again, as they had before he'd blacked out. "I'm broke."

In one sense, Win could say that he had beaten cancer, but in another, there was no question it had gotten the better of him. In more ways than one. Most entertainment health insurance is granted on an earned-income basis, so an actor needs to maintain a certain level of income each year to be continually covered. The year before Win's surgery had been a lean one, and his coverage had lapsed.

The worst part of it was that he hadn't even been aware he was no longer covered. All the notices the union had sent offering him the option to buy the insurance on his own dime had gone to his old PO box in Silver Lake. Most of the time, he was good about checking the mail, but he had gotten out of the habit of dropping by, and missed the notices. All of them.

"At least you hung up before you said it," said Teddy. "That coulda blown this thing up in ways you never get back."

"Actually, there's more . . ."

During that lean year that had preceded his diagnosis, around a decade after his wife's death, Win was struggling. He was five years sober, and the endless heat, the lack of work, the unrelenting parade of regrets—all of it had conspired to awaken the demon within.

One Saturday evening, halfway through the summer, he was lying awake in his upstairs bedroom with the windows open, listening to the forest, wanting to feel something besides loneliness. Eyes wide open, he couldn't stop thinking about his late wife. Joan. *Joanie.*

Their life together ended on a day that should have been a moment of peace. Clare had plans to spend the weekend with a friend from middle school, so Joan had suggested they spend a quiet couple of days at the Wrightwood house. Just the two of them.

Win's drinking had taken a shocking turn of late. Whenever he had a start date looming (he was scheduled to start a new picture in less than a month), he would begin to taper off. But for weeks leading up to this trip, he'd been skipping his diet and exercise routine and increasing his daily intake of booze. He would launch in the late mornings with beer or wine and then work up to the hard stuff. By dinnertime, Joanie would have to wake him from the "nap" brought on by his crashing blood sugar levels.

But by their second night at the big old house, he'd gotten into the swing, and he put together a candlelit dinner. They'd laughed a lot, easy in the way parents are when their child is out of the house, pretending for a moment they were still carefree. They'd gone to bed, the dishes left in the sink till morning. As they had lain tangled in each other's arms, Joanie had said her plan for the morning was to make breakfast and then spend the day walking the hills.

That had sounded like a fine plan to Win the night before, but he'd woken up on Sunday morning with a hangover, already thinking about his first drink. He'd come into the kitchen as Joan was slicing potatoes, onions, and bell pepper for her special home fries. She'd said good morning and reminded him about their planned walk. But instead of saying, "Great," or "Can't wait," he'd snapped at her.

"How about you just hand me some hair of the dog," he'd said, followed by words he'd obsessed over ever since: "And you can do that walk on your own. Maybe give me a little peace in this life."

He'd known as they left his lips his words were inexcusable, but his hangover was leading the charge, and he'd followed it.

"No reason to ruin this perfectly fine day before it even starts."

She'd dropped the spatula on the counter and turned off the burner beneath the pan.

"You know what?" she'd said as she wiped her hands. "Today might be a good day to spend on your own. In fact, why don't we make it a whole week."

Joan had swiped up her purse and keys and headed for the front door. Stunned at his own callousness, Win heard the door slam behind her, followed by the sound of the Mazda RX7 he'd bought her for her fortieth birthday, firing up.

She might have intended to head back to their Silver Lake condo or to pick up Clare early, but he'd never know. She'd driven straight down the mountain to Highway 138 and taken a right, which would bring her into LA from the east, usually the fastest route on the weekends. But an exhausted trucker coming from the opposite direction fell asleep at the wheel and drifted across the freeway into her lane. The loaded eighteen-wheeler struck her car head on, demolishing the little Mazda and killing her instantly.

When the highway patrol called, Win was drinking an ice-cold lager at the breakfast table, trying to convince himself the fight had been her fault. He hung up the Trimline phone, went to the downstairs bathroom behind the kitchen, and threw up. Shaking and numb, he called the parents of Clare's friend and asked if she could stay for a little longer while he went to the hospital to identify Joanie's remains. Two days later, father and daughter accompanied Joan's body to her hometown of Madison, Wisconsin, to be buried next to her parents and maternal grandparents.

Somehow, *Look, Don't Touch!* learned about the funeral plans and sent a reporter to cover the event. The next day, photos of a grieving Winston Greene generated the highest volume of online traffic their website had ever seen.

So, instead of staying put that hot, lonely Saturday night, Win made the mistake that so many addicts make, especially those who isolate themselves in a mountain home far away from any kind of support system. By that point he had been sober for so long he believed he was over the hump, that he could have a drink now and then without fear of relapse. He made a choice then that has haunted him in the way all his other bad choices have: he got up, dressed in T-shirt and jeans, and headed out. It was only around nine thirty PM, so he knew something would be open.

He wound up at the Midnight Caller, a popular spot near the center of town, known for its pizza, burgers, and strong drinks. Once someone's home, the large A-frame had an ample rectangular main room with tongue-and-groove flooring and exposed beams in the ceiling. Scattered among the vintage hunting and ski artifacts on the walls were several flat screens, silently broadcasting everything from college sports to TCM. The "bandstand" was a cleared space at one end of the room. The menu encouraged patrons to "Munch, Gulp, 'n' Giggle."

A four-piece cover band was just getting through its improvisational take on the Doobies' "Black Water," replete with electric guitar and keyboard solos. The aroma of hamburger, pepperoni, and bacon grease mixed with the pungent aerosol of beer was seductive. Win slipped into the room and found a place at one end of the crowded bar.

Seated next to him was a local, a scrappy older fellow known as Cookie. He wore a faded denim vest over a black motorcycle jacket, his full white beard half covering a face of deep lines and blotchy skin. A red bandana covered his bald pate. Cookie, who had a smile full of alcoholic levity, liked to boast that he could be found on this same bar stool pretty much any night of the week.

He flashed a faint look of surprise at seeing Win in the bar at this hour. Win might grab lunch or a late breakfast there, but never showed up on a packed Saturday night, when food was hardly uppermost on patrons' minds. Plus, everyone in town was aware of Win's sobriety.

The bartender, Wanda, her bleached-blond hair cascading over her pear-shaped body, walked over and asked in a scratchy voice, "Whatcha' have, honey?"

Win leaned over and self-consciously whispered his order, which Wanda couldn't hear over the din. She cocked her head in that way that said *"Come again?"* He repeated himself and she poured a healthy Maker's Mark bourbon, neat, along with an ice-cold Sierra Nevada Pale Ale from the tap and set them on the bar in front of him.

Cookie raised his own mug in a toast, and they clinked their glasses together. Win took his first sip of beer in five years, relishing the crisp, frothy brew as it rolled over his tongue and down his gullet. Then he gazed down at the glass of whiskey, lifted it, pausing to appreciate the woody aroma, and took a nip.

The caramel liquid stung the inside of his mouth, bringing with it a flood of memories and sensations. He downed the remainder in one gulp and felt the satisfying heat as it spread across his chest.

Cookie grinned and stroked his beard. "Another?"

Win nodded.

Cookie raised a hand to Wanda, pointed down and wagged his index finger back and forth in the sign language of the barfly: *"Another round for me and my friend."*

By closing time, Win was wearing Cookie's bandana and denim vest, and regaling him, Wanda, and the few remaining stragglers with insider stories of Hollywood. Why, on one of Win's first shoots, it took six takes to get one shot of him galloping a horse through the front gate of a replica of the Alamo that John Wayne had built near the Rio Grande back in the 1960s. The spirited stallion had been featured as a champion racehorse in a Robert Redford movie and just kept bolting past the gate. After five feeble attempts by Win, a stunt rider in a dirty-blond wig and hat pulled low had to be called in to finish the scene.

The next morning, his head feeling simultaneously crushed and on fire, he wondered how he'd made it home. He fought his hangover with eggs, coffee, and Advil, then got in his car and dropped by Hanson's Market for a twelve-pack of Sierra Nevada and a fifth of Maker's.

Two months later, as autumn finally arrived, Teddy drove him to a detox facility in Pasadena for an extended rehab. Winston left clean and sober and determined to make it stick this time. His determination was tested almost immediately afterward when he received his cancer diagnosis and then had surgery, followed by the radiation treatment.

Then the bills began to arrive, more than two hundred thousand dollars' worth, and he was forced to confront the terrible mistake he'd made by letting his insurance lapse during his backslide into inebriation. He bit the bullet and paid it all off, clearing out both his savings and retirement accounts (including a hefty penalty for early withdrawal) and leaving him with credit card debt to the tune of thirty grand. He'd finally cleared that one just a few months ago.

On the plus side, he had oodles of airline miles he could use someday.

Lauren, Grover, and Teddy just stared at Win, astonished, wondering how he could have allowed himself to end up in this predicament.

Win ran through his bank accounts in his mind as he lay there on Grover's couch, but it didn't amount to much more than walking-around money. What little extra income he did make he spent on Clare, Zeke, and Amy, to ensure his granddaughter had three squares and a roof over her head. *Thank God I paid off that big ol' house back when I could.*

After a minute of enduring their stunned silence, Win spoke: "These people think I'm loaded."

And those same people must have thought the dead man from Santa Fe Springs was loaded too. And would they deal with Clare the same way they had with him when they found out how little Win could cough up?

"Oh Jesus," said Win, "what am I gonna do?"

19

SYLMAR

C LARE WAS GOING to need the bucket soon.
   The shakes had gotten so bad at one point that she
thought she might crack her teeth. The tremors in her torso and
extremities were violent enough that she couldn't get off the floor
for a good long while. But once that passed, the nausea welled up.
She hadn't had to use the bucket for anything else yet, so if she
had to boot, at least it would be into a clean receptacle.

   As she lay there fighting the withdrawal symptoms, she regretted with all her heart the moment she and Zeke had met Rocket.
At first it had been great: they'd buy a folded paper bindle of heroin from Rocket and head into the bowling alley's bathroom for a
couple of snorts.

   They were never shooters—needles freaked them out. Limit-
ing themselves to snorting it bolstered their delusion they weren't
junkies. They'd say, "Junkies use needles. We just like to party."

   Now she lay shaking and shivering on the floor of this cellar, imagining which end of her body would empty out first. She
wondered how Zeke was holding up. Bitterly, she imagined he was
just fine, probably high at this very moment. *Dad was right—I
should've left him.*

   Hot saliva rose in her throat, and she barely crawled to the
bucket in time. As her body convulsed, she thought back to the

days when she'd drag those black garbage bags full of puke out of her father's bedroom. She wished she had a plastic bag to pull over her head and suffocate herself right now. When she was done throwing up, she gazed at the puddle of clear gastric acid at the bottom of the bucket and tried to remember when she'd last eaten. *What I really need is water.* And soon she would need a real bathroom.

She tried to remember who she used to be. Before Zeke. Before Amy. After her mother died, she tried different creative outlets, hoping to fill the painful void with something constructive. Though both her parents were thespians, she'd never once considered acting, preferring to find something outside of her father's shadow. The last thing she wanted was to ask him for help. She'd tried painting, which she had some aptitude for, but realized if she made it in her vocation, she'd likely move to the desert and become a rageful Georgia O'Keeffe. She picked up the guitar, tried her hand at writing songs, and even started a girl band with some friends from school. They started getting some small gigs, mostly private beach and pool parties, but one of them got pregnant and dropped out, another got into college early, and the momentum fizzled. She didn't know if it was a character flaw or just the natural course of things, but when the breaks didn't come fast enough, she lost interest. It was around that time that Clare started using with intention. *I guess that's what they mean by "youth is wasted on the young,"* she thought.

At that very moment, perhaps the lowest point in her life, a simple, desperate plan of escape began to form in her mind, kindling a tiny flicker of hope.

PART 5

KATE: "I mean, it's like you cain't never win!"

FRANK: "Yeah. An' I'm sure gettin' tired o' losin'."

—Bettye Allen and Winston Greene
in *Angel Star* (2012)

CHAPTER

20

VENICE BEACH

"YOU HAVE *NOTHING*?" Lauren asked.

The three faces staring down at Win made him feel cornered.

"I have some . . . just not a whole lot," Win answered.

"Win," said Grover, "you've been working as long as I've known you. Even with everything that's happened, I'd think you'd have a pretty good pile."

"I sure didn't expect the hospital to be so much," Win said.

"Yeah, but still . . ."

Still prone on the sofa, Win looked at the ceiling in weary vexation—he'd had this conversation with himself for years and always arrived at the same conclusion. "It's not like I was ever top ten," he said, referring to the status of what had to be, outside of being an astronaut, about the most exclusive club in the world: The Top 10 Box Office Draw. It was a room that only allowed entrance to a rarefied few, perpetually recognizable surnames like Redford, Fonda, Newman, Streep. "I've been banging out B-movies for the last twenty years," Win continued. "I'm still lucky to be the guy on the poster, but this business has been the land of diminishing returns for a long time now. Nobody makes what people think we do. The last strike proved that."

Grover, even with his highly specialized profession that mostly sustained his level of income, nodded in agreement. They'd all seen a lot of successful, experienced colleagues truly struggle over the last several years.

"And you let your insurance lapse?" Lauren asked, forcing Win's attention back to the problem at hand. He could tell she was trying to keep the judgment out of her tone, but a hint came through anyway. He had always admired how she put her family ahead of everything, and the disappointment in Lauren's voice wounded him. Failing to do everything you could to protect your loved ones—including taking care of yourself, especially if you were the sole provider—was anathema to her.

Ever since his operation, he had lived with the worry that something might catch him by surprise again, though his daughter being kidnapped would have been far down that list. Writing the check to the hospital that had cleaned out his accounts had given him both a sense of relief and introduced a low hum of foreboding that had dogged his everyday existence since.

"I kept it pretty quiet. You know how it is in this town: You get a hangnail, and then a rumor goes around that you lost a leg. It's hard to get work again."

Lauren sighed, then nodded. "Yeah."

"I screwed up," Win said. "Been putting it all back together ever since." She looked sympathetic, but he noticed she didn't try to reassure him. He'd fucked up, big-time. No two ways about it.

Teddy chimed in. "Well, there's proof to the phrase 'When it rains, it pours.' So, if it comes to it, how much *do* you have?"

Win raised himself up on one elbow. His head swirled. "Probably twenty-five, thirty thousand? Maybe I could unload my car quick . . . And there's always the house."

Win watched his three friends' heads pivot as they glanced at each other.

"We should see about supper," said Lauren, standing up from the sofa. "The kids'll be getting famished. How about we order in? And I think our guests should join us."

"Good idea," Grover replied, pulling out his cell phone to open a food delivery app. "You guys okay with Indian? The kids love it."

"Sure," Teddy said. "That's very kind of you."

"I know Amy would love that," Win said.

"Speaking of, you might want to try to keep that house," said Grover. "I got a feeling she's going to need a place to live when this is done."

CHAPTER

21

SYLMAR

"**F**OR FUCK'S SAKE!" Clare screamed. *"I need to take a shit!"*
"So use the bucket," she heard Ozzie say from the other side of the door. He sounded like his patience with her was running short. "That what it's for."

"I threw up in it. It's bad enough in here already." She drew in a breath. *"Please!"* She knew why they kept her down here in the cellar—they figured she wouldn't be heard outside. She hoped they were wrong.

"Look, I'll pee in it, but you can't ask me to do that, too," Clare said. "I mean, would you want to come down here after I did that? I have to eat sometime, and you're going to have to bring it to me . . . You can even watch me, just don't make me do it in here!"

"Who says you're gonna eat?"

She heard him chuckle at his own joke, then waited, hoping for an answer. When she didn't get one, she said quietly, "Please? Just let me use the bathroom."

Ozzie sighed. "You stay there until I tell you to come up. Got it?"

"Yeah. Okay," she answered. Then she heard a dead-bolt slide.

She watched the door from the bottom of the steps and followed the sound of the locks as each bolt retracted, three evenly spaced gadgets in a vertical row, iron bolts sliding out of the door's frame, top to bottom. The knob turned and the door opened just enough to reveal the barrel of the pistol Ozzie was aiming down the stairwell.

"You stay in front of me," Ozzie commanded. "No bullshit."

Her hand quivered as she took hold of the railing to pull herself up the steps. Her legs felt weak under her, like her bones might crack under her own weight. She took the stairs one step at a time, her eyes glued to Ozzie's pistol.

It was a large-caliber automatic, similar to the kind her father often carried when he portrayed yet another of his "world-weary" B-movie detectives. Actors always bandied them about like they knew how to use one, and made the viewer believe that they would. She hated them. To her, they represented what a phony her father was. But she knew that in Ozzie's hand, it meant death. She also knew her chances of taking it from him, skinny as he was, were too low to contemplate.

Ozzie stepped back as she reached the doorway and came into the hall. He directed her with his free hand, his other keeping the barrel trained on her torso. His face had an oily sheen that made his acne scars even more pronounced.

"Left," he said as she reached a doorway a few feet down the hall.

She glimpsed the living room at the end of the hall, a few more feet down and to the right, cluttered with worn furniture and its windows covered by aging Levolors. What if she made a run for the front door? It was no more than twelve, fifteen feet from where she stood, just on the other side the living room. *No.* Too much ground to cover, plenty of space for Ozzie to shoot her in the back.

"What're you waiting for?" Ozzie said. "I thought you were in such a fucking hurry."

She looked into the bathroom and saw immediately that the one small window was closed, and there were bars on the outside. Must not be a great neighborhood if someone felt the washroom had to be protected like that.

"Don't even think about the window," Ozzie said from behind her. "I'll kill you."

Clare knew he liked to mess with people—she'd seen him torment the druggie clientele at the bowling alley plenty of times—but this felt different. Vicious. "I won't."

Ozzie gave her a humorless smile as she went into the bathroom.

It was a step back in time, maybe even worse than the bathroom at her and Zeke's place, if that was possible. Everything had once been a bright and cheery hue of green, yellow, or red. A small linen closet. Worn, cracked Formica across the counter and around the stained sink bowl. An oxidized faucet flanked by rusty hot and cold handles over a cabinet with flimsy, uneven doors. The mirror above the sink had small flowers engraved around the edge, in defiance of the pervasive stench. Black mold was working its way toward the center of the mirror glass, breaking up the ancient silvering.

Two ratted lace window curtains held back no light and offered little privacy. The commode was beyond the tub, against the wall to the right of the window. It was dark outside. She looked back at Ozzie.

"Get it over with," he said, and surprised her by pulling the door partially shut. Not closed, but enough to give her a semblance of separateness.

She turned and dropped her pants, suddenly nervous he might change his mind and drag her, jeans around her knees, back to the cellar and throw her down the stairs. She sat and got settled, took a breath and . . . nothing.

"C'mon!" he commanded.

"I'm sorry," she answered. "Just give me a minute. I've never done this with someone right there."

The door swung closed even more. Apparently, Ozzie didn't want to experience this kind of sharing either.

"Can I turn on the water? Sometimes that helps."

"*Jesus.* Okay."

She raised up and stretched to reach the faucet. The pressure wasn't great, but it ran. She sat back down and told herself to relax. It worked. The relief came in a cascade, and suddenly she was done. Her heart fell a notch when she looked to the paper holder and saw an empty cardboard roll, a fingernail-sized remnant of tissue stuck to it. She glanced around and found a half-used roll on the floor, next to her feet, and snatched it up.

"Almost done," she said, but then remembered this meant she was going back to that cellar. She tried to think of something, anything to keep the conversation going. She flushed and pulled up her jeans. "So, why did you guys do this? You didn't have to—we had it all worked out."

They were supposed to fake this whole thing! She was supposed to just stay out of sight until they got the money. She'd been certain her father was so guilt-ridden over her mother's death that he'd pay anything to get his daughter back, no questions asked.

"Insurance. Now get out here."

"Just gotta wash my hands," she said, and turned on the hot faucet. "Insurance? It's not like I was going anywhere."

"I said hurry up."

She dried her hands on a stiff towel hanging on a ring, took a cursory look in the mirror to steel herself, and left the bathroom.

"Thank you," she said, and then glanced again into the living room. "Where's Rocket?"

"Oh, he's over at none-of-your-fucking-business," said Ozzie. "Now move."

Her mind raced as she walked down the hallway. If she could get around that coffee table in the middle of that front room, she could use it as an obstacle to anyone chasing her and maybe give herself time to get out the front door. She'd have to wait for the right opportunity.

She heard a squeaking sound, rhythmic and light, followed by two quick shuffles—*squeak chh-chh, squeak chh-chh*—coming from the far end of the hallway, beyond the cellar, where two bedroom doorways separated at the end of the hall.

An old person's voice, too scratchy for Clare to be able to identify its gender, mumbled on about something, and she realized what she was hearing: Someone was using a walker on the other side of one of those doors, the two wobbly front wheels chirping under the weight and overuse. As she and Ozzie approached the cellar door, she could just make out the words, "What's going on out there? Who's here?"

Clare turned and looked at Ozzie, who aimed his gun at her chest and then cocked his head toward the basement.

She went down a few steps and turned to see the door swing shut, followed by the clank of dead bolts. She tiptoed back up and put her ear against the door, trying to listen. A couple seconds later she heard Ozzie's voice, sounding far away and with a different tone to it.

"I told you, you shouldn't be out of bed. C'mon, let's get you back in there . . ."

Then his voice trailed off, leaving her alone again.

22

Venice Beach

Throughout dinner, the Washingtons were all chatter and laughter. Extra chairs were brought in by the older kids to accommodate everyone at the dining table: Lauren, Grover, their four children, Teddy, and Winston, with Amy seated next to him.

At one point there was a heated discussion among the Washington children about who deserved more saag, citing examples from the previous night's dinner, when *someone* had apparently had more than their fair share of lasagna. The guests found it amusing, but then Grover announced that if they couldn't work it out pronto, he'd just eat it all, which they knew he could and would. A bargain was quickly made, and dinner carried on.

"If you don't mind my asking," Teddy said to Lauren, who was seated next to him, "how is it that your children are at home on a school day?"

Lauren smiled in a way that suggested she was used to answering this question. "We made the decision to homeschool our kids, *Officer*."

"I apologize, ma'am," Teddy said, his face beginning to flush. "I meant no disrespect—"

"Oh, hush—I'm just teasing. Asking questions must be in your DNA. Honestly, we have nothing against public education, but while I was carrying our first, I read several studies that showed children educated at home tended to do better as adults. Grover was doing quite well with his career, so by the time kindergarten was approaching, I didn't have to work. And that's why our children are sometimes mistaken as truants."

Teddy chuckled, both at her explanation and at her accurate observation of him.

Amy spread tikka masala sauce over her mound of yellow saffron rice, carefully removing the chunks of chicken. She slathered some of the sweet brown chutney on top, smushed it all together, and scooped up a big mouthful. She was hungry, having only snacked since the bowl of cereal Win had given her that morning. Win stared at the food on his plate.

"Do you want some of mine, Grandpa?"

"What's that, honey?"

"I thought you liked this stuff."

He forced a smile. "I do, honey. I guess I'm just not that hungry. You go ahead and gobble yours up."

CHAPTER

23

SCOTT BRANOVICH STRODE into the *Look, Don't Touch!* offices, annoyed with himself. He was known to have the well-honed instincts of a bloodhound, and they had failed him.

With his own eyes he'd seen Winston Greene, his granddaughter, and another man he was pretty sure was a disgraced LAPD cop from somewhere down South go into Greene's daughter's house, stay awhile, and come back out and leave. Then he'd wasted his opportunity to get a scoop by talking to Greene's useless son-in-law.

He should have followed Greene. He knew something was up. Just the day before he'd gotten an email from someone calling themselves IndecentExposure@anonymousemail.me containing a tip about the actor: *Winston Greene is about to have some BIG trouble with his kid. I bet someone like you would like to know what it is.*

"IndecentExposure" had clearly been onto something. Maybe even knew more about what was going on than their vague email suggested, though they hadn't responded to any of the questions Branovich had sent in response.

Branovich was the most productive reporter *LDT* had. He'd broken more stories about broken stars than anyone here. He was, at thirty-two, becoming something of a legend among the gossipmongers. And he was well paid. The more dirt he dug up, the bigger the paychecks. And the yearly bonuses made all the hard work—and, yes, the occasional moral compromises—worth it. His casual-chic Rodeo Drive wardrobe sure didn't suffer.

He'd cultivated an image as a "reporter of the people," having years earlier made the decision not to be ostentatious when he was interviewing people, celebrities or everyday joes. That kind of behavior might be fine for the cheaper class of his profession, but it wasn't his style, and he was sure he'd risen as quickly and as far as he had because of his modest approach. Sure, he had a nice, quiet house in the hills, with a pool and a gym and a sauna, but the Tesla stayed in the garage until he had a hot date. He drove the decade-old blue coupe to work.

These days, most of his stories were about those in the public eye, celebrities. *That's* where the money was, in exposés of somewhat talented, spoiled, self-indulgent stars. They acted badly in plain sight, practically begging people to point their cell phones at them and let the world know about their embarrassments. And *LDT* was happy to send Branovich over with a satchel of cash to purchase the footage. And he'd nailed all kinds: a TV actor involved in a hit-and-run, a rock star secretly entering rehab, a smitten actress sending nude selfies to her intended, to list a few.

But he blew it, failed to follow his instincts. Winston Greene, the once-bright star who'd pretty much flamed out, was the story here, not the screwed-up daughter. She might be the linchpin, the inciting event, but Winston was clearly the lead actor in this drama. Something may have happened to her—her brain-dead husband Zeke was definitely hiding something—but the star is the one the world wants to hear about, not the supporting cast. *Hell, she could be dead, and she's* still *not the story.*

Sure, people would want to know what stupid thing she did, but only in the context of how it screwed up Winston Greene's career. And Branovich had let him get away! *What the hell was I thinking?*

Branovich decided to stop beating himself up. He checked his watch and saw it was almost seven o'clock. Day thirty-four of his P90X class was starting soon. He could make it if he left now. *No.* He had to get to work, be the crackerjack newsman he knew he was.

He punched up Greene's file on his computer and started scanning through it.

Now, who would Winston Greene turn to if he needed help?

24

VENICE BEACH

As HE INFLATED the blow-up bed Grover had rolled out for him, Win could feel Amy's eyes on him. She was sitting on the sofa, outfitted by Lauren with bedclothes and a pillow, watching him work. He'd moved the coffee table across the living room and placed the bed parallel to the sofa, so if Amy woke up in the night from bad dreams or because she had to use the bathroom, he would be right there, next to her.

Win could tell that Amy knew something was very wrong in her world, and why wouldn't she? Her mother had been ripped away from her early that morning, and her daddy hadn't stopped it. Then she'd been dumped by a scary man at Grandpa's house. He might be the only anchor she had left. By the end of dinner, everyone had noticed that she only wanted to talk to him. And though he had been preoccupied by thoughts of what Clare was going through, and how ill-prepared he was to save her, Win had done his best to answer his granddaughter's questions and give her all the attention he could muster.

Now, Amy wouldn't let him leave her sight. There was no way she was going to let him disappear on her too. Win was doing everything he could to ease her anxiety, but tomorrow he was going to have to leave her with the Washingtons. He was sure they would make her feel safe and secure, and welcome, but he felt terrible for the kid. Who at her age could be expected to handle this kind of trauma?

And the constant worry was making him sick. No wonder he had no appetite, imagining how this horror show might end. He had envisioned all manner of outcomes, including multiple scenarios that featured his daughter's dead body lying on a roadside. Or what if she just disappeared, and he never learned what had happened to her? That, he feared, would drive him mad. And even if he was able to come up with a ransom and save Clare by selling his house and all his belongings, that would just mean more disruption and poverty for Amy. It enraged him to think that these people, who wouldn't give a donkey's ass if Amy ever had another bite to eat or a place to sleep, had such power over him. Whatever happened to Clare or him (or Zeke, he grudgingly thought), he had to make sure Amy would be cared for.

Amy. So many years ahead for her. So many he wouldn't see, even if he survived what was coming for them.

He smoothed the top blanket on her makeshift bed with his palm. "This gonna work for you? I can make it softer if you want."

She answered him by hugging him as hard as she could. Then he sent her on her last bathroom visit for the night and tucked her in when she returned. Last of all, he handed her the threadbare, stuffed puppy she always kept by her side, but Amy pushed it back at him.

"You keep it," she said.

"What?"

"You take her. She'll watch over you."

"It's okay, honey, you can—"

"No! *You* take her!"

He realized then that her insistence was a desperate attempt to exert some control over a situation that was, even to her little mind, uncontrollable. He felt his throat constrict.

"Okay. She'll keep an eye on me, and I'll keep an eye on you. Deal?"

"Deal."

"Now try to sleep. I'll be right here. If you need something, just say so. Okay?"

"Okay. 'Night, Grandpa."

"'Night, Amy."

Grover settled his kids into bed, then went upstairs, where Lauren was finishing the last of her nightly beauty routine.

Their spacious bedroom offered spectacular sunset views, but after dark they pulled the drapes for privacy from the neighbors. Normally, it was his routine to pull them shut, but he saw Lauren had already done it.

The foundation of Lauren and Grover's relationship had been laid more than two decades earlier, when they'd fallen in love as juniors at Venice High. It had only gotten stronger as they took their first steps into adulthood together, Lauren to Loyola Marymount College a few miles south, Grover to Hollywood success. In all the years since, nothing had unsettled their stable world, not really. But today they'd opened their home to an old friend, and he had brought with him his granddaughter and a jolting dose of uncertainty.

"I'm thinking I should go with him tomorrow," Grover said. He'd closed the door so they could talk privately, and taken a seat on the bed.

"I know you are," said Lauren, without turning around. "I think so too."

Her back was to him, but Grover could see her face in the mirror as she applied moisturizer. Her skin was like umber cream as it was, with no wrinkles even as she approached her forty-fifth birthday. He still felt the blind love for her that he had back in high school.

"You're a good friend," she said, digging through a drawer. "And he sure needs one right now."

"I would say take them all to your mom's," said Grover, "but since your dad's stroke . . ."

She shook her head in agreement. "He can't take the excitement." She stood and went to sit next to him on the bed. "Don't worry, we all know what to do. We'll be all right."

He nodded, then put his arm around her as she nestled into him. "Win's lost his way from time to time. I hope this isn't one of them."

"I don't think it is." She sighed. "But this feels like the universe just up and decided to rain on us."

Grover looked at her, as impressed as ever by her wisdom. "I admit this whole thing makes me a little edgy."

"It damn well should," she said. "His daughter's been kidnapped, and you know as well as I do that never turns out well, even when it does."

He searched her eyes, really looking at her. "Thank you."

"I didn't do anything."

"Yes, you did. You always do." He drew a breath and let it out in a rush, releasing some of the tension he was feeling with it. She always had that effect on him too. He got up to open the door. "Sometimes I wish there were two of me."

"Tell me about it," she said with a flirtatious wink.

25

THE 10 FREEWAY (EAST), 5 MILES SOUTH OF HOLLYWOOD

TEDDY ROLLED DOWN the 10 Freeway eastbound from Venice on his way to his Echo Park neighborhood. Even late on a Wednesday, the traffic was heavy. As he navigated the other vehicles, his attention drifted back to his evening with the Washington family.

He imagined what life would be like, grounded like theirs seemed to be. He hadn't known a family life since his older brother, Chuck, had been gunned down on Elysian Fields Avenue one night by a small-time dope addict and petty crook. "Home" had disintegrated quickly after that. His father had disappeared into a swamp of alcohol, and his mother had just plain disappeared.

Teddy came home from high school one day, and she was gone, having taken only a coat, her purse, and a framed picture of Chuck that had hung in the hallway of their Bywater house. For all Teddy knew, she had spent the rest of her life mourning her older son's death while waitressing at a diner in the bayou, ignoring the fact that she had left another son behind. By the time he graduated from high school and got a job bagging groceries at a local supermarket, his father was dead from cirrhosis.

Chuck's death and its aftermath had shaped Teddy's worldview: He hated crooks. Big-time, small-time, he hated them all equally. And he would've done just about anything to bring them down.

The detective who had first responded to his mother's missing person's report took an interest in the teenager, dropping by now and again to check on him in the weeks and months afterward. He even brought Teddy to a station look-see. Teddy got interested in the job, the interest held, and on his twentieth birthday he successfully applied to the NOPD. By working hard as a rookie and then as a beat cop, solving hot cases and cold ones, Teddy made detective before turning thirty.

But he never caught the scumbag who'd killed his brother and destroyed his family.

When a new movie began filming in town, Teddy—being young, decorated, and dashing (in a Big Easy sort of way)—was given the plum assignment of technical advisor to the film and its star, Winston Greene.

They hit it off, finding acres of common ground in their childhood experiences and appetites. Teddy enjoyed the work, helping trace the arc of Win's character, and together they worked through the best ways to play every step of the story's plot points. And this being pre-sobriety for them both, Teddy delighted in introducing his new friend to the best local watering holes.

One day on set, Teddy broached the idea of making a move west, and Win offered to help. Maybe scare him up some more advisory work to bridge the gap until he found something steady. Teddy made the leap and moved to LA, joining the LAPD. Within two years, he was a detective in his new city, assigned to the Highland Park Division.

Then his rigid worldview got him in trouble.

It was a simple case to make: a small-time dealer and addict named Rodney Willis had left behind a DNA sample while robbing a Bank of America branch in Highland Park. Sweat had dripped under his plastic Halloween mask and off his chin onto the counter. Rodney's extensive rap sheet made identifying him a cinch—Teddy had him locked up in no time. While Rodney was awaiting trial, Teddy went to interview Rodney's live-in girlfriend, Deborah. A transplant from New York's Upper West Side (and also an addict), she made Teddy an offer: "Lean back and let me take care of you." In return, Teddy would make the DNA evidence disappear. Then she'd take care of Teddy again. And again, if he liked.

Teddy took her up on it because . . . well, because she and Rodney were crooks. And because he never intended to shitcan the DNA—that would go against his worldview, cutting a crook loose like that. And because he decided he wanted to punish them both, not just one of them. So, he testified at the trial with his trademark, crusading-crime-fighter-with-a-drawl act, and Rodney was convicted.

Turned out Deborah wasn't as dense as Teddy had thought (dumb assumption on his part) as she had collected some DNA evidence of her own, causing quite a reaction in the DA's office. Rodney's case was thrown out, and he was released with a nice payout (far larger than the bank haul). Teddy was fired, a shame to the force. He tried to make the case that, technically, he hadn't actually been bribed since he hadn't tampered with the evidence, but he knew it was hopeless. He'd screwed the pooch and his LAPD career was over.

Red lights! Teddy snapped out of his reverie just in time to stomp on the brakes, nearly rear-ending a stopped car in front of him. The traffic had slowed to a near-standstill at the downtown interchange, as usual. He could feel his heart pounding all the way up to his temples. He took a breath and caught a glimpse of himself in his rearview mirror. *You look tired, Teddy boy. You're only forty-seven, and you look tired and overweight and used up.*

Then he reminded himself that he was good at this. The job. Always had been.

Winston Greene was one of the few true friends he had. He wanted to help him through this, recover his daughter unharmed, and get their lives back to normal. But he was also in it for himself: Unlike the sordid gigs that came his way these days, this case made him feel like a cop again.

PART 6

Okay, numb nuts, how is it you won two world championships, and now you can't even make your rent?

—Winston Greene in *Warrior Son* (2015)

26

VENICE BEACH

S UNRISE HAD ALWAYS been Win's favorite time of day. Today he dreaded it.

He'd lain awake most of the night, listening to Amy's soft snoring and seeking relief from the thoughts swirling in his head. He desperately needed sleep, but then the morning light would arrive that much sooner. By staying awake, he told himself he was holding off the dawn as long as possible. Now that it was here, he wished he had gotten some rest.

He pulled his jeans on over his boxers, picked up his smartphone from where it was charging on the coffee table, and crept to the bathroom, stopping to set Amy's stuffed puppy next to her. Without waking, she rolled her little body and wrapped a tiny arm around it.

He could only imagine the dreams she was having, but at least she was asleep. That counted for something.

They'd stayed awake well past her bedtime as he answered her questions about everything that had happened to her: Mommy was with some bad people, and he didn't know when she might come back. That her daddy needed to stay home for now, and that she was better off right here, with her grandpa and their friends who love them. Now was no time for false assurances that her world would soon go back to the way it was, but he wanted her to know that no matter what happened, she'd be safe.

He pulled the bathroom door shut behind him, then sat on the edge of the tub and swiped open his phone. Today was Thursday. He had to find a way to get these assholes what they wanted, probably before end of business Friday. He was worried about what could happen to Clare if he tried to put them off over the weekend.

He launched the web browser and typed in his bank website, which loaded almost instantly. The Washingtons had three children of web-browsing age, so they had monster Wi-Fi. He quickly found his branch: business hours, nine to six. Traffic permitting, he could be there by nine thirty latest, and have an answer as to what he could liquidate by ten. Not having an exact amount made all this much more difficult—how much would he need? He figured he would just clear out the account and hope it would be enough.

He cracked the door and peeked out. Amy was still sleeping, so he decided to grab the shower he didn't get yesterday. He found a clean towel in the cabinet under the sink, turned on the water, stripped, and stepped in. It felt better than he expected. His current haircut was stick-up-straight short, and he could probably go another day without needing to wash it, but he loved the sense of renewal a shower brought. He lathered up and rinsed, then used the sliver thin bar of soap, which was one shower away from being replaced, to clean the rest of his body.

Before shutting off the stream, he turned off the hot flow and braced himself for a cold jolt. In the lowlands of Southern California, house water was never frigid enough to cause a heart attack, but it served this morning's purpose: to snap the lack of sleep out of him and launch him into what he knew would be a long and trying day.

He dried himself and dressed, balling up the towel to wrap up with his linens. He wanted to get his and Amy's laundry into the washer before the Washingtons insisted on doing it themselves.

He opened the door to find Amy standing outside, holding her stuffed pup and bouncing slightly on her toes. "Did I wake you, honey?"

"I need the bathroom."

"Okay."

He stepped out and she went in. He closed the door behind her, dreading how her life might change again by the end of the day.

27

SYLMAR

CLARE'S EYES OPENED directly into the single lightbulb above her. She squinted, wondering how on earth she could've slept with it on.

She was surprised to have slept at all. With no window to gauge the time, she guessed it was morning. She pushed up to a sitting position. She needed to pee and was relieved to find her appetite had returned somewhat. Good thing she still had the sandwich Ozzie had brought her sometime last night. It sat untouched on a paper plate, and the two paper cups of water next to it were still full.

But the sleep had helped. The shakes had stopped, and she felt steadier, even a little stronger. She relieved herself in the bucket, then dribbled some water from one of the cups into her palms and rubbed them together. She figured a little bit cleaner was better than completely gross. Then she drank the rest of the cup, swishing it around to moisten her mouth before swallowing.

She picked up the sandwich and sniffed. *Tuna.* She hated tuna. She wondered if she'd ever mentioned that to Ozzie, and this was his way of tormenting her. Her stomach growled, reminding her she was a beggar, not a chooser. She unwrapped the sandwich, the bread dry from sitting overnight, and choked it down before chugging the other cup of water.

Then she heard the dead bolts being clicked back, making her heart pound against her ribcage. From her vantage point on the floor, she could see up the stairs to the lower half of the door. It opened and the faint light silhouetted two denim-clad legs. Then a folded newspaper thudded onto the concrete floor at the base of the steps and skidded to a stop.

"Get over here," Rocket demanded.

28

VENICE BEACH

AMY SAT NEXT to Win on the sofa, peering at her tablet while Win scrolled through his bank accounts, adding up his cash and his barely started again IRAs. It wasn't a whole lot. If he could convert everything to cash today, it came to just under twenty-eight thousand dollars.

He'd seen two bad guys, but he figured someone had to keep an eye on Clare, so there had to be at least one more. Split three ways, it wasn't even ten grand each. He couldn't imagine pulling something like this for a payday that wouldn't even buy a decent used car. He was going to have to come up with more, something that would make them walk away once and for all. And the only thing he had that could translate to that kind of money was his house.

Ever since he'd screwed up on his health insurance coverage, he'd come to view his home as his retirement account. It was his, free and clear. Before this, he figured when the time came, he could sell it for a profit, move back to a condo in town or even to the Motion Picture Home out in Woodland Hills (though the idea of assisted living made his skin crawl). He might even be able to leave something for Amy's college fund. He never planned to die in the house—just keep it until it made sense to sell it. Now he was going to have to use it to get his daughter back alive.

His thoughts were interrupted by Lauren's soft voice. "Hey, little girl, there's some waffles in here with your name on 'em."

Win looked up and saw Lauren and Grover in the dining room doorway. He had heard them rummaging around in the kitchen, moving quietly in case Win and Amy might still be asleep. He'd called out to them that they were both up and dressed, and Lauren had come in almost immediately with a steaming mug of black coffee for him and a small glass of apple juice for Amy. Then just as quickly she'd disappeared, and the house began to fill with the inviting aroma of waffle batter, syrup, and bacon.

Amy looked at Win and he said, "Get 'em while they're hot. I want to talk to Uncle Grover."

Grover smiled at Amy as she passed; then he strode into the living room and sat in one of the overstuffed chairs across from Win.

Grover took a beat. "I think I better stick with you today."

"I'd appreciate it but . . . you sure?" Win indicated the kitchen, where they could hear Lauren and Amy debating the best topping for a waffle.

"She'll keep Amy here all day. We talked about it."

Win exhaled a sigh of relief. He'd been hoping they would offer, having felt he'd asked enough favors already. "Thanks. I think it's gonna be a busy one."

Grover nodded. "Then let's get some chow."

29

Echo Park, 5 miles east of Hollywood

TEDDY POURED HIS third cup of chicory coffee. He had been raised on this bitter stuff and never could get used to anything else, which was funny since none of his friends here could ever get used to it. He secretly enjoyed slipping someone a cup of it.

It was one of the few luxuries he allowed himself, paying extra for it at the old Farmer's Market in the Fairfax district, where he also could get a taste of old LA in the form of a slice of Du-par's delectable raspberry pie à la mode.

He went out to the small deck off his front entrance. He had chosen this modest, rustic apartment complex in the hills of Echo Park because it was an easy commute to his old beat in Highland Park but was still distant enough to not feel like he lived where he worked.

He was too tense to sit, so he stood at the railing. If he went to the corner of the deck and craned his neck a bit, he could just see the crest of the fountains down in Echo Park Lake to the south, where Jack Nicholson stole photos of Mr. Mulwray and a young mystery girl in *Chinatown*. Teddy had known from the start that his PI career would never be as glamorous as that (no one like Faye Dunaway ever called him with a case) or as satisfying as his work as a detective, but at least he was still in the business of investigating, solving something, of helping people. And every now and then, one of those people was a friend.

Teddy blinked against a dry gust off the hills. Some days, the cool Pacific Ocean breeze could be felt this far inland, but when the wind was blowing in the other direction, it came in from the high desert in Nevada and Utah. Then it was known as the Santa Ana winds, which according to legend could affect everything from your health to your mood. Some months, in September especially, it became unnaturally hot and dry, elevating the risk of fire and, some said, earthquakes and murder. Could be why he felt so tight this morning, his neck tingling. Raymond Chandler and Joan Didion wrote about the Santa Anas as the harbinger of something dangerous and deadly. *So different from the splendid humidity back home.*

He heard a rustle in the brush below him. A coyote was scuttling back to safer territory, probably Elysian Park just to his east, to the undeveloped land below Dodger Stadium. It was scrawny and looked desperate. Like many of the perps Teddy had known.

He opened his phone and texted Win: *Where and when?*

A moment later Win's reply buzzed with an address and a time: nine thirty. Teddy's map app opened to a corner on Sunset, not even a mile from his apartment. He knew it was a bank and that it must be Win's. He was looking for a way to pay these dirtbags off with whatever cash he could scrape up.

Teddy hated that Win had to do that, but he also knew that a situation like this could go sideways in a Tokyo second. Kidnappers were jittery by nature and easily spooked, which didn't improve the chances of survival for the victim. If he were still a cop, there would be a professional negotiator involved, someone who knew how to keep the conversation going in a way that could lead to a positive outcome. But in this case, he didn't want the cops involved, as much for Win's reputation as for Clare's safety. When he allowed himself to fantasize, Teddy pictured the pricks dropped by gunfire during the handoff and the safe recovery of Clare and the ransom. He'd never admit it to Win, but such a result was unlikely.

Still, he would do anything for Win, not just because they were friends but because of the way Win had shown up for Teddy during his troubles with the LAPD, frustrating the press by refusing to pile on to the smear campaign against a disgraced officer. When badgered for comment, without hesitation Win had said, "The man you're describing is not the man I know. The man I know is one of the best people I've ever met. He's my friend and I stand by him."

Not everyone would have done that. Win took some heat for this remark, especially when the full weight of the evidence against Teddy had come out, but he never retracted it, and their friendship never wavered. Making a real friend is never easy, especially in LA, but Win might be the best friend he'd ever had, anywhere. He was going to do everything he could to help get the man's daughter back, safe and sound.

Teddy texted back: *C u there*

Just shy of two hours later, Win, Grover, and Teddy emerged from the Chase bank at Sunset and Echo Park Boulevards and walked to their cars. Win had left his in Grover's driveway.

A sealed envelope in Win's inside pocket held twenty-seven thousand three hundred and forty-one dollars, everything he had in cash, after closing his longtime account over the objections of his bank officer. Win fibbed that his daughter was getting a divorce and needed the money to help her and his granddaughter make a new start. Folded in his hand was a Quit Claim form, unsigned, but filled out and ready to go. His plan was to sell his house to a quick-turnaround developer and add that to the cash he'd just withdrawn. It meant getting a lot less than full value for the home, but he could feasibly have all the money in hand before end of business Friday. *Tomorrow.*

He just hoped he could hold them off that long without risking them harming Clare.

"So," Win asked them both, "who wants to drive me back so I can sell my car?"

"I will," said Grover.

"I'll follow," said Teddy. "You and I should trade numbers, just in case."

As Teddy and Grover exchanged their contact info, Win said, "I was thinking I could unload it at one of those used-car lots down on Lincoln Boulevard. It's clean, pretty low miles, I figure I could get a few thousand for it. Thirty grand in hand might buy me a little more time to sell the house, right?"

Grover asked Teddy, "You think they'd be satisfied with the thirty grand as a down payment?"

"Unlikely," said Teddy. "I've only seen multiple payoffs in blackmail cases, never in a ransom. And every day they hang on to her increases their risk of discovery, so they'll be gettin' jumpier by the minute. A delay could piss 'em off enough to cut and run, despite the thirty grand." He glanced at Win, immediately sorry he'd said that out loud.

"Let's get going," said Grover. "We'll think about it on the way. All we can do now is wait for them to call again."

"And" said Win, "see if anyone might be interested in a well-kept two-story in Wrightwood."

30

G ROVER BROKE THE silence that had settled in the car as he and Win drove east on Sunset to access an on-ramp to the 101, back to Venice.

"You have a chance to think about what happens when all this is over?"

"No," Win said, surprised by the question. "I haven't thought much past pulling my pants on this morning."

"Things aren't going to be the same, no matter what," Grover said. "Things were tough before, but when Clare comes back, she's going to be different. You all are."

Win looked out the window. At street level, LA was a mostly two-story town. It was as average-looking a city as anywhere in the world, with apartments and single-family homes built during the great postwar boom of the 1940s, now interspersed with functional storefronts, trendy restaurants, and coffee bars. If you didn't know you were on the storied Sunset Boulevard, you'd mistake it for practically any gentrifying street in America. Occasionally, you'd pass a relic of a once-beautiful home, someone's long-past dream house, built after making a better than expected living, perhaps by providing lumber to the movie studio construction departments. These days, many of those had been converted to boutique offices or small post-production houses, offering low-cost editing, sound mixing, or color-correction services to indie filmmakers.

An acting teacher Win had once studied with, a refined and erudite Englishman named John Abbott, had come to Hollywood after WWII and lived in a small bungalow he'd bought from Cecil B. DeMille's casting director. Surrounded by a colorful, blooming garden, the cottage sat like a bird's nest in the Hollywood Hills above Franklin and Ivar (made famous as the location of William Holden's apartment in *Sunset Boulevard*). Abbott had a million-dollar view down to Hollywood proper, the foothills giving way to green palms, Spanish architecture, and vintage streetlamps. He said he'd never seen anything so beautiful as Los Angeles in the 1940s, that England on its best day couldn't compare (which Win found hard to believe, having once seen the Cotswolds in early summer). Clean air, street cars and trolleys, plenty of sun, and the ocean always nearby.

"Paradise," Abbott had called it. "You could see *aaallll* the way to Baldwin Hills," he said, referring to an affluent enclave eight miles due south.

Grover made a right toward a freeway on-ramp a few streets down and had to slow as they passed through a series of long white trucks and trailers lining both sides of the street for nearly a block, the telltale sign of a movie or TV company on a local location shoot. The trucks hauled all the necessary equipment: cameras, dolly tracks, sound recording, lights and stands, wardrobe, makeup and hair. The trailers, referred to in the biz as "honeywagons," would have short stairwells on the sidewalk side that allowed access to individual dressing rooms for that day's performers or to makeshift production offices. There would also be assorted support vehicles supplying craft services (snacks and drinks) and full catering for meal breaks, and whatever else the staff and talent might need while on set.

These convoys were as much a part of the LA landscape as the rolling hills and palm trees, and whenever Win passed one, he couldn't help but wonder what project it might be, if it were something he'd want to be a part of. He'd habitually try to spot someone he knew, but today he didn't. Whenever he was between jobs (like at this moment), the insecurity of *not working* made him wonder if he had reached the dreaded fourth stage of the Hollywood Actor's Career Arc:

Stage 1. Who's Winston Greene?
Stage 2. Get me Winston Greene.
Stage 3. Get me a Winston Greene type.
Stage 4. Who's Winston Greene?

"People used to say I could've had Costner's career," Win said suddenly.

"I don't follow," said Grover, eyebrows raised.

"I have become an 'actor of note.' I mean, c'mon, my career arc is like Jan-Michael Vincent's if Jan had just cleaned up before it was too late." Win sighed. "I still drove it off a cliff."

"You're not being fair to yourself, Win," said Grover. "You're a lot better off than he was at this stage—in *every way*. Let's not forget how it ended for him."

Grover had a point. Jan-Michael Vincent had been, like Winston Greene at one time, the next big thing. And then Jan-Michael had left a trail of bar fights and car wrecks, and arrests for drunk driving and domestic abuse in his wake. After breaking his neck and losing much of his ability to speak, and then half a leg to amputation, he'd died in North Carolina, thousands of miles from the town where he'd made, and lost, his fortune. He'd been a huge star, a household name, and it was a month before the news of his death was reported to the public. Even *LDT* didn't think his passing was much of a news item, giving him only half a column on their Obituary page.

Win felt a tightness in his chest. It was the internal scars, reminding him that he hadn't worked out yet this week and it was time he did, if only for sanity's sake. He leaned toward the dashboard and pushed his chest forward while pulling his shoulders back. The stretch lessened the discomfort.

As he settled back in the seat, he said, "All I really did was rescue what little was left of my reputation. Seems like that's what I'm doing right now with my family."

He turned and looked out the window at the passing landscape of Los Angeles. He suddenly felt exhausted.

PART 7

"My head and my heart's had all kindsa arguments.
Head always loses."

—Winston Greene in *The Last Ride* (2016)

31

VENICE BEACH

WIN'S CELL PHONE rang. Despite the blocked number, his instincts told him it was the skinny prick. Win had just collected five thousand in cash from the used car dealer and pocketed it. The call came in as he, Grover, and Teddy were walking across the lot to the sidewalk.

Win answered. "Yeah?"

"Hey, cabrón. You got something for me?"

"Yeah," said Win. "Everything I could get my hands on since yesterday. I should be able to get more later."

Win glanced at Teddy and could practically *see* his heart drop. Earlier Teddy had admitted that he'd started second-guessing himself, and that now he wished he'd brought in a negotiator. Someone who knew how to talk to the kidnappers, establish their trust, get the exact ransom amount, then whittle them down from there. But he'd also said it was too late for that now. That the best they could hope for was that the perps would take what Win had collected so far and call it quits. But they all knew better. Their demand would be more than Win had, no matter what. But Win felt he had much more decisive clarity than yesterday, and he was determined to get Clare back safely. He *wanted* them to know they had a better payday coming. And Teddy could only do what he could do. He'll just have to live with that.

"Don't fuck with me," said the voice on the phone.

Winston drew a breath. "I'm not! I'll give you everything I have. I just need a little more time to get it all together. C'mon, it hasn't even been twenty-four hours!"

"How much you got so far?"

"This minute?" Win said. "About thirty-two grand. Cash."

"Thirty-two grand. I wouldn't give back your *dog* for thirty-two grand! What do you take us for?"

"I understand," Win said quickly. Teddy had also instructed him to anticipate that the perps would ask for a certain amount, which, strangely, they still hadn't done. (To Teddy, it was almost as if these guys were making up their kidnapping as they went.) But once they named a price, Win would at least know how much further he had to go. Even if what he had didn't equal what they wanted, he'd know how what he *could* raise would compare to what they demanded from him. "I'm going to sell my house. Hopefully today, but tomorrow at the latest. Should be able to get another hundred thousand. Maybe more."

In fact, Win had no idea what his house could bring in a quick turnaround. He thought his best option would be an equity purchaser. These companies normally paid around sixty-five percent of a home's value, but with a waiting period of anywhere from seven to thirty days. Obviously, Win needed a much faster settlement than that, which meant even less money. Possibly fifty percent, but likely closer to thirty-five or forty percent on the dollar. In a good real estate year, which this was, his house could conceivably bring north of $800,000, free and clear. In a fire sale, he'd be lucky to get two hundred grand. Probably not even that much. One hundred was probably a safe bet.

"What about the rest?"

"The rest?" Win looked at his friends, confusion on his face.

"Of your money, cabrón! We don't give a shit about your fucking house. We want all that *movie money* you got stashed away."

"I . . . don't have anything stashed," he said, dumbfounded. Grover and Teddy leaned in closer. "I'm telling you what I got. My house. What I got in my hand. That's it!"

"You think you can bargain over your own *daughter?*" said Ozzie. His tone had changed. He sounded disgusted. "You know what? We're gonna send her home in a *bag.*"

"No, wait! Listen to me! I lost *everything*, like, a year ago. I had *cancer*! It all went to the hospital! Clare doesn't know that, but she knows I was sick. Ask her." He paused, panicking that the little psycho had just gone off to kill his daughter. "Are you there?"

"I'm here."

"This is all I've got. Jesus, I just sold my fucking car!" He paused again. "Maybe I can borrow something. Cash out my credit cards, I don't know—whatever I can get."

Teddy, who had never been a hostage negotiator, stared at Win as if he'd never seen anything like this. He waved at Win and mouthed, "Proof of life."

Win nodded. "And I want to talk to her."

"No," Ozzie said. "You can talk to her when you get the money. You have until midnight tonight. If you can't get it together by then, you'll be getting a bag a week, each one with a different body part. Ever see that old movie, *Frankenstein*? You can put her back together like that."

The line went dead, then Win's phone vibrated with an incoming text. It was a picture of Clare at the bottom of what looked like a basement stairwell, maybe the same basement where they'd shot the video of her. She was holding up a newspaper, opened flat so the front page was recognizable. It was that morning's *Los Angeles Times*. Proof of life.

32

SYLMAR

ROCKET, BASEBALL CAP askew, watched Ozzie end the call from the sofa across the room. Ozzie sighed and hunched forward, elbows on knees. Jordy had been pacing back and forth through the doorway between the living room and kitchen but stopped when Ozzie ended the call.

"What?" Rocket said.

"We got . . . conflicting information," said Ozzie. "Said he has to sell his house. That he just sold his car. That all in, he can get maybe . . . a hundred thirty K."

"The fuck!" exclaimed Jordy.

Rocket winced. "Do you think he's trying to chisel us? Maybe that cop is coaching him."

"*Ex*-cop," said Ozzie. He shook his head. "He sounded like he meant it."

"The guy's an *actor*," Jordy said. "It's his *job* to sound like he means it. *Fuck!*"

"Jordy," said Rocket, "take it down a notch." Then to Ozzie, "So you think he's being straight."

"Says he got sick and the hospital took it all, and that the puta didn't know. Knew he was sick," Ozzie corrected himself. "Didn't know it cleaned him out. Or close to it."

"So, he had it, but now he doesn't." Rocket looked down. "Well, shit."

"That's just great." said Jordy, pacing again. "Let's shake down a rich movie star. The kicker is, *he's not rich!*" He turned to Rocket. "I told you, go for a million. But *nooooo*. 'I got it all figured,' you said. 'Keep him off his pins,' you said. Like you're going fucking *bowling!*" Then, his voice laced with sarcasm: "Don't *this* sound familiar."

Rocket had to take a beat, then he returned Jordy's look. "Or *maybe* . . . he's just trying to keep some of it," he said, letting some sarcasm of his own through. "To start over with. I would if I thought I could get away with it."

Ozzie chimed in. "Then tonight we'll know what he's really got. But what about the puta—you think she knew he was busted?"

Rocket shook his head. "No. She really thinks he has it. And"—he said for Jordy's benefit—"maybe he does." Back to Ozzie. "We'll have to wait and see, like you said." He paused. "Might be the weekend before we're done. You guys better go stock up, get supplies in case we have to wait it out here a couple days."

"Janette'll wonder where I am," said Jordy. "Might ask around."

"You two lovebirds got plans?" said Ozzie. "Sunday picnic at the beach?"

Jordy looked at Ozzie. "It's called an alibi, fuckhead."

"Would anybody miss her before Monday?" asked Rocket. Clearly there was an idea behind his question.

Jordy knew what he was implying, but unlike Edvina, Janette didn't deserve that. Jordy had to think on his feet. "Maybe. Could be planning to see her dad. She does that on the weekend sometimes. I could get some stuff from her place, leave a note that I went surfing for the weekend. That should do it."

They heard a scratchy voice, muffled as it traveled through the walls from the back of the house, calling for something. Jordy and Ozzie looked at Rocket.

"Yeah, yeah, my turn," he said, and got up as Ozzie and Jordy filed out the front door to trek to the supermarket a few blocks away.

Rocket locked the door behind them and headed to the back bedroom.

Clare sat on the basement floor, lost in a swirl of serrated thoughts.

This whole kidnapping thing had been her idea, so she really had no one to blame but herself.

But what the hell was she thinking? She knew they were small-time hoods with a proclivity for violence. Seen them go after dead-beat druggies, beat the shit out of them, and steal anything they could carry. What the hell had she expected?

Still, she'd been skeptical of Ozzie's story about that guy up in the desert, the one they supposedly killed, figured they just told her that story to make it clear they would go through with the plan. But locking her up and treating her like a damn animal?

Maybe they really *had* murdered that guy . . .

No, that's just a story. Zeke did that kind of thing, puffed himself up so people would think he was tougher than he was. He wasn't fooling her—she knew he was just a five-foot-six man-boy, glomming on to someone who would do the hard stuff for him. God, was she so conditioned by her father *acting* like a tough guy that she was attracted to men with bravado instead of balls? It made sense. Enough to make her stomach turn just a bit.

She closed her eyes, as she'd been doing since she'd awoken because, suddenly, every time she did, she'd see Amy's face. *Is this as close as I'll be to her again? A vision in my head . . . that's already starting to fade?* She realized she was holding her eyelids closed tight, like a child who refuses to look. When she opened them, the tears spilled onto her cheek. It had a cooling effect. And then it all became clear:

Jesus! She was finally getting the picture. They'd *never* planned to divvy up the proceeds with her. Taking her picture with the newspaper this morning was to prove she was still alive, but as soon as they got her father's money, they'd probably leave her dead in this very basement. Maybe that's what they were yelling about up there.

"Ozzie!" she shouted. "*Ozzie!*"

She heard shuffling above her, followed by steps thumping toward the cellar door.

"Quiet!" It was Rocket.

"I gotta pee," she said.

"Use the bucket."

"Okay, I gotta do more than pee. I went through this with Ozzie yesterday."

"Yeah, and I told him not to do it again. Use the bucket."

Clare kept her voice calm, measured. "You don't empty the bucket. You make me eat with it down here. What do you expect? C'mon, it'll only take a minute." She paused, tried another tack. "I've done everything you asked, even though you locked me up in here. Can't you meet me halfway on this one thing?"

After an interminable moment, the locks turned. She'd guessed right that, even if he planned to do her in when this was over, Rocket didn't want to be dodging dookies spread across the floor to do it. The door cracked open, and Rocket stood at the top of the stairs, glaring at her, holding a gun in his hand.

"Move it."

She came up the steps, gauging her legs' stability as she went, moved down the hall, and turned into the bathroom, swinging the door partially closed behind her like Ozzie had the night before. This time she turned on the faucet as she passed it, not too strong, so Rocket wouldn't think she was trying to cover an escape. She noticed someone had put a fresh roll in the wall dispenser. She dropped her drawers and sat.

She didn't really need to go. She'd emptied her bowels the day before and then thrown up whatever was left, including what hadn't digested of that disgusting tuna sandwich they'd given her. But she figured she should try anyway, just in case, but all she managed was number one. She pictured Rocket standing outside the door, tense, his hand gripping his gun. She stood up and flushed, ran her fingers under the faucet, shook them to air dry, and opened the door to the bathroom.

She was surprised to find that Rocket wasn't in the hallway. Then she heard sounds coming from the far bedroom, where she had heard the aluminum walker the day before. She heard Rocket mumbling something, followed by a louder voice, old and cracking and indecipherable. Muffled, like something was covering the person's mouth. Perhaps it was the last of the drugs in her blood-stream that slowed her decision-making abilities, but before she realized this was her opportunity to bolt, Rocket was back in the hallway, looking pissed. He aimed his gun at her.

"Get in here."

She raised her hands, her palms forward in submission, and went into the bedroom.

A very thin, very old man lay prostrate on the bed. His chest was concave, his extremities pencil like, so bony Clare could make out the ridges on his kneecaps through his threadbare trousers. He wore an old cotton tank top, and his belt was faded leather, the silver buckle oxidized. The walker was parked against the wall by the window. Someone must have put it there, out of the man's reach. The sagging queen-sized mattress lay in a vintage brass frame with rounded pipe head and footrest. Military decorations, ribbons and stars encased in frames, hung on the walls. This old man must've been a hero back in the day, maybe World War II, or Korea.

His left wrist was tied to the bed frame with what looked like a white electric cord, the paleness harsh against his gray-pink skin. He was reaching to untie it with his free hand. Rocket yanked the old guy's loose wrist to tie it to the frame on the opposite side. He set his gun on a rickety nightstand. The man was livid and confused at the same time; his weak legs thrashed with what little energy he could muster. Clare stood frozen, aghast at the cruelty Rocket was inflicting on the man. And then it hit her: he'd put the gun down.

She turned and bolted out the door.

33

CLARE HEARD A thump behind her at the other end of the hall-way but wouldn't allow herself to look at anything but the front door, coming closer to her in what seemed like slow motion.

She felt like she was wearing fifty-pound ankle weights, her legs weakened by the withdrawals and lack of sleep, but she pressed forward. The chairs and sofa, the TV, all just *things* to go around, over, or through. She was vaguely aware of her foot catching on a coffee table, and a wild smack to knock a floor lamp out of her way. She could hear Rocket's feet stomping down the hallway behind her. If he caught her, there would be no second chance, no opportunity to make her case, no plea for forgiveness. She had convinced him to grant her a tiny act of compassion by letting her use a bathroom like a human being, and then she'd taken advantage of it. She was certain he would kill her.

She reached for the front doorknob and heard another crash behind her, closer this time. He was gaining on her. As she turned the knob, she heard a blast from Rocket's gun, and felt the door-jamb splinter inches from her head. Wood slivers stung her face.

She yanked the door open, and her eyes screamed at the bright sunlight. She burst straight through the old screen door, its edges curling and the frame long since out of square, going through it easily as it broke from the hinges. The rusty old screen curled and tangled around her foot, and she kicked it away. She'd made it to the front yard. She ran for the sidewalk.

"Clare!"

She heard him but didn't stop.

It was a residential street, not a cul-de-sac. Small, single-story houses with sad front yards feeling the drought, windows barred for security. Working-class neighborhood, fallen on hard times. There was light traffic on the street. A few cars whizzed by, the drivers oblivious to (or afraid of) the distraught woman wildly waving her arms. And no pedestrians.

"Clare!" she heard Rocket scream again, louder this time.

She glanced over her shoulder and saw him standing on the small porch, the screen door's frame dangling next to him, gun at his side. Her lungs heaved, and her skin flushed with heat, but adrenaline coursed through her veins, and she was determined not to get dragged back to that house.

She spotted a gas station on the corner, across the street, about five hundred feet away. She was sure she could make it, go to the attendant, and beg him to call the police. She started sprinting down the sidewalk. The passenger window of a parked sedan imploded as she ran past it, the glass shattering behind her. She made a hard right between it and the next parked car as a bullet ricocheted off a windshield.

As she darted to the street side of the cars, she felt another gunshot whine past her head. She ducked, but she knew she couldn't stay there for long. She had to keep moving or he'd chase her down. Random thoughts bounced through her head: *I'll get rid of Zeke. I'll be a mother to my daughter. I'll apologize to my father. I'll prove I can make something of myself.* She snuck a look at the gas station again and willed herself to believe she could make it.

She took a breath, sprang up, and ran into the street.

Rocket sensed movement out of the corner of his eye. He grabbed the gun and spun around, aiming at where she'd stood in the doorway. But she was gone, running toward the front of the house. He went after her in such a hurry he banged into the opposite wall in the hallway. He saw her disappear into the living room to the right. She was going to break for the front yard.

Rocket had dropped the ball, thanks to that old bastard who just wouldn't do what he was told. He barreled down the hall into the living room to see Clare reaching for the front door. He raised his pistol, but banged into the coffee table that minutes earlier had been in front of the sofa and was now toppled on its side in the middle of the room. He stumbled as he fired and the bullet went wild, shattering the doorjamb.

He called to her, but she was already out the door. He followed her into the bright sunlight and screamed her name again, stopping on the porch to let his eyes adjust. He held the gun tight to his side, hoping to draw as little attention as possible. Scenarios of how this might end flashed like lightning. Rocket believed his chief talent as a businessman was analyzing a given situation and deducing the best outcome, and he was already considering the possibilities now. He doubted he could get her back inside. Then again, if he promised not to hurt her and to pick up where they left off, she *might* come back. The plan only worked if she was under lock and key. If she escaped—

Fuck it. She's done. Take her out, then get in the car and go. He raised the Glock and fired. A car window exploded just behind her. He fired again but it ricocheted off another car's windshield.

He tracked her movements as she ran to the street side of the parked cars and popped off another shot (he thought he heard it land with a *crack* in the wood siding of a house across the street). She disappeared behind a car. He walked toward her, his gaze focused on where she'd dived out of sight. Then there she was again, starting in the direction of the gas station on the corner. If he chased her there, they could recognize him—he'd filled his car up there yesterday. He had to do it now. He aimed for the wide spot between her shoulders, the easiest place to hit a moving target (he'd heard that in a movie once). As he tightened his squeeze on the trigger, a blur of purple appeared from the left side of his vision.

Clare charged out in front of the deep fuchsia Angel City ice-cream truck, giving the driver no time to hit the brakes. One more step and Rocket thought she'd have cleared it, but the truck caught her on her left side. The force of colliding with the grille sent her airborne, propelling her to the opposite side of the street, her trajectory interrupted by a parked car, leaving a sizeable dent in its side. Her body thumped onto the blacktop, motionless.

Rocket hustled to the sidewalk to get a better look, thinking he might have to finish her off. Her left arm and leg lay at odd angles—broken, for sure. Who knew what else? Even from across the street he could see blood running from her mouth and nose. He sighed and lowered the gun. He had to leave. Now.

He went inside the house, walked to the bedroom to find the old man had nearly freed himself, and fired. Once. Twice. Then a third time, because he was pissed.

When Rocket emerged from the house, an athletic bag in his left hand, the pistol in his right, and his baseball cap angled on his head, he saw a woman in a yellow sundress with a tiny, impeccably groomed Pomeranian on a leash. She was on her phone, standing next to where Clare's body lay in the street, giving information to whichever emergency service she had on the line. Her free hand rested on the shoulder of the truck driver next to her, in an effort to comfort the distraught young man. He had covered his face with his hands, and Rocket could hear him moaning.

The woman's dog started barking in Rocket's direction almost as soon as he stepped out of the house. Rocket considered taking both her and the driver out (and that yappy little dog too) but decided it was too risky to stay any longer. He calmly walked to his car, got in, backed out into the street, and drove away in the opposite direction. He opened his phone and dialed Ozzie's burner, having memorized the number. Ozzie answered.

"Bitch tried to rabbit," said Rocket. "Didn't get far but it's gonna make the news. Go to Jordy's."

He hung up and with his free hand pulled apart the phone, taking out the SIM card and the battery, and tossed the phone pieces out the car window, one by one. With no ID on her body (and nothing and no one to identify his crew left behind at that house), they should be clear for at least another several hours.

That might be just enough time.

PART 8

"Have you been checked for a heart?
Or did they just find a big dollar sign,
all lit up like a Vegas casino?"

—Winston Greene in *Killtime* (2018)

CHAPTER

34

VENICE BEACH

WIN, TEDDY, LAUREN, and Grover were seated around the dining table. Amy was with the Washington girls in their room while they did their schoolwork. At eleven thirty AM, the midday sun lit up the indoors in warm creams and tans.

After emptying his bank account and selling his car, Win had called four companies that specialized in real estate equity purchases. Only one would even consider paying cash for his house inside of twenty-four hours, and only then after an inspection. He couldn't argue, given the catastrophic fires in the last few years, when the guy said he wanted to be sure he wasn't just buying a concrete foundation. They agreed to meet in Wrightwood in two hours.

"You know, Win," said Lauren, "it's possible Clare's in on this."

Win rubbed the stubble on his chin, leaned forward, and crossed his arms on the table in front of him. "Yeah, it's occurred to me," he said. "Addicts can do strange things."

For all the times Clare had torn his heart apart, she had always done it on impulse. He had never imagined she would, or even could, put into motion a plan deliberately designed to harm him. He *wanted* to presume that this was not premeditated on her part. Thanks to his own struggles, he knew as well as anyone how wily addiction could be.

"What about the husband?" asked Teddy. Everyone looked at him. "Might even been his idea. It was like pullin' teeth gettin' anything out of him yesterday. He might be hangin' on to a secret."

"No," said Win. "Zeke couldn't take a shit if someone didn't show him how."

"Jesus, Win," said Grover, "tell us what you really think."

"If this started with them, it was Clare's idea." Tears started to pool in his eyes. "Zeke was scared, yeah, but not of us. He's scared of these guys who've been calling," he said, holding up his cell phone for emphasis. "They're the ones in charge." He looked at Teddy. "Right?"

"Yeah," Teddy said, looking at his watch. "You got an appointment back at your house to make some money. In the meantime, I'm gonna hit that bowling alley again, just in case the famous Rocket shows. As I expect he will not, I'll have another go at said son-in-law. See if the boy's got somethin' he's just dyin' to add."

35

SYLMAR

B RANOVICH WAS SPEEDING. He'd exited the freeway and was
almost to Zeke's house, his tires chirping around every corner.
When he'd woken this morning, he was no closer to cracking the
story of Clarissa Greene-Montgomery's troubles than he'd been
when he finally conked out last night, he thought around halfway
between midnight and sunrise.

He'd stayed up trying to find evidence of Winston Greene's
daughter's supposed misfortune, alluded to in the mystery email
he'd received. He had done everything that a motivated tabloid
reporter could do to uncover the secret in a city that, on a Wednesday, rolled up the sidewalks at ten pm, but was fruitless in finding
anyone who would talk to him. He'd hit every bar and restaurant
he could think of, even that place where Greene's brother worked.
The guy had thrown him out.

The search had begun with him sitting outside on his back
deck, the pool lamp throwing a watery chiaroscuro on the house
and trees, and combing the internet, looking for arrest reports
in the LA metro area. He'd made phone calls to his sources
around Hollywood's gyms, bars, and clothing boutiques. He'd
even kept his Whistler TRX-1 portable police scanner on, even
though it could only monitor his immediate area, just in case he
heard something that smacked of the actor's daughter getting into

trouble. Cops would occasionally refer to someone famous they'd cuffed that day during idle banter over the airwaves, though never by name. "I got a biggie" could be code for a star pulled over for a DUI, for example. He'd kept the scanner on all night, and still had it with him now. But so far, nothing.

But Branovich wasn't about to let this matter drop. A lesser muckraker might suspect that the anonymous email was a bum lead, a carrot dangled for the tipster's amusement. But he had a feeling that this particular tip was solid, and he was not going to let it get away.

His last encounter with—or more precisely, regarding—Winston Greene was when he'd paid Zeke for some trivial information, so picayune he couldn't remember the details. But he'd spent some time last night going through *LDT*'s digital records and learned that Greene had been on their "hit list" for quite some time, in equal parts for his own rise-and-fall story, for his wife's tragic death, and for his association with that disgraced ex-LAPD detective, Theodore Beauregard.

What set Greene apart was that the actor had never taken any money for his story. Over the last decade, *LDT* had tempted him with many thousands of dollars, but he had never accepted a dime. That gave him a "most wanted" standing at *LDT*. The staff, never famous for their own integrity, actually respected Winston Greene's, and if any one of them could get him to talk, then that reporter's standing at the publication would skyrocket. Anyone who could land Greene (or any other coveted target known for not cooperating with the tabloid) would be rewarded with the best assignments, the best perks, and the biggest bonuses.

Branovich had owned that rarified realm at *LDT* for the last couple of years, always delivering on his reputation for getting the story, no matter what he had to do to get it. Scott Branovich was the man who got it D-U-N, done. As great as this exalted position was, though, he was acutely aware that if some other reporter were to land this scoop, at *LDT* or any of the other tell-all rags, he would get knocked down a few pegs and have to double his efforts just to crawl back up to the top. He was not about to allow that to happen.

When Branovich arrived at Zeke's home, he didn't bother hiding down the street. He parked in front of the house and trotted to the front door, pounding on it with an insistence that telegraphed his determination.

"I don't want to talk to you!" he heard Zeke say from inside.

"Well, I want to talk to you, Zachary, and I can make it worth your while. I'll give you a grand right now, just for answering a couple simple questions."

The silence meant Zeke was thinking it over, imagining what a grand would look like, feel like, in his hand, which was the muckraker's first hurdle in making a deal. Now he just had to close.

"That's one thousand dollars. All yours. And no one has to know."

After a moment, Zeke said, "Let me see it."

Branovich pulled an envelope from inside his jacket and opened the flap. Inside were fifty crisp, twenty-dollar bills. The door slivered open.

Branovich held up the envelope and ran his thumb across the top of the bundle so Zeke could see he wasn't just hiding a stack of singles between two twenties. "C'mon, let me in."

The door opened wider, and he slipped inside.

Branovich turned around as Zeke closed the door behind him, wincing at the musky odor. His eyes adjusted to the gloom, and he could see the place was a mess. He wondered what Winston Greene had thought about that when he'd been here yesterday.

Branovich could see that the anxiety preventing Zeke from speaking to him yesterday was no match for the sight of the cash he was offering. He shook the envelope. "This is yours . . . *if* you give me what I need."

"What do you want?" said Zeke, though Branovich could see the young druggie's eyes were lasered on the envelope.

"I saw your father-in-law was here yesterday." Zeke's hand absentmindedly rose to the stubble on his left cheek. "Your daughter left with him. Along with that friend of his, the ex-cop."

Creases burrowed across Zeke's forehead.

See, I think you're my tipster. You sent an anonymous email a couple days ago. I think you wanted to make a little extra cake by giving me a heads-up about a big story. Because you knew I'd come sniffing around, and you figured you could collect a little something on the side when I did. Well, here it is." He held up the envelope in front of Zeke's face. "But not until you deliver."

"Email?" said Zeke. Now Branovich saw his eyes wander, as if the answer was floating somewhere in the air in front of him.

"You know, the little missives people send back and forth over the internet? Do it right and you can do it anonymously, like you did with that handle. 'IndecentExposure'?"

"I don't know what—"

"Hey! You're not getting this money unless you give me something I can use! Now, tell me what this is all about, or I walk outta here. And you better pray I don't turn right around and tell your daddy-in-law about this."

Zeke's eyes were locked on the dingy carpet, when a bright fan of sunlight spread across the floor, broken by the shadows of his own legs. Someone had opened the front door behind him. Branovich squinted against the brightness. A man wearing a tilted baseball cap was standing in the open doorway.

"You're not supposed to be here," Zeke said.

The man looked from Zeke to Branovich. "Who the fuck are you?"

"Scott Branovich, *LDT* magazine, and just who the fuck are *you* who doesn't know how to knock?"

"Oh, right," the man said with a chuckle as he shut the door behind him. "Guess you got my email."

He reached behind his back, pulled a pistol from his waistband, and fired twice.

"Anonymousemail." *Silly name for such a useful invention.* Rocket counted the money from the envelope that Branovich had dropped when the bullet hit his skull. *In fact,* Rocket thought, *the internet is pretty fricking awesome.*

It had taken about five minutes to set up an untraceable email account on Anonymousemail.me and send the message to Scott Branovich at *LDT.* All he'd needed was a valid email address to send it to, which was easily found on the *LDT* website:

> Got a hot tip? Click HERE! Or contact one of our experienced reporters. Click HERE for our DIRECTORY. If you have a newsworthy story, we'll put our best people on it and make it worth

your while. You won't be sorry! (But someone else might be.)
Or call our toll-free hotline: (888) 555-TELL.

Rocket counted out a thousand dollars, even. If this was for Zeke, Branovich had definitely overpaid. *At least there's no blood on it. Damn, a head shot makes a helluva mess.*

He slipped the cash back into the envelope and tucked his pistol back into his waistband. If this was all he came away with, it would at least be enough to get to Mexico. *A man can start over down there.* If you believed the papers, the drug trade was booming. Then again, it was dangerous. US couldn't even compare. People got killed just for *looking* at el jefe the wrong way. Mass graves, torture chambers, bodies lining the streets of vacation hotspots. Corrupt police. On the other hand, there was a lot of money to be made, and money can buy protection. If he could make something happen, then his Hollywood career would just be a cashier's check away. But he'd need a bigger stake than a grand to get anything going.

That fucking actor is going to pay, whether he finds out about Clare or not. He didn't like it when he was wrong, but Rocket had to admit Ozzie had nailed it. *We should have grabbed the kid instead.* No good bitching about it now. Rocket needed to get to the guy—and the money—*before* he found out his daughter was dead.

Rocket stepped over Zeke's body. He thought he saw a twitch but decided it must be the dim light playing games with his eyes. That funnel-shaped hole in Zeke's head had put a definitive end to that waste of a life.

In a way, Rocket felt worse for the *LDT* reporter than he did for Zeke. He'd always gotten a kick out of the articles the guy wrote. Too bad there wouldn't be any more.

Gotta go. Still got work to do.

36

THE 405 FREEWAY, NEAR SYLMAR

A FTER A CAREER spent conjuring emotions, Winston knew he
had met his match in the hatred rising inside him like a molten bubble. But it wasn't directed at Clare or Zeke or even the
skinny prick who'd brought Amy to his home yesterday. It was
aimed squarely at himself.

He and Grover were caravanning behind Teddy. Win looked
out the passenger window and stared blankly at the passing San
Fernando Valley.

From the elevated freeway (if the smog allowed), one could
see the Angeles Mountains, on the other side of which lay
Wrightwood. Nestled on this side was his hometown of La
Crescenta, known as "The Balcony of Southern California." In
reality it was the shaggy-dog next-door neighbor to privileged,
manicured La Cañada/Flintridge, which bordered the Angeles
National Forest and boasted the beautiful botanical park Des-
canso Gardens. The La Cañada Flintridge Country Club, with
its glorious view of LA to the south, had employed his father
as the golf-course greenskeeper. From here on the freeway to
those foothills, though, was nothing but bland buildings, sun-
bleached and unremarkable. It was, to Win, the perfect visual
example of "a vast wasteland of mediocrity," Newton Minow's
1961 statement about television.

Recently he'd taken to distracting himself during traffic jams by imagining an alternate future, one where he'd relocated to New York or Portland, or even London or Paris. Some place that delivered on what he believed every human on the planet is entitled to: clean air to breathe, clean water to drink, and decent architecture to look at. All three were a challenge here, on top of trying to raise well-adjusted children amid the pervasive celebrity culture.

He'd fantasize about making trips to LA only because someone was paying him to. He'd see some old friends, have them over for dinner at the oceanside hotel he'd been put up in for the duration of the gig, and then head home to that someplace else when he'd wrapped.

Staring out at the familiar landscape sent his mind back to when he was just starting out: a friend had landed him a job changing brake pads and doing tune-ups at a service station out in Northridge. In those days he hadn't known shit about cars (and was still occasionally haunted by some of the shoddy brake work he might've done). But it had been a valuable learning experience. He would commute to and from his new single apartment in Hollywood in his '67 Ford pickup, which sported a three-on-the-tree shifter and a hodgepodge paint job of army green, oxidized tan, and primer gray, a holdover from his teens in La Crescenta. The eighteen-mile drive was often a one-hour ride each way, his introduction to the reality of metropolitan Los Angeles traffic life.

He had felt so adult, paying his rent on his studio apartment, working his job, flirting with the girl at the fast-food drive-through window on his lunch break. And he had his first professional-level acting classes two nights a week, Tuesdays and Thursdays.

Truth was, he had been scared shitless most of the time. When the freeway traffic would slow to a crawl, he'd look out at this very same boundless expanse of megacity and wonder how he would ever make even a small dent in it.

In those days, many of the emotions he experienced were new, and often terrifying. Fear, ambition, defeat, confidence, insecurity, loathing . . . self-loathing. But there was one other feeling, which had always followed on the heels of the others: hope.

He could still recall one particular night, trying to sleep on the fold-out sofa bed he'd had to strip down and spray with Lysol to clear the scent of mildew. He'd just turned twenty-one, finally street legal to drink, but couldn't afford a six-pack of beer. He was folded into a fetal position, staring at a blank wall lit blue by moonlight, and questioning his choices, his very existence. Why? Jesus, why had he decided on what had to be the world's most demoralizing profession? The attrition rate in Hollywood was astronomical. He'd been there for nearly a year, and he hadn't gotten even a single audition, let alone a bit part in something.

He had no college degree, no special talents. In other words, he had no safety net or proverbial "something to fall back on." Anyone he knew who did have one, wound up doing that thing instead and then "falling back" on an acting career when time allowed. (Or worse: One guy in his class he used to hang with—*Jason? Jake?*—spent his bartending money on coke, then moonlighted as a gigolo, and then went to prison for a robbery gone bad. Might even still be there.)

Win had lain there that cold January night and felt the chill through the socks he always wore to bed. The cost of gasoline required to get him to and from his damn job, and those acting classes, left him wondering if he would make his rent that month. Overwhelmed by a sense of failure, he had wished someone were next to him, to pull close for comfort. Instead, he was cold and alone in the dark, with no idea what would come next.

But then a small shred of hope would rise, like a chance encounter with an old friend, accompanied by a pleasant ache in his heart. And the hope would give him purpose, and the purpose would give him strength. And energy. And direction. And he persevered. And in the end, he'd made it in an industry where statistically *no one* succeeded.

As far as he knew, he was the only one from those days who had stuck it out. Of all those faces—from all those classes and barrooms and shitty jobs, all the cast members of early plays in tiny, near-empty theaters, most just acquaintances, all of them colleagues—not one had dug in for the long haul. Not the way he had. He guessed they'd lost hope and detoured into other lives.

Hope. If you had asked Win before yesterday, he would've said "hope" is an abstract belief in the future. Today, he wouldn't know *what* to answer. But was that what had kept him going for all those years? Hope? It was like a good friend that gave him that little push when he needed it.

Once during an extended dry spell, Winston had researched a few industry averages and found that more than seventy percent of all movies made included an actor who could claim exactly one film credit and that most Hollywood careers didn't last more than a decade. Even for big stars the average was around twenty-five years. (And if you were a woman, careers were even shorter.) Winston had passed that mark ages ago. The common moniker people would use to refer to him and others like him was "a survivor." As if they'd lived through combat or something (and sometimes he felt like he had). This in a business with a worse success rate than restaurants, where failure was practically guaranteed. He and his contemporaries would joke that to still have a career at this stage you just had to be the last man in the room. El último hombre en pie—the last man standing.

Winston believed another reason for his longevity had to do with consistency. Throughout his career, even through all the turmoil caused by his addiction, he had worked with the same agents and managers. For a short time he was lured to one of the three letter mega-agencies, but their impersonal nature (and addiction to sequel paychecks) drove him right back to his original team, who were generous enough not to hold his brief affair against him. Because his reps knew him so well, and were honestly committed to his professional standing, Winston was more often than not matched with roles and directors that suited him. Nowadays, the movies he appeared in made him look like a Cadillac engine dropped into a Volkswagen beetle, but they kept him working. He'd never been able to say, "I'd like to thank the Academy," but he was usually singled out as the best thing in the picture. The glory days might be over, but those working relationships were as strong as ever.

And he still felt hopeful most days. Felt it, wanted it, for Clare and for Amy. Even occasionally felt it for Zeke, that alone giving proof to the saying "Hope springs eternal."

But today, looking out Grover's car window, all he had room for was anger.

He watched as Teddy took the exit into Sylmar, then checked his iPhone for about the twenty-eighth time today.

"You have a charger in here?" he asked.

Grover opened the console between the seats. Win pulled out a cable, plugged in his phone, and placed it on his thigh, where he could keep an eye on it.

37

SYLMAR

TEDDY SWUNG AROUND the dead-end circle where Clare and Zeke's bungalow sat, braked to a stop, and killed the engine.

Like the cop he had once been, Teddy always took a mental picture of where he went, and yesterday that sedan hadn't been sitting in the driveway—and that blue coupe hadn't been parked in front either. Otherwise, the place seemed unchanged.

He swiped his palm back and forth across his mouth, a habit he'd developed in New Orleans when working a case. He reached under his jacket and felt the handle of the .38 snub he always carried, holstered and looped into his belt on his right side. Same spot since he'd first walked a beat. He might not be a cop anymore, but having been law enforcement and a PI pretty much guaranteed he passed the state requirements for a concealed carry permit despite his public disgrace.

He drew the pistol and clicked open the cylinder. One of his rules: Always double-check the load. Six bullets. Full. He snapped it back into place, holstered the gun, then reached over and popped open the glove box. He worked his fingers under the stack of owner's manuals and the AAA map kit until he found the six-cylinder reloader. Another rule: Carry extra ammo just in case.

He dropped the reloader into his left jacket pocket and got out of the car.

38

14 Freeway (East), 45 miles north of Hollywood

Grover sped across the 14 Freeway nearing Acton. Brown boulders and dry scrub brush spread over the hills on either side of the road. At this time of day and this far from the city, there was hardly any traffic, so he rode the gas a little harder than usual, just over the limit.

"You know, I'd have to talk it over with Lauren first," Grover said. "With four college funds to plan for, we don't have a lot of extra cash. But maybe we can add to what you have, front you until you get to the other side of this. Then sell your house properly, get what it's really worth, and pay us back."

Win stared at the dashboard in front of him in silence a moment, then looked at his friend. "You have no idea how much that means to me. Normally I'd say no, but I'm desperate. Let's see what happens with this guy first, okay? Who knows, maybe he'll save the day."

"If it's okay with you, it's okay with me," Grover assured him. Then he said, "You know, you could've told us you were sick."

Win sighed. "I know. I wish I had."

"Why didn't you?"

Win thought for a moment, as if he were considering it for the first time. "I guess between that and losing my money . . . I don't know." He shook his head. "You ever feel like the world's biggest loser?"

"Nope. Can't say that I have."

Win looked at him, then saw the glint in his eye. He laughed out loud, grateful for a friend like Grover who could take his mind off his predicament, even for a moment. "Prick."

"Biggest in four counties."

"I'm sorry."

"You should be. You're the one that missed out on Lauren's chicken soup and apple cobbler."

"Aw, shit, you're right." Win squeezed his temples with his thumbs, his face locked in a grimace. "You wouldn't have any aspirin in the car, would you?"

"Bad one?" Grover asked.

"Yeah." Win dropped his hands and looked up. "Damn head's gonna explode."

Grover saw they were approaching a sign with the blue and white gas, food, and lodging symbols and remembered there was an am-pm market (basically your garden variety convenience store) located not far from the off-ramp that was used by film and TV crews as the stereotypical "last chance for gas" location. Everything from TV's *Moonlighting* to at least one of the *Terminator* flicks had filmed there.

"We're making good time. Let's get you something," he said as he slowed and took the exit. He guided the car down the ramp and onto the boulevard, then into an empty space near the front door. "You wanna wait in the car?"

"No. I need some air." They got out and went inside.

The cashier was a plump young woman wearing a uniform smock. She looked up when they entered, and Grover could see circles under her eyes. *Looks like she hasn't slept in a week.* She sat on a stool with a large textbook open on her lap, which she went back to reading. Probably a student at Antelope Valley College over in Palmdale, maybe fifteen, twenty minutes away. She had to be at least twenty-one years old to ring up the alcohol that likely made up half the sales here. Win headed for the nonalcoholic cooler.

Grover tried to block out the scratchy Muzak pumped in from a radio station that sounded like it was tuned just off its mark on the dial. He heard the door open with a jingle, and a seventeen- or eighteen-year-old boy bounced in.

"Hey, Connie! Top of the morn'!" he called to the cashier.

She gave him a small but polite smile and went back to her book.

The kid grabbed a couple PowerBars and went to the register. "Man, that sunrise shift is hard to get used to," he said to no one, though he must've meant it for the cashier.

Win, who'd picked an orange Gatorade, found the aspirin at the front of an aisle near the register. "Here we go," Grover heard Win say as he grabbed a packet and joined Grover in line behind the energetic teenager.

The kid turned, surprised, as if he hadn't realized there were other customers in the store.

Grover saw the kid do a double-take. He knew the body language: Win had been recognized. The register beeped as the cashier rang the kid up. Grover was relieved when he paid for the bars with his smartphone, scooped them up, and went out the door.

"'Til next time!" he called to Connie over his shoulder.

Win stepped to the register and put his items on the counter.

"I got it," Grover said, and scanned his own phone over the electronic pad before Win could protest.

They stepped outside and both flinched as the PowerBar kid pushed off the wall where he'd been waiting to ambush them.

"I *knew* it! You're that *actor*!" he exclaimed. "My mom thinks you're the *bomb*, man!"

This was something all working actors came to know well: encounters with excited fans. Some can become so focused on the famous person in front of them that they forget to monitor their own behavior.

"She is going to be so *jazzed*," he exclaimed, pulling his phone from his back pocket. "Seriously, she is not going to *believe* this!"

Grover saw a guy at the gas pumps take notice. He wanted to head the kid off before he went in for the selfie he seemed to think he was entitled to. He'd seen Win handle this kind of thing before, and he was always patient and gracious, but Grover also knew that, today of all days, Win probably had as much interest in having a stranger take his picture as he did in having his dick slammed in a sliding glass door.

The kid was about three feet away and closing, and all Grover had time to get out was, "Son, right now might not be—" before the boy plopped one arm around Winston's neck and brought up his phone with the other.

Grover imagined a disaster in the making: Winston flipping the kid over his hip to land flat on his back on the blacktop. The boy making a *huuggh* sound as the wind was knocked out of his lungs, and then a cascade of legal actions would befall Winston for everything from assault to "intentional humiliation" or some bullshit like that. All of it corroborated by the guy at the pumps who, of course, was probably recording it all on his phone.

But then he was surprised when Winston simply swung his free arm over the kid's shoulder. What he could muster of a smile was barely there, but he let the kid take the picture. Then he dropped his arm and said, "Give your mom my best," and made a smooth exit to Grover's car and got in.

Grover went to the car and backed out. They passed the kid as he stared at his phone, a smile on his face.

Win pried open the aspirin bottle.

When they got back onto the freeway, Grover said, "You know, you'd be forgiven if you disappointed a random fan once in a while."

"I feel bad enough for the few that I have in the past," Win said. "And I'm not taking any chances with my karma today."

CHAPTER

39

TEDDY STOOD ON the sidewalk facing the house. The only sounds were the passing cars on San Fernando Road and the occasional jet passing overhead on approach to Burbank Airport.

Something was definitely off. The cul-de-sac had looked as deserted of life yesterday as it was today, but it felt different somehow. Something about the dark blue coupe in front rang a faint bell, but he couldn't place it either. Maybe it was a neighbor's car and had been parked across the street the day before, but he wasn't convinced.

He went to the car in the driveway and looked in the driver's side. Outside of needing a cleaning, it looked normal. A few gum and candy wrappers strewn around, open ashtray holding a few coins instead of cigarette butts and ash. Nothing that would suggest it belonged to anyone but your average citizen in need of a trade-in.

He glanced at the big living room window, maybe to catch Zeke holding the drapes apart, but they were still and straight. He circled around the car to look in from the passenger side. Again, nothing unusual. Zeke had said the kidnappers came in from the back, so he headed around the house toward the backyard.

What was left of the gate wouldn't keep anyone out. It hung at a slope on its hinges, the bottom slat resting on what was left of the back lawn, which, like the front, was mostly dirt and dead grass. The hook and pin of the gravity latch hadn't met each other in years. Teddy lifted the gate open and slipped through.

The backyard smelled like dry sweat and dog shit, even though they had no pets. A six-foot-high wooden fence enclosed the yard, and there were a couple of skeletal fruit trees, with no leaves and no fruit. It surprised him to see a pile of trash heaped in the far corner of the yard. A lot of it was bagged, but there was plenty that wasn't: newspapers, magazines, plastic cups and plates, disposable utensils, stained clothing and old towels, a rusted microwave.

Can't believe anyone would let a child play back here. No wonder Win held out hope that someday Clare and Amy would come to live with him.

Teddy pressed against the house and drew his weapon, then moved toward the glass kitchen door. Standing at the edge of the glass, he poked his head out once and quickly drew back. No one. He took another look, this time taking in the room. The table where Win had slapped Zeke yesterday was still there, as was the splotch of creamed coffee on the wall and floor. *Jesus, he had all night to clean that up.*

His .38 in his right hand, Teddy reached up with his left and nudged the mortise-style handle to see if it was locked. It slid open easily, nearly silent.

He raised his pistol, gripping it with both hands, and stepped inside.

40

WRIGHTWOOD

THE EQUITY-PURCHASE GUY was at the house when Winston and Grover arrived. He wore dark gray slacks and a powder-blue dress shirt, cuffs rolled to his elbows. The knot of his pale yellow tie was open. He was carrying an aluminum clip box and was heading for his car, a sleek, black, late-model luxury sedan that, like the man's black loafers, was powdered with driveway dust.

"This guy does all right," said Win.

"Uh-huh. And sometimes a ride like that is just for show."

The man had parked his car just behind the filthy roadster the kidnapper had left in the driveway yesterday. Grover pulled off the dirt drive onto the open yard, and they both hopped out.

"Mr. Greene," the man said. "I'm Bob Conrad. We spoke on the phone."

"Thanks for coming out on such short notice," said Win. "This is Grover."

"No problem. It's often the way this business works," he said, tucking the aluminum box under his arm and shaking both men's hands. He reached into his shirt pocket and pulled out his business cards, handing one to each.

"You probably want to see inside," Win said, starting for the porch.

"Actually, there's no need," Conrad said, spreading his hands as if to show they were empty. He cleared his throat. "I'm sorry, I wish I had better news for you."

Win blinked at him. "Come again?"

"I'm afraid I can't buy your house."

For a beat, Winston thought the man was joking. "You haven't even looked at it!"

His voice had a note of apology in it. "I've seen what I need to see . . ."

Win and Grover waited.

"Well, there's a few very basic requirements that any structure needs to meet for a company like mine to be able to invest in it." He started counting with his fingers. "It has to be free of mold. And not too terribly vandalized, and I can presume your house meets those conditions, no problem."

"Then what *is* the problem?"

"Well, when I got here, I went up to knock on the door, and I noticed there's a couple boards on your steps that are really loose."

"Yeah, I keep forgetting. Some twelve-bys and nails should do it," said Win.

Conrad nodded in agreement. "Usually that's all it takes, but it can also be an indicator of something more serious. You see, when a part of a house that's meant to be immoveable, like a staircase, whether indoor or outdoor," he motioned toward the steps, "becomes unstable, that could be due to something else, like the ground shifting."

"What?" Win couldn't see where the guy was going with this.

"Obviously I haven't done a geological," the man said, bringing his palm to his chest, "but then, I don't have to. When I felt that, I took the liberty of checking under your house. You can do it from the crawl space in back. All I had to do was lift the screen, and there it was."

"There *what* was?"

"It's your foundation, Mr. Greene. Your house is slipping off it. It's not too bad now, and you can fix it if you get on it soon. But I'm afraid it turns your property into a money-losing venture for me," he explained. "I'm really sorry. It's a beautiful house."

"But the doors and windows all close just fine," Win protested. "Please, come inside, see for yourself. There's nothing wrong with the house."

"There isn't right *now*. I mean . . . there *is*, but you just don't notice it yet. Except for those," he said, indicating the front steps again.

Win rubbed his face and glanced at Grover, who was beginning to glare at the man. They were both getting an idea of where this guy was leading them.

"Look, Mr. Conrad," Win said. "I'm a little desperate right now, so I'll probably meet whatever you want to pay—"

"Believe me, Mr. Greene," Conrad said, cutting him off, "that's not it. I'm not trying to whittle you down. This is a great house and you deserve to get some real money for it. But this is what I do. Your home needs a substantial investment before it can be turned around. I mean, yes, you could sell it to someone willing to take on the problem at a drastically cut rate, but you said you needed to do this quickly, and that would take time. For inspections, negotiations, estimates. And for someone like me, I mean, I *am* the company . . . it just doesn't make sense." He looked at the ground, then back up again, genuinely regretful. "Sorry."

He walked to his car, but before getting in, he turned and said, "Look, it really is a beautiful home. If things change and you decide to sell after doing the work, please give me a call. I can refer you to a great realtor. Good luck."

He hopped in, and as he backed out, he rolled down his window and called to Win, "Big fan, by the way."

41

Sylmar

O ZZIE PARKED ACROSS the four-lane boulevard from Janette's apartment building, taking in the rectangular three-story. It had wide, brightly colored vertical stripes that demarcated each unit's small balcony. Day-Glo colors of orange, yellow, and green were meant to make the facade seem tropically inviting, a lure to younger tenants. Meanwhile, the sides and rear of the building were the off-white beige color typical of affordable rentals all over Los Angeles.

"Looks like a box of candy," Ozzie said to Jordy in the passenger seat. "It got a pool? We could barbecue. Call up some chi-qui-*taaas*."

Jordy stared at a corner apartment on the second floor.

Ozzie followed his eyes to where Jordy was looking, then turned back. "Your girlfriend home?" Ozzie knew that Rocket's instruction to meet at Jordy's meant that they needed a new place to hide out for a few days, and Jordy's (Janette's) was the only place left available to them. They also all knew that it meant Jordy's girlfriend would have to go, after all.

"Number two-nineteen. Wait two minutes, then hit the buzzer. I'll let you in." Jordy started to get out.

Ozzie grabbed his arm. "Why don't you want me to come with you?"

Jordy pointed to the entrance. "You see the front door? See the camera over it?" Ozzie looked back at him, blank. "They know me here. They don't know you. I don't think they should get video of us going in together to commit murder. Do you?"

Ozzie hadn't noticed this side of Jordy before. There was a clarity, an ability to look down the road at the outcome and predict the consequences. *Inside that albondiga he calls a head, Jordy's a planner.* That impressed Ozzie. A little. But Jordy's condescending tone pissed him off. He decided to go along—for now.

"Yeah. Okay."

"Number two-nineteen," Jordy said again as he got out and started across the street.

Ozzie rolled down his window. "Hey! What about the chiquitas?"

Jordy kept walking.

Ozzie watched him as he got to the sunken "moderne" entryway, went down the three steps, reached into his pocket, and unlocked the secured front door with a key fob. Jordy stepped in, and the door closed behind him.

Ozzie looked at his watch. Two minutes later, he was standing in front of the sunken entrance to the building. He scanned the instructions next to the LED panel and keypad. He pressed #, which prompted a dial tone, and punched in the numbers two-one-nine. A line rang, then clicked, as if a phone had been answered and a high tone came through a speaker next to the panel. The front door audibly unlocked.

Inside the lobby was a small sitting area sparsely furnished with two sleek chairs and a matching coffee table. The walls had vertical, two-foot-wide stripes that matched the sunny exterior colors, offset by cooler blue and green stripes in the floor tiles.

He started for the elevator across the lobby and heard the jingling of keys coming from somewhere. He passed a mailbox alcove on his right, where a middle-aged woman was fumbling with a key ring. She didn't look up as he passed.

He punched the "Up" button and heard the mechanism start with a clunk. The car came down with a *swoosh.* As he waited for the doors to open, Ozzie wondered if that lady had seen Jordy.

Ozzie stepped into the second-floor hallway, looked in both directions. *Deserted.* A floor-to-ceiling window across from the elevator offered a view of the courtyard garden. He was disappointed to see there was no pool.

The unit numbers were etched into tiny metal plates on the apartment doors, and he had to stop and squint at the first couple to get his bearings. He realized 219 was at the end and started for it, muttering to himself, "Pendejo jerkoff. Talk to me like I'm a fucking idiot. 'See the camera?' Yeah, idiota, I know what a camera is for. You and me are going to have a talk when this is over."

Though he hadn't yet crossed the metaphorical Rubicon into murder, Ozzie had fantasized many times about killing Jordy when the big man least expected it. *Maybe today is the day?* But best right now to switch things up: *Take it easy on him for a bit, get his guard down, make him like you.* Then a bullet to the head. But not from behind, like they did that car guy last year. He wanted Jordy to see it coming, to know it was Osvaldo López-Famosa y Fernández-García who did him in. The better man who got the better of him.

He reached apartment 219 and knocked.

42

THE ODOR OF day-old coffee and rancid dairy filled Teddy's nose as he stepped inside. He left the door open behind him for ventilation and felt the inside air pull past him as it wafted toward the opening.

He took another step into the kitchen, letting his eyes adjust. Then he detected another smell, one he recognized from murder scenes he'd worked, metallic and slightly sweet. *Blood.* If he could smell it from here, where there was no visual evidence of it, then there had to be a lot of it nearby.

Someone had been cut and bled out or suffered some other fatal wound. He sniffed, checking for other telltale odors, and there it was: the faint, acrid smell of expended gunpowder. He also caught a whiff of shit in the air.

He dropped to a defensive crouch, his gun extended in front of him. There was no movement in either of the open doorways that bookended the wall, but he was able to see into the living room via the Vu Thru fireplace in the center. He could make out two sneakered feet, pointing at the ceiling.

Teddy held his breath, listening for any sound. He had a feeling he was not the only one still breathing in this house.

43

J ORDY OPENED THE door.

"We alone?" Ozzie asked.

"Yeah, get in here. Anybody see you?"

"Nah, man. There was some old puta getting her mail, but she was fucking with her keys too much to notice."

Ozzie looked around the apartment. A corner unit with an open floor plan, spacious living room and kitchen area, pale yellow walls, and faux hardwood floors. Tasteful but affordable kit furniture and arty wall posters. Apparently Janette liked things clean and well ordered.

"This ain't so bad," said Ozzie. "You made it sound like a dump, a place you wouldn't want your mami to sleep."

"It's okay," Jordy said behind him.

Ozzie was about to lay on the charm, tell Jordy how smart he was to have such a great setup, when a belt dropped past his eyes and tightened around his neck. His reflexes sent his hands up to grab it, but the belt was already too taut to get his fingers under it. His feet rose off the floor. Jordy was using his considerable height and strength to essentially hang Ozzie. He started kicking his legs.

His vision began to shrink, like the iris of a lens closing, his consciousness fading more quickly than he would have imagined possible. He lifted his right knee, reached down toward his boot where he kept his secret friend. Jordy yanked upward, lifting him higher.

Ozzie raised his knee until his fingers reached inside the top of the boot. At first, he couldn't feel it where he always dropped it, right behind his ankle bone. Then, there it was, the ivory handle of his switchblade, the one he bought in Tijuana a few years ago. Jordy jerked him again, and he lost contact with the knife, but he reached deeper and got a grip on it. He pulled it out, his fingers turning the handle and feeling their way to the button release. The click of the blade opening filled the room.

He felt Jordy pause for an instant. He must've heard it.

Ozzie flipped the knife in his palm, the blade now under his fist, and jabbed as hard as he could, sinking the knife deep into Jordy's thigh, once, twice before the belt loosened. Jordy's shriek assaulted his ears.

Spurred by the sudden agony in his thigh, Jordy raised Ozzie higher, then twisted to one side and dropped to the floor on top of him, forcing Ozzie's oily, twisted face to take the full weight of his body in the fall. He heard Ozzie's teeth shatter as his mouth hit the faux wood flooring.

The belt around Ozzie's neck loosened a bit when they landed, and Jordy felt him pull in a desperate breath. He raised his knee and pushed it sharply between Ozzie's shoulder blades, then grabbed his head under the chin. With his fingers interlaced, he craned Ozzie's head sharply toward him. He pulled hard, wrenching his head back until the neck bones wouldn't go any farther, and then pulled a little harder. He felt the bones snap. It sounded like a trip to the chiropractor gone wrong.

He'd seen it done in a movie once, *Marathon Man*. It took more muscle than he'd thought it would. It had seemed so effortless onscreen. But he thought it was funny how things like that can stick with you and then pop into your head right when you need them.

44

TEDDY STAYED LOW, his pistol aimed through the fireplace, as he made his way to the doorway on the left, which was the farthest point from the rest of the house and the shortest path to the open kitchen door.

He glanced into the living room and quickly drew back, surprised by the sight of two bodies instead of just the one he'd spotted through the fireplace. He swung his gun around the door-jamb, bringing his body around after it, using the wall to shield himself, if necessary.

The bodies of two men lay on the floor. One of them, the far-thest from him, was Zeke, eyes open, his head lying in a pool of blood. Teddy could make out a neat hole in his forehead, and that his mouth was frozen open in a gape of surprise.

The other man, the one closer to him, he didn't recognize. He looked about the same age as Zeke, maybe a little older, and though casually dressed, his clothes were expensive. He was also on his back, with a hole in his forehead. Not as centered as the one that had hit Zeke, probably because he had been farther away from the shooter. Upon death, both men's bowels had emptied.

From where he stood, Teddy could see spray patterns of blood and brain matter on the wall and carpet around the fireplace. The killer had used a large-caliber weapon.

Rather than contaminate the scene, he stepped back and went through the kitchen to the other doorway. From here he was directly across from the front door. Ahead of him and to his right was the hall that led to the rest of the house, where yesterday Win had sent Amy to collect her things. He listened. Nothing. The killer had either just left or was hiding in the house.

Teddy had a choice: He could leave the way he'd come, right now, and make an anonymous call to the police, or he could check the rest of the house. If the perp was still there, he might be able to take him down and get some answers that could lead them to Clare. He'd have to report it, regardless.

The fact that one of the bodies belonged to the kidnap victim's husband meant this whole thing had gone sideways. Clare was running out of time—if she was even still alive. He decided to try and bag the shooter, give her the best chance of coming home alive.

The decision to search the rest of the house made, his senses went into overdrive, especially the sixth sense every law enforcement officer in the world develops: a heightened awareness of your surroundings for those moments when every swinging door or creak in a floorboard could be signaling danger.

For the first time in a really long time, he remembered what it was like in the old days, when he was on a foot chase through the back alleys of New Orleans or LA. He felt like a cop again.

Teddy stepped into the hallway and moved toward the back of the house. Reaching the bathroom on the right, he nudged the door open all the way to the wall and scanned the room from the open doorway. Clear.

On the left was the door to Amy's room, also open. The layout meant the small room's space was to the right of the door, and the closet was inside on the left. He could see Amy's bed set against the back wall, and her dresser under the window that faced the street. There were worn stuffed animals lined up on it and across the pillows of the bed. He crouched to see under the bed frame, even though it was too low to be a viable hiding spot for an adult. *Better safe than shot in the back.* Amy had left her closet door open, so he could see inside. He crossed the room and made a cursory glance into the corners of the closet anyway, just to be certain. *Clear again.* That left the master bedroom.

Teddy went back to the hallway. This is when it gets most dangerous for anyone clearing a crime scene on their own. If all the other spots have been cleared, the nervous suspect knows you're closing in. And if he's armed, like this one obviously was, death is potentially right around the next corner.

The door to the master bedroom was closed. Teddy felt a dribble of sweat coursing down the side of his head and another start down his forehead. He wiped them away with his jacket sleeve before they reached his eyes. He took the last step to the closed door, silently gripped the knob with his left hand, and in one move turned it, pushed the door open wide, and dropped into a firing stance.

Unlike in the rest of the house, the curtains were wide open, and bright light flooded the room. The hair on the back of Teddy's neck stood on end.

The head of the queen-size bed was against the wall that faced the backyard. It was unmade, and there was men's clothing strewn about the room, across the floor, and on the rumpled bed linens. The musty odor that filled the rest of the house was more evident back here. He dropped low to get a look under the bed frame and saw what looked like an old suitcase and a clumsily folded blanket, but not a person. He straightened up, and a hint of fresh air hit his face. He stepped farther in and saw the window that faced the side of the house was wide open.

The home's design meant that the footprint of Amy's room intruded into this room's space, leaving an alcove to the left of the window. Someone could be hiding there.

"Toss your weapon out. Do it now," he said. "Come out with your hands where I can see them."

The only reply came through the open window: sounds from the neighborhood, distant traffic, a few kids. He crept forward, checking the walls and floor around the mouth of the alcove for any sign of movement—a shadow, any sign of a person hiding there. He quickly stepped into the room, swinging the gun around to cover the alcove. Nothing there but a small table with a lamp and an aging modem attached to the phone line.

He turned to the window, inspected it for shoe marks on the sill. He didn't see any but figured he was too late. The shooter must have heard him come in from the kitchen, so he went out this way. His shoulders drooped as he lowered his gun.

"Shit," he drawled.

"I hear ya," said someone behind him. Teddy turned.

A young man wearing a baseball cap was standing in the closet on the opposite side of the bed, the sliding mirrored door open just enough to aim his pistol through.

Teddy could see his own reflection, slack-jawed and vulnerable. "I must be slippin'."

The bullet hit his chest and sent him backward, where the window frame clipped him behind the knees and pitched him out to land hard on the ground below.

45

JORDY UNDID HIS fly and slowly lowered his jeans until he exposed the two gashes in his leg.

The blood had started coagulating, so now the denim was stuck to his skin. He yanked it out of the wounds and gasped in pain as the blood started to flow again. Each puncture was more than an inch across, and had been made worse by Ozzie's flailing, turning what would have been a simple cut into a ragged, jagged gape. It felt like the blade had nicked his thigh bone.

"Damn," he said. If only Ozzie had stuck his forearm, or even his side, he'd have an easier time recovering. *Gonna be tough to get up on a board for a while.*

He found a first-aid kit in the bathroom cabinet alongside Janette's special towels and chick shit. He stripped off his jeans, swabbed the wounds with cotton balls doused in Bactine, then glopped on some Neosporin cream, grateful it was the pain-relieving kind. He used several large adhesive strips to pull the holes closed (poor man's stitches, which wouldn't hold for long), then finished it off with a few gauze pads held tight to his thigh with the rest of the tape.

He choked down a handful of Aleve, followed by a gulp of coppery water from the faucet. Without proper sutures and a compression setup, it was the best he could do for now.

He limped to the bedroom and opened his side of the closet, grabbed an Aloha shirt and chinos, and pulled them on. He checked himself in the full-length mirror that stood in the corner, the one that he liked to watch himself bonk Janette in. Then he grabbed a few more shirts and a jacket and pulled his duffel down from the top shelf. He went to the dresser and opened the bottom drawer, taking some extra jeans, skivvies, and socks. He stuffed everything into the duffel, zipped it closed, then headed to the front room to clean up the mess.

From under the kitchen sink, he retrieved a sponge, a spray bottle of Formula 409, and a roll of paper towels and inspected the scene. The jeans he'd had on were ruined, but at least they'd kept his wound from dripping too much. A small puddle of saliva and blood had trickled from Ozzie's mouth where his lip had split open, and there was the smattering of shattered teeth where his face had met the floor. He flipped Ozzie onto his back and slid him out of the way, then wiped it all up. Nothing he could do about the tiny divot Ozzie's teeth had made in the faux wood.

Janette wouldn't be back until tonight so he wasn't worried about her coming in while he worked. Instead, he felt concern for her, bothered that this could implicate her. But Ozzie and Rocket? They would have killed her, no problem. In the end, Jordy just couldn't accept that. Edvina was one thing—she'd tossed him out like so much garbage. But Janette had put a roof over his head and never asked for anything but a little of his attention and time. The impulse to shield her surprised him.

Jordy fished his wallet and keys from his bloody jeans, then rifled Ozzie's pockets and took his car keys, wallet, cash, and everything else, and stuffed it all into his chinos.

He grabbed a paper grocery bag and a plastic produce bag from under the sink. The bloody paper towels and sponge went into the paper bag, along with his own bloodstained shirt and denims. He slipped the produce bag over Ozzie's head, to keep from leaving a crimson trail of DNA behind him. It fit perfectly, even leaving enough slack at the neck for Jordy to use a twist tie to secure it. He chuckled when he noticed the word printed in bold letters across Ozzie's bagged face: "Organic."

He opened the door to peek down the hallway. This would be the riskiest part: getting down the hall to the trash chute in the janitor's storeroom with Ozzie hanging over his shoulder. Once he got the body into the chute (which should be wide enough for the skinny little fuck), it would drop three floors to the big receptacle hidden behind a steel double door in the sub-terranean garage. Hopefully no one would be crawling around down there, looking for a lost contact lens case or something when Ozzie dropped in.

It was Thursday. Trash pickup wasn't until Monday. He could even swing down there and cover him up. With the garbage mask-ing the smell of his rotting corpse, hopefully no one would notice until the truck came to empty the dumpster, and he'd just get hauled away to the dump. *"Desaparecido,"* as Ozzie would have said.

Jordy took hold of Ozzie's wrists and pulled him to a sitting position. With the broken neck no longer providing support for his head, it flopped backward and dangled between his shoulder blades. Wrestling Ozzie's corpse up from the floor was like lifting a loosely tied bunch of sandbags.

Between the cleaning and the pain and shock from his leg wounds, Jordy was starting to sweat, his palms becoming clammy. He lost his grip, and Ozzie fell to the floor, making a thud as he landed.

"C'mon, you got this," he grumbled.

He peeled off a paper towel to dry his hands, dropped it into the paper bag, grabbed Ozzie's wrists again, and pulled. He quickly grabbed him under the armpits, widened his stance to set his weight, and lifted him all the way to his feet. Ozzie's arms hung limply at his sides, and his head jostled back and forth behind him, making it difficult to hold him steady.

Jordy felt dampness under Ozzie's arms, and he got a strong whiff of shit.

"Crapped your pants, huh?" he said. "I'da thought you were better than that . . . cabrón."

He worried that Ozzie's poop might leave a stain on his shirt. *But a shirt is easily replaced. A murder rap is forever.* He readied himself again, and in one swift move crouched to catch the body and plant his shoulder under Ozzie's midsection. It folded over his right shoulder. He stood up straight and shifted the body to bal-ance it. If he could barely smell that shit before, he sure could now.

He cracked opened the front door and listened for any sound: footsteps, a TV or stereo, the elevator moving. Nothing. Typical midday of a workweek. He moved quickly down the hall keeping a firm hold on Ozzie. He couldn't risk dropping him and having to waste time trying to lift him again. He could drag him, but Ozzie would leave a trail in the carpet and it would just be too weird for someone to happen upon Jordy vacuuming and scrubbing the hallway.

He passed the elevator just as its motor started. Someone was calling it, maybe someone in the lobby headed to this very floor. He could see the door to the janitor's room at the end. *Twenty yards to go.* He picked up the pace.

He reached the door and pushed it open with his free shoulder. Stepping inside, he breathed easier when he saw no one was dumping garbage or sorting recycling. The overhead fluorescence hurt his eyes.

He went to the garbage chute and pulled open the hatch. Hinged at the bottom, it swung out, its downward motion stopped by chains screwed into the wall on either side. With the chains fully extended, the door stopped evenly at Jordy's navel, like a shelf.

He faced the hatch, guiding Ozzie's feet into the chute, then made a little hop to toss the rest of him down the shaft. But the soft midsection of Ozzie's limp body caught on the hatch opening, the dead weight ripping the chains from the wall and the heavier upper half of the body pulling the rest of him back into the room.

"Fuuuck," said Jordy. Ozzie's face landed on the concrete floor with a splat, but luckily, the plastic bag had done its job of catching the ooze from his mouth.

He got a grip on Ozzie's jacket collar and lifted. Ozzie's arms flopped up lifelessly, and his jacket started to slip off. Jordy reached down with one hand and got a firm grip on the back of Ozzie's belt, his other hand still gripping the collar. He shifted the body around and lifted, this time aiming Ozzie's head and shoulders into the open chute. With the hatch hanging flat against the wall, Jordy got the upper torso in.

Ozzie hung folded from the waist in the opening, his legs limp to the floor, the shit stain in the seat of his pants facing out. Jordy held his breath as he bent down, grabbed Ozzie's ankles, and lifted. The body disappeared into the dark chute. Jordy froze and listened. He heard it banging into the sheet metal walls as it gained speed on its way down. The corpse came to a crunching stop in the trash bin far below.

Jordy closed the chute door until it latched, then pushed the screws back into the holes they'd left when Ozzie's weight had yanked them out of the drywall. *Someone will open it and think they broke it.* He smiled, proud of his work.

He had been formulating his own plan B for the last few hours, and with Ozzie toast and no way for Rocket to find him, there was nothing to slow him down.

He wondered how long it would take him to get to the Washington home in Venice.

46

WRIGHTWOOD

WIN AND GROVER watched the ass end of the sleek black sedan carrying Bob Conrad roll away down the dirt drive. At least he hadn't mentioned the filthy car in the driveway.

Without a word, Win pocketed the business card and hurried toward his home. When he reached the front porch, he stepped too hard on one of the problem boards. It shifted under his feet, and he lost his balance. He tried to get his other foot under himself in time to catch his fall, but the toe of his boot caught on a step, and he went down, sprawling across the boards to the ground. A cloud of dust rose when he landed, like a movie pratfall.

He heard Grover run to him. "Win!"

Win lay on his stomach, propped on his elbows, his body and face covered in dust.

"C'mon," said Grover. He got a hand under Win's arm as he pushed up from the dirt and got to his feet. "You okay?"

"I'm fine. You believe that? We were just talking about those goddamn stairs!"

"Not like you haven't had a lot on your mind," said Grover.

Win brushed himself off with angry swipes, then climbed the steps again, this time more carefully, and went inside.

He headed across the living room to the grand staircase that framed the fireplace, and went upstairs. In his bedroom he yanked open a dresser drawer, pulled out another pair of faded jeans, and grabbed a clean flannel shirt from the closet. He could hear Grover down in the kitchen, running water and opening and closing cabinets. Win made a quick stop in the bathroom to rinse his face and run his wet fingers over his scalp to clear off the driveway dust.

He came downstairs and went through the kitchen, the dusty clothes rolled under his arm, his cowboy boots clomping on the wood floor. He saw that Grover had started the coffeemaker and taken a seat at the foldaway dinette table just inside the doorway.

Win stepped into the garage to the washer/dryer and dumped in his clothes. After pouring in some soap and starting the machine, he went back to the kitchen; opened a cabinet; produced two mugs, a thermos, and two travel cups; and set them all on the counter by the sink.

Grover watched Win as he pulled his cell phone from his back pocket and connected it to a charger cord at one end of the counter, then checked the Trimline phone for voicemails on his landline. He sighed and set it back onto its cradle.

Win leaned on the edge of the sink and looked out the window above it. On a normal morning, as he made his coffee and got his bearings for the day, he would stand here and look out at the undeveloped landscape. Most days a slight breeze would be nudging the tree leaves. There was none. Stillness. He felt a strip of fear course through his body. *The calm before the catastrophe?*

Win switched his gaze to the black circle of the garbage disposal, which always reminded him of the movie *Rolling Thunder*. The house of a Vietnam veteran played by William Devane is invaded by a gang of criminal hicks determined to steal the valuable coin collection his community had given him after he returned home from a North Vietnamese POW camp—a thanks-of-a-grateful-nation kind of thing. What the bad guys don't realize is that the soldier had endured relentless torture in the prison, and it takes a long time for him to give in. It's only when the criminals grind off his hand in a garbage disposal that he relents and tells them where the coins are hidden. After taking the coins, the robbers shoot him and his wife and son, leaving them for dead. But Devane survives, contacts a fellow prisoner he met in the POW camp, played by Tommy Lee Jones, and together they take revenge on the gang. Win never looked at a garbage disposal the same way again.

Ironically, it had been one of the movies that inspired him to be an actor, and he used to joke that the perennial ups and downs of showbiz made him feel like William Devane's character. Right now, he'd shove his own hand into the InSinkErator if he thought it would bring his daughter back to him. But he was no closer today to bringing Clare home than he had been at this time yesterday. It felt like every minute that went by without her found was a wasted one, and that every tick of the clock was bringing them all closer to a tragic finale. If that happened, he wondered if he would be tempted to enlist Grover or Teddy to be his Tommy Lee Jones, and together they would deliver bloody, vengeful justice. He wondered if he was even capable of that . . . and then he decided that he was.

He thought of when Amy was born. He'd invited Clare and Zeke to bring her here during their initial recovery and adjustment to parenting and had been happily surprised when they accepted. They'd spent a lot of time in this very room while Win cooked meals and they all cooed over the new arrival.

The custom-built kitchen, like the rest of the home, hadn't been changed much over the years. The original cabinetry was well oiled against the high-altitude dryness. Square, built-in cubbies above the refrigerator were meant for wine storage, but Win used them for the carbonated juice drinks he liked. Even the dinette table was created to be part of the wall, hinged to it below a paned window.

"They'll get in touch. Nothing to do now but wait," Grover said from his spot in the kitchen nook, right where Clare used to sit while she breastfed Amy. "You're an actor—you should be good at that—sitting around, waiting for the action to start."

Win looked at him, a slight smile cracking his face. "You'd think."

The coffeemaker made a gurgling sound, followed by three subtle beeps. Win filled the mugs with coffee, brought them over, and sat across from his old friend. Grover reached for a small bowl of sugar and powdered creamer packets Win kept by the window. He chose two of the creamers.

"I got the real thing," Win offered, and started up.

"Nah, I actually like this shit."

Win settled back into his chair, sipped the black coffee. He appreciated that Grover had made it strong. After a beat he said, "I never got used to it."

"What's that?"

"The waiting," said Win. "All this time, I never did."

"You've been doing this a while, Win."

"Yeah," Win said with a touch of irony. "Somebody told me a long time ago that to be an actor in Hollywood, you need to figure out how to handle the waiting. What to do with yourself in the downtime."

"That's pretty true for all of us," said Grover. "Whether you're waiting on a call for a job or a call to the set, you're waiting."

"I think it was easier when I still had a family at home." Win got a picture in his mind, of himself and Grover and several crew members crowded around the U-shaped dining area in his Winnebago, a pile of wooden matches in the middle of the table. "Remember how we used to play matchstick poker at lunch?"

Grover grinned and nodded back. "You bet."

Win's face changed. "You know, when things happen for you in this business, you just . . . follow 'em. It's like being dragged around by the heels." Win looked out the window. "The only thing I ever really did right was marry Joanie."

Grover looked at him hard. "Don't do that to yourself. *You* didn't kidnap your daughter. And you didn't kill your wife either, for that matter."

"I've had enough therapy to know I was a codependent clown," Win said. "She went out of her way to make sure I had everything I needed to keep on being a functionally drunk asshole. Until she didn't. And then she died."

"And then you cleaned up. You didn't fall apart like a lot of guys would. You salvaged your career. Raised your kid as best you could. Never asked for charity or sympathy from anyone." Grover leaned in. "I've seen more than a few come and go in this business myself, Win. *You* put your shit back together. How many can say that?"

Win sighed. "Maybe you're right."

"I know I'm right."

Win had long ago lost count of the colleagues who had dropped off the radar entirely due to their inability to conquer their substance abuse. He had even developed a theory that most actors are, at least initially, driven by a deep sense of self-loathing. The prospect of becoming someone else, if only for a little while, was better than living in your own skin full-time. Especially in

LA, where actors were always encouraged to dig into their personal experience and use what's already there. It's practical in that it's honest and reads well on camera. But if you landed some jobs, got that industry acceptance, you learned that the elements of your personality you don't like can be gifts. Gifts you could turn to gold if you were willing to exploit them. And *if* you could avoid being consumed by them.

"Maybe I should call Teddy, see if he has anything."

"I think he'd let us know if he did."

"True, but it gives me *something* to do before I go completely out of my skull."

Win stood up and retrieved his cell from where he'd just plugged it in. He opened the screen and tapped Teddy's number. The distinctive drawl came on after a few rings: "You've reached Theodore Beauregard, Esquire, Private Investigations. Your call is important to us, so please leave a detailed message and someone will get back to you as soon as possible." *Beep!*

"It's Win. Who else, right? Just wondering if Zeke gave you anything. We're at my house . . . which turned out to be a dead end. Call me." He hung up and set the phone on the table.

As they sat there staring at each other, they heard a *tha-thum-thump*, followed by a loud buzz, coming from the garage.

"What the hell's that?" Grover said, rising to his feet.

"It's just the washer, does that sometimes." Win got up and went to the garage, the buzzing becoming louder as he opened the door.

He lifted the washer lid, and the buzzing stopped, its echo bouncing off the hard garage surfaces. His jeans had balled up to one side, forcing the basket to tip in the spin cycle, shutting it down and tripping the buzzer. The last spin cycle was nearly finished anyway, so he pulled the clothes out, stuffed them into the dryer, and started it. Then he went back toward the door that led to the kitchen, grabbed the handle . . . and froze, his mouth hanging slightly open.

From the kitchen, Grover had an unobstructed view to where Win stood.

"What is it?"

Win turned slowly to the garage, then back to Grover. "Come in here."

47

SYLMAR

ROCKET WENT TO the front window and pulled back the curtain to see if a crowd had gathered after those gunshots. Not a soul. That was a part of LA that never ceased to amaze him, the lack of connection between neighbors. Sylmar was no exception, apparently, not even when gunfire breaks the quiet.

His shoved his pistol back in his waistband, his shirt covering it, and felt for the thousand in cash stuffed in his pocket. Satisfied, he went out the front door, calmly strode to his car in the driveway, backed into the circle, and drove away.

48

WRIGHTWOOD

GROVER FOLLOWED AS Win stepped into the garage and punched the garage door button.

The mechanism churned to life, and bright sunlight filled the windowless space, illuminating the tool collection lining the walls, organized on hooks set into perforated peg boards. He kept his skis and camping equipment stowed on plywood sheets spread across the rafters, and the back wall opposite the yawning door was lined with white laminate kit cabinets from the Home Depot over in Victorville.

In the center, hidden under a custom-made waterproof cover, was the silhouette of an automobile.

"Damn," said Grover. "I forgot all about that."

Win looked at him over his shoulder. "So did I."

He went over and grabbed a handful of the fabric that was drawn tight under the front bumper, pulling out the elastic hem to expose the grille. Grover moved to the other side and together they rolled the cover back to reveal a 1968 Ford Mustang 390 GT 2+2 Fastback.

The *Bullitt* car.

Well, not the actual *Bullitt* car, but the same model and make. The original had disappeared into middle America before popping up for auction in early 2020, fetching a cool three million four hundred thousand dollars. And why not? Steve McQueen himself had driven it in the grandaddy of all movie car chases.

"When was the last time you took it out?" Grover asked.

"Year before last, I think. Maybe longer."

Win had picked it up dirt cheap at a police auction many years earlier. It had been seized from a convicted coke dealer. He had read in the *Los Angeles Times* that these auctions sometimes yielded amazing deals on exotic vehicles seized from criminals, so for fun Win started scanning the auction listings and eventually came across the description for the Mustang. He went down to the police lot, hiding under a baseball cap and sunglasses (code in LA for "famous person here"), and outbid everyone, landing the car "as is" for two thousand five hundred and seventy-five dollars in cash. The paint was oxidized and flaking, the chromed bumpers were rusting, the upholstery was ripped and stained, and the ceiling cloth was hanging down in tatters. He then undertook a mission to restore the car to look exactly like the centerpiece of his all-time favorite movie.

First, he had the engine rebuilt with the help of a crusty mechanic in Wrightwood named Manny. The old guy was stunned when the town's one local celebrity towed the vehicle in and asked him to work on it.

The factory transmission was fine, but they decided it needed a Borg-Warner T-10 heavy-duty, four-speed with matching heavy-duty clutch, just like McQueen's. A new drive train; differential and axles; and wide, oval nylon tires installed, and suddenly it was street legal.

And no cutting corners with the paint. A Ford dealership arranged to have the car repainted in the same Dark Highland Green as Detective Frank Bullitt's vehicle. When he dropped the Mustang off for its new paint job, salespeople and mechanics alike came over to meet the movie star and get a look at the vintage gem in process.

It took him a few years to get all the finishes restored, a process that accelerated once he got clean. He taught himself how to replace carpeting and rocker panels, head lamps, and the dash cluster. He even revitalized the trunk and weatherized the undercarriage (most cars in SoCal didn't need that, but Wrightwood has real winters). He taught himself how to calibrate the carburetor, spark plugs and valves, and how to adjust the distributor to mix the fuel and air to perfection. He accepted his limitations when it came to restoring the upholstery, but by then he had done so much himself it didn't feel like defeat to hand the job over to a specialist.

In the end, everything on the car was as it was at the time it was built. No concessions to modernity, no surround sound or even an FM radio (that would interfere with the defiant roar of the engine). Spending time in the garage, lovingly returning this jewel to its original badass glory, had given him something to do with his hands instead of filling a glass with liquor or popping open a beer. Restoring it became a form of therapy, a way to distract himself from the sorrow after Joanie's death.

And driving it along those open, uncrowded mountain roads was a kind of celebration.

At first, he had taken it out often, but then less and less so. It no longer brought him joy, but he couldn't place why. One day he came into the garage, intending to take a drive in the mountains. As he sat there in the driver's seat, listening to the low rumble of the idling engine, he could no longer separate it from a sense of loss. He twisted the power knob on the radio, and nothing but static came through. It felt like a metaphor, as if the broadcast of this episode of his life had ended, and the station had signed off. He shut down the engine, rolled up the windows, and covered it. He arranged for a local kid to swing by once every couple of months to check the battery and charge it, if needed. That had been two years ago.

"You wouldn't have a Blue Book in your car, would you?"

"Not hardly. But you got internet, don't you?"

They went back into the house, leaving the garage door open, the Mustang getting its first sunlight in years.

Win opened the center desk drawer and retrieved the thumb drive that Amy had brought to him yesterday. He handed it to Grover.

"Hold on to that. In case something happens to me."

Grover gave his friend a look and stuffed it into his pocket. "Okay."

Within minutes they'd found a website, Hemmings.com, dedicated to collectible automobiles, and were staring at an identical 1968 Mustang, also restored to replicate the *Bullitt* model, for sale in Rochester, New York. Asking price: one hundred and twenty-five thousand dollars.

"I've been tearing all over creation trying to raise a few grand, and all this time I had a frickin' fortune collecting dust in my garage." He shook his head, looked at Grover. "You know anybody who wants to buy a classic car—like, today?"

"Not in the time you have," said Grover. "But if you sign over the pink slip, couldn't you just give them the car?"

Win looked back at the screen. "Holy shit."

49

SYLMAR

Rocket dialed Ozzie, then put the phone on speaker while negotiating turns through residential neighborhoods. He'd decided to avoid the crowded boulevards just in case one of Zeke's neighbors had reported seeing his car parked there.

Ring, ring, ring, ring. The line went dead. They had deliberately not set up any voicemail. He dialed again. Again, no answer. He dialed Jordy. Same thing.

Something was wrong. It dawned on him that those two might have finally gone after each other. Ozzie was always popping off at Jordy, needling him, and the mutual animosity between them had only gotten worse since they'd come back from the actor's house yesterday. And given the take wasn't going to be anywhere near what they had been promised (at least that bitch Clare had paid for *that* mistake, big-time), now the rest of them would have to scramble twice as hard if they were going to salvage what they could.

Rocket knew that the apartment Jordy currently called home was on the second floor and faced the boulevard, so when he arrived, he drove slowly down the busy street to get a look at the place. There seemed to be no activity at all up there. The windows were closed, but the drapes were open, which was weird. The backup plan was, if they needed somewhere else to hole up, this was the only safe spot left, so if they had gone in and found Jordy's girl, they would've pulled the shades and taken care of her. Then they'd lie low for a couple of days, and they'd be long gone by the time anybody found her. He decided to drive around the block, see if he could spot Ozzie's clunker.

He circled the building. Ozzie's car was nowhere on the street, and he didn't think they would've driven it into the garage—too many surveillance cameras recording license plates nowadays.

He cruised back onto the thoroughfare facing the building, spotted an open space across the street, and parked. He needed to think for a minute. He let the engine idle while he dropped his head and closed his eyes, rubbing his temples to concentrate. He tried to picture a scenario that could explain why neither guy was answering the phone. He came up with two:

First, Ozzie and Jordy had patched up their differences while grocery shopping, then went after the kid on their own, cutting Rocket out altogether. Second, Ozzie and Jordy had had their inevitable showdown. One had taken the other out, and the survivor went to grab the kid on his own. All he would need was wheels and one of the burner phones to set up the exchange.

The former was unlikely. Those two hated each other like a junkie hates to pay his dealer. But the latter sounded right.

One thing was for sure: this was turning to shit. He needed to take control now or lose any stake in the plan for good.

Rocket was about to pull back onto the street, when a police cruiser appeared in his side mirror, creeping up the boulevard behind him. He touched the pistol in his waistband, then opened his phone as if he were looking for directions.

The cruiser slowed as it pulled parallel to his car. Rocket stiffened. He kept his eyes on the phone screen, feeling the cruiser slide past him. When he looked up, he saw two officers, a man and a woman, each scanning their side of the street. They were looking for someone, but not him. The cruiser stopped for the red light at the corner ahead, sat idle until the light turned green, and continued on. He let out a breath. It was a reminder he had to be careful now.

He flicked on his turn signal, made a point to look over his shoulder, and pulled out.

CHAPTER

50

WRIGHTWOOD

W INSTON HAD RIFLED through six cardboard bankers boxes
from the high shelves in the garage already.

Storing them up there was a great way to keep them out of
the way but made them even more of a pain in the ass to look
through. But at this point he didn't care. Since Grover gave him
the idea to use the Mustang as lucre, all he could think about was
finding what he needed. He had to set up his articulated ladder,
go up, grab a box, pass it down to Grover, go through it until he
knew it was the wrong one, tamp down his rising anxiety, go back
up, put it back, grab another, pass it down, going further and further back in years until he found the one that held the Mustang's
certificate of title. The coveted pink slip.

He always kept at least seven years of financial records, ever
since the first accountant he could afford, who had once worked
for the IRS, advised it. Conventional wisdom recommends keeping the last three years of records, but Win was told by the accountant that it was almost a certainty that a contested year would go
back further, leaving most taxpayers with no records to defend
themselves with. Ever since, he'd kept seven years.

The seventh box he hauled down wasn't a tax box, but one
where he kept memories and mementos: anniversary and birthday
cards from his late wife, childhood photos, passes to award shows

and film festivals, news clippings. And there it was. It should have been in a file with a handwritten label called "Legal Docs," which he always kept in his office drawer. He had no idea how this little wrinkled slip of paper, which had the power to set his daughter free from this waking nightmare, had ended up in here.

When he saw the corner of it peeking out from behind a postcard his brother sent him from Cabo one year, he snatched it and held it triumphantly over his head.

"Well, my friend," said Grover, "how does it feel to hold one hundred and twenty-five thousand dollars in your hand?"

Win smiled his first real smile in days. "Chicken feed."

Then his cell phone rang.

51

Rocket held the burner to his ear. "Hey, superstar. Everything coming along?"

"I'm doing the best I can." The voice coming through the phone sounded thin. Rocket realized he was on speaker.

"I don't like people eavesdropping on my conversations," he said.

"Sorry," Win said. "I'm with a friend. You didn't give me much time, so he's helping me out."

"It isn't that private *dick*, is it?"

"No."

Rocket sensed that Win didn't know about the ex-cop yet. "What's his name?"

"Doesn't matter. You don't know him. He doesn't know you. Let's leave it at that."

That surprised Rocket. So far, there'd been nothing but eager cooperation from the actor. In fact, he didn't give a flying fuck who was on the line as long as it wasn't law enforcement. But he needed to keep the mark on his heels, not let the power balance shift, especially now that he had a lot less leverage. But the actor didn't know that. Not yet.

"Maybe I'll just hang up. Be on my way."

"No!" said Win. "I just want this done. Tell me what to do."

Rocket let that hang in the air for a moment. "I'll call again later. Tell you where to bring the money."

"Where's the other guy?" Win asked.

"Which other guy?" He knew Win had seen two men yesterday.

"The one that's been calling me. The little prick that came to my house."

"Don't worry. He's with . . . what's he call her? Oh, yeah, the puta madre. Now, how's my money coming?"

"Probably not as much as you expect."

"I *expect* not to be fucked with."

"I'm not. I'm just not Tom Hanks living in Malibu Colony! I'll give you everything I have. I just want my daughter back," Win said. "I'd like to talk to her."

"No can do, Kemo Sabe. You can talk at the handoff."

"I want to talk to her *now.*" Win's voice cracked.

"Well, you *can't!*" Rocket said, his anger rising. He took a breath to steady himself. "I'm not there right now. Just wait. It'll be done in a few hours. And be ready. You'll need to move when I tell you."

He hung up.

PART 9

"There's nothing as dangerous as a man with a family to protect."
—Winston Greene in *Eaten Alive* (2019)

PART 9

52

SHERMAN OAKS—9 MILES NORTHWEST OF HOLLYWOOD

ROCKET STROLLED DOWN the sidewalk on Ventura Boulevard like a tourist. He was pretending to window-shop like any other pedestrian, hoping it would clear his head. It had no effect, so he headed back to where he'd parked on the next block.

Just where the *fuck* were Ozzie and Jordy? He decided to give them another half hour, but only to allow for the off chance that they'd had to get new burners. He picked up the pace to his car as more questions filled his head: Had Ozzie or Jordy, or both, split and left him to take the fall? Had the actor found out that his daughter was a grease spot and called in the cops, and now they were *all* conspiring to reel him in?

He reached his car, barely slowing to pull the keys from his pocket. Once in, he left the windows up and started the engine. The AC had never worked in this piece of shit car, so the best he could do was to crank up the fans. The airflow felt cool on his skin, and the white noise helped. He wished he could play his video game, just for a little while—he needed to calm the fuck down. If those guys would just give him a phone call, a text . . . *something*.

Rocket had been in charge of this crew from jump, and right when they needed to stick together, to follow the plan or it all falls apart, those guys make a left turn? On the other hand, if he was in their shoes, he knew what he would do: he'd make a play for himself, go for the lion's share. *That's why I can't get these pricks on the phone.* No avoiding it: one's dead, the other's in the wind. If he had to bet, he'd put that kind of move on Ozzie. It'd be just like him to put a hole in Jordy's head, then make a play for himself. Especially since he knew he wouldn't be getting the jackpot he'd thought he would.

Then he remembered something Music Man had once told him: *"You want to give God a good laugh, just tell Him your plans."* Meaning, there was *always* some unanticipated X factor. Music Man was doing time thanks to just that kind of unexpected outcome. With that in mind, he considered the less likely alternative, that Jordy had gotten the drop on Ozzie. With Clare dead, and knowing that Jordy (like Ozzie) didn't share Rocket's feelings about kidnapping kids, there was no reason to think the big dumb surf nut wouldn't try to grab the little girl and get the money for himself.

And what's the difference if it was Ozzie or Jordy? If they weren't going to show him any loyalty, then why be loyal to them? He should just go get the money from the old man before he found out that his daughter was dead (and before his granddaughter might go missing). As for his crew? They'd made their choice. They could fucking figure it out.

Now Rocket needed to see what to do about the old man.

53

WRIGHTWOOD

THE TENSION INSIDE Win's house had thickened like a dense fog as the two friends waited—waited for the phone to ring, waited for instructions, waited for news from Teddy. Waited for something, anything, to happen. Any conversation had ended a while ago, and a hyperalertness to sound had settled in.

Grover could hear not only the tiny snaps and pops of the chair underneath him, but every crackle of the rug fabric under Win's feet as he paced in the next room. Jesus, it seemed like he could hear the very air flowing through the house.

At one point he got up and went to the sink for a glass of water. The squeak of the tap turning and the water splashing in the sink as he ran the faucet pierced the silence with such force, he turned it off after pouring only half a glassful. He looked through the doorway at Win in the big front room, who was staring at his cell phone as if willing it to ring. Grover returned to his seat and drank down what he'd poured and decided that was enough for now.

Not even two hours had passed, but it felt like days. Win had paced from the kitchen to the living room and back countless times, and gone upstairs more than once to check his emails. On his last trip upstairs, Win had brought back a laptop, plugged it in, and set it on the dinette table, offering it to Grover in case he needed to go online.

At around three o'clock, Win said, "Traffic's going to be getting bad around now. Maybe we should start driving toward the city, so we can make it there quicker when they call?"

"These guys know where you live, so they could just as well do the swap somewhere up here, in which case going to LA would be counterproductive. Didn't Teddy say they'd try to rattle you by keeping you in the dark?" He shrugged. "Or maybe I just saw that in a movie once."

"There's got to be something we can *do* besides sit around!"

"It's not too late to call in the cops."

Win shook his head. "No. I'm not going to risk that." Grover wasn't surprised—Win's past experience with Teddy made it clear that when it came to celebrity cases that could generate publicity (and this one certainly would), cops were only human, and could make mistakes in judgment like anybody else.

Grover called Lauren to check in at home. She assured him everything was all right and that she'd even gotten Amy down for a nap. They had been texting each other all afternoon, but he brought her up to speed on what they'd been doing anyway.

"Sounds like you're doing all you can, although . . ." She paused. "Listen, you know I'm no fan of the police, but—"

"I mentioned it," Grover said. "He won't. I think he trusts them less than we do."

They wrapped up the call, and he promised to keep in touch, either by text or voice. She promised to do the same. Then he told her he loved her and hung up. Win came back to the kitchen and half sat on one of the chairs, as if he needed to be ready to leap into action at any moment. He placed his cell phone on the table in front of him.

Grover could see the strain on his friend's face. The circles under Win's eyes had become noticeably darker, somehow pulling the brightness from his blue eyes, and the lines around his mouth seemed visibly deeper than they had been just yesterday. *What a difference a day makes.* Grover wondered if he would see the same in his own face if he looked in a mirror.

Win's cell phone rang, and they both jumped at the sound. In the tense stillness of the house, it had the shock of a fire alarm. Win grabbed the phone and stood, so Grover did the same. They leaned over the device, and Win answered in speaker mode.

"This is Winston!" he said, not sure why he'd answered like that. He never had before.

"Hey, superstar. Wanna make a trade?"

"Yes!"

"Six o'clock. You'll get a map with a pin texted to you about an hour before. When you get there, you'll get another one. When you get *there*, you might get another—you might not. If we decide we're safe, you'll give someone the money. Might be me, might not. You clear?"

"Yes."

"If I get even a whiff that something is off, we're done. And you know what that means."

"Yes. I understand."

"Where are you?"

"At my house," said Win, as if there were no other place he could be.

"Good. And I don't care how many fucking friends you got. You come alone."

The line went dead.

54

NORTH HOLLYWOOD, 7 MILES NORTH OF HOLLYWOOD

ROCKET ONLY HAD a couple of hours to get this thing right, figure out how to get the money and *not* hand over a live body.
And, of course, how to escape.

He'd been driving around the valley, trying to think of every
angle and how to stay one step ahead of each. Turned out driving
in LA was almost as good a way to think as playing video games—
and after all that time behind the wheel, he'd come up with a plan
that might make it possible to pull this off alone.

Rocket went to the drive-through at an In-N-Out in North
Hollywood and ordered a Double-Double with cheese, no onions.
Because there were cameras everywhere, he wore his sunglasses and
baseball cap, then steered to the back lot to a spot facing a brick wall.
His stomach had been roiling all day (four murders and a mangled
body before noon will do that to a guy), and he tried to settle it with
sips of root beer and the burger. It didn't work. Instead, it felt like
there was a hot coal in his gut. He feared he might be getting an ulcer.

Rocket decided he probably wouldn't feel better until he was
safely across the border, so he should just get on with it. He'd
snatched his phone from the cup holder and called the actor and
gave him instructions for delivering the money. With that done,
he needed to figure his escape plan now that he knew where the
exchange was going to be, more or less.

It would be better to do the swap in the city, where he could get to a freeway on-ramp and just disappear in the dark. Then again, the mountains were sparsely populated, and he would be less likely to get stuck in traffic. Up there, if he handled the grab without his car being made, it would be a smooth ride down the hill, and then he could take a less obvious route to the border.

He plotted a route on his GPS and started the engine.

Pearblossom Highway, 60 miles from Hollywood

Rocket reached the turnoff that took him up the mountain. Thirty minutes later he'd ascended from the desert to the forest. At the top, he made a left at a stop sign, following the directions.

There were barely any other vehicles going in either direction, so he took a chance and pulled off at a wide spot in the road. He hopped out and trotted into the trees to milk the cow.

As he stood, a breeze blew through and rustled the leaves. It made him hyperaware that he was going solo up here. No one to back him up. He decided he liked it.

He noticed that the tree's shadows were now as long as the trees were high. Even a city boy like him knew that meant darkness would soon drop. He went back to the car.

A little farther on, he passed a deserted ski resort. A sign read "Mountain High." He'd never been on a pair of skis in his life, but he deduced that those ribbons of clear space running top to bottom in the hillside must be ski runs. Patches of snow were still visible, but the Great California Drought had hit this area harder than most, and the resort had closed early this year. The motionless, empty ski lifts looked lonely. Ominous.

He passed a stone tower on his left, maybe fifteen, twenty feet tall, with those notches in the top. At Hollygrove, he and the other kids used to rip movies and TV shows from the Torrent sites, and that tower looked like it came out of one of their faves, *Game of Thrones*. It was like the shape of a chess piece. A rook. Only this one was square instead of round.

The final moves of the game were about to begin.

CHAPTER

55

JORDY PARKED OZZIE's car around the corner from the Washington home. The day before, he'd been surprised at how easy it was to tail both the actor and the ex-cop. Maybe because they were caravanning in separate cars, the PI kept his eyes on Winston in the car in front of him, instead of in his rearview, where Jordy might've been spotted trailing a few cars behind and a lane over. They'd led him right here.

Now he needed to chill, wait for night to fall. Given the spotty, aging streetlamps, darkness gave good cover down here. Even if someone saw him, they'd never be able to identify him unless they passed him on the sidewalk and looked him right in the eyes.

The wounds in his leg had begun to throb. He'd changed the bandage an hour or so ago and saw that the ragged gashes had coagulated into weepy, bloody scabs. He knew he needed stitches, but for now he was just going to have to gut it out. His leg had stiffened because of the trauma, and just the act of using his right foot on the gas pedal—he managed to use his left foot to brake—had become torturous. Straightening the leg would be an exercise in determination, but he had to do it. He could get proper treatment once this was all done. He knew a guy, a fellow rider who happened to be an EMT, who would stitch up surfers who couldn't go to a hospital when they got cut on the coral in protected coastlines.

He reached for the small paper bag on the seat next to him and retrieved the bottle of Aleve he'd picked up at a tiny market on Lincoln Boulevard. He popped the top, poured several more pills straight into his mouth and chewed them down. The directions limited you to three every twenty-four hours, but the father of a girl he once dated, an MD, told him that when it came to over-the-counter drugs, "You can take a homeopathic dose or you can take a *real* dose." The guy had been an arrogant prick, but he was right. With the walk from here to the Washington house, the pills should be kicking in at just the right time.

He gulped from a lemon-lime energy drink to wash away the bitter taste and, in his head, ran through the route to the house.

CHAPTER

56

ONE HOUR AND forty-two minutes after leaving North Hollywood, Rocket arrived in Wrightwood. It was late dusk. It felt like night fell sooner up here than it did down in the flats.

The last of the magic hour was lighting up the mountainside to his left, causing the entire slope to shine with an intense orange and pink glow. It reflected down on the village like a giant, radiant lantern. The beautiful spectacle caught him by surprise, and he slowed the car so he could watch it a little longer.

When he hit the town, he made a right at a gas station/convenience market, which put him in the town's small commercial center. He looked around to get his bearings. Both sides of the wide street were lined with diagonal parking spaces, and the mostly single-story buildings were occupied by the usual assortment of businesses: an ice-cream parlor, a real estate office, a florist, a bookstore, and a handful of restaurants, the most popular of which looked to be a place called the Midnight Caller. Despite the cold creeping in with the darkness, people were crammed onto the small front patio, huddling under heat lamps, clutching cold beers and mixed drinks. He could hear music coming from inside.

The street ended at a pizza parlor, where he made a U-turn and went back down the block. It was almost six o'clock and nearly dark.

He pulled into one of the diagonal spaces at the curb, opened his phone's GPS map, and found the street he was on: Park Drive. He tapped a business, an independent bookstore, and a Yelp screen opened. "Great place for the classics, if that's your thing." He tapped another icon, a vintage motel on the next street over.

This time the Yelp screen opened with a mosaic of three photos, one of which caught his eye. It was of two boys who looked to be about ten years old, hunched over a diner counter, scooping blue sherbet into their mouths. Perfect boy logic: Pick the strangest color of food and eat it. By the looks on their faces they had made a good choice. They were both laughing, their mouths wide, exposing their blue tongues.

Rocket's mind wandered to an imaginary history where he had grown up somewhere like this, where you could go with your best friend to the local ice-cream joint and eat blue stuff together. He wished he'd had the chance.

"Well, I didn't, did I?" he heard someone say. Then he realized it was his own voice.

That brought him back. To inside his shitty car. He looked around, made sure no one was watching him talk to himself. *Maybe when this is done, there'll be enough for a spot to land.* He'd never had any use whatsoever for small towns (especially ones that reminded him of what he'd missed in life). But this one, this one was special: it would be a launchpad into his bright and shiny future.

He opened his phone to Google Maps, slid the map around on the screen, and zeroed in on the location he had in mind. He pressed his thumb to it until a pin dropped on it. He snapped a screenshot, cropping out any symbols on his phone. He didn't want to share the service provider or the signal bars, not even the battery level. He clicked the arrow symbol in the lower left, and two rows of options appeared, the top being the few people he'd sent a text to in the last few days. He sent the photo with the pin to Winston Greene, Hollywood star.

Now he had to make his final preparations. He started the car and backed out, rolled down to the highway, made a right, went one block, then made another right.

He was headed up—into the residential section of Wrightwood.

CHAPTER

57

VENICE BEACH

JORDY REACHED INTO his duffel in the darkness until his fingers found the gun. He'd made sure to bring it with his other things after dumping Ozzie's body down the trash chute.

He took out the snub-nosed .22 revolver he'd lifted from Edvina before she kicked him out. She'd hated guns, but her father had bought it for her protection down in edgy old Venice. *A lot of good that did.* He opened the cylinder, checked it was loaded, gave it a spin for fun, then snapped it home with a flick of his wrist. In his large hand it could've been mistaken for a toy.

He used his arms to heave himself up and out of the car, taking some of the weight off his throbbing leg. He shut the door and left it unlocked. If he were a car thief, he wouldn't bother with this rolling piece of shit, and he had to be able to make a quick getaway with a squirming child in his arms.

The evening mist that the ocean had pushed into the neighborhood enveloped everything in a blurry vapor. He looked up at the blooms swaying at the tops of the palms lining the street. To him, they seemed like fingers gently unfurling from a fist. He felt the breeze that brought the ocean's aroma and drew it in. He took a deep breath. The salty smell made him forget the pain in his thigh for a moment.

He squared his shoulders and limped toward the house.

58

WRIGHTWOOD

THE WALL CLOCK above the kitchen doorway was approaching six PM, and still no word from the kidnappers.

The incessant ticking of the battery-powered clock on the wall was like a nail being tapped into Win's forehead. At one point, he nearly ripped it off its hook and threw it out, but it really was the easiest way to keep track of the agonizing passage of time. He kept glancing up at it as he and Grover finished off the TV dinners Win had found in the back of the freezer. He'd chosen chicken nuggets, and as he mowed through them, he pondered what part of the bird he was eating (or if it had ever even seen a chicken). Grover went with the pasta, spinach, and ricotta, mainly because the alternative was a dicey-looking, stir-fried steak-and-vegetable dish.

"You know," Grover said, "if your girls end up living here, you might have to consider the plant-based thing," referring to Amy's culinary preferences.

"I know, I know." He looked at the streaks of grease on his empty plate and wondered if it was possible to feel your own arteries harden, when his thoughts were interrupted by a *ding-ding* from his phone.

Win unlocked the screen in one quick move and saw there was no text, only a screen grab: a map with a red pin in the center.

The predominant background of pale green was divided diagonally by a solid yellow line, Highway 2, where it ran through town. The green was the Angeles National Forest. He recognized the top of the image as the north side of the highway, mostly undeveloped land. The location of the red pin, at the end of a single curved white line on the south side of the highway, made his neck tighten. He used his thumb and forefinger to expand the picture to get a better look. His eyes narrowed.

"What is it?" asked Grover.

He turned the phone around for Grover to see. "That pin is *this* house."

"He said it would be an hour after the first text," said Grover. "And that he might send another one, directing you somewhere else. But if not, we should assume he has eyes on this place and can see there's no police. And if he already knows I'm here, I wouldn't have to hide."

Win had been struggling with this all afternoon, driving himself and his friend bananas with his endless pacing and fretting. He had expected that fear and uncertainty would make his decision for him. Instead, when he imagined the imminent showdown he was facing with the kidnappers, he was strangely calm. How could he involve the best friend he'd ever had in a life-and-death situation when he had a family of his own to worry about? He knew the answer.

Win looked at his friend.

"You have to leave."

59

VENICE BEACH

J ORDY LIMPED ACROSS the street and stood in front of the Wash-ington house.

The city streetlamp that should have been illuminating this section of sidewalk wasn't functioning, and the fog had thickened, dropping a dark veil over everything. And with not much beach traffic, the neighborhood was quiet. Only the occasional passing vehicle, the slow-moving drivers focused on navigating through the thick haze. No one would see him.

Jordy checked up and down the block for the two SUVs he saw parked here yesterday. Both trucks were gone, and he was pretty sure the ex-cop's sedan was gone too, though he couldn't remember the color or model. Only the Jaguar was still in the driveway. Luckily, it seemed the man of the house was out and about somewhere. That was a relief—he was a concern, a big man like himself, toned, well muscled.

And he had kids. *"There's nothing as dangerous as a man with a family to protect,"* echoed in his head. He'd heard it somewhere, maybe in a movie.

But unless someone had come over sometime today to help out, it was likely just the mother and a bunch of kids in there. If he was going to do it, now was the time.

He headed across the yard to the side of the house.

Lauren glanced at the clock on the kitchen wall. 6:03 PM. As usual, she was a little disappointed that it was already getting dark out. She'd be grateful when daylight savings arrived, and the days got longer.

She was rinsing the last of the dinnerware for the dishwasher when, over the sound of the running water, she heard something: *pling!* She turned off the faucet and listened more intently. *Pling!* There it was again. It could easily be mistaken for an arriving text on one of the many smartphones in the house, but it wasn't. It was the alarm system.

A neighbor's dog or cat had probably triggered the motion detectors that ringed the house, providing three-hundred-and-sixty-degree coverage around the property. That wasn't unusual. But her instincts told her something else. She wiped her hands on a dish towel and went into the former pantry immediately off the kitchen, where the brains of the system were installed.

Lauren took a seat at a small table set against the wall in front of a flat-screen monitor. The screen was filled with two rows of three rectangular windows, images showing overlapping views of the entire perimeter of the house. If you tapped one of the windows, it enlarged to fill the screen with a crisp HD image from the corresponding camera.

Though these alerts were usually due to neighborhood pets, every now and then a skunk made its way into their backyard, and they had to call animal control. The next *pling!* confirmed there was something moving out there.

It was a man, coming over the wooden fence at the side of the house. She tapped the small image, and it filled the screen. The man was big—tall and muscular—with a surfer's long blond locks. His furtive behavior could only mean one thing: he was doing something he shouldn't be. He was going to break into her house.

When the man's feet hit the ground, the motion detector tripped the light on that side of the fence, lighting him up like a deer on a dark mountain road. He crouched slightly and grabbed his right leg as if he was in pain. *Pull a muscle, sugar?*

When the man straightened up, she could make out the handle of a gun sticking out of the waistband of his pants. He drew it and held it out in front of him, aiming at nothing. His flummoxed expression showed he hadn't expected the house to be so well defended. He started moving toward the backyard, quickly now, as if he knew a stopwatch had begun and that he had only a short time to do whatever he had in mind. Lauren's gut told her his target was Amy.

Well, I might have something to say about that.

Goddamn, that fucking light is bright.

Jordy rounded the corner to the rear of the house, blinking as he tried to adjust to the sudden changes in lighting, from dark to *bright* and back to dark. He tripped on a sprinkler head and barely caught himself before going down.

That'd be perfect—fall on my gun and shoot myself. He looked around. There was no movement, but he couldn't help but notice how nice it was back there. The yard was spotless, practically manicured, and the outdoor furniture looked like it was solid wood—handmade, maybe. Even the kids' toys were primo. *Who are these people? Shoulda hit them instead of that loser actor.*

His eyes landed on the patio covered with immaculate Spanish tiles that led to a French double door, mostly glass panes. *And there's my way in.*

Lauren stood up from the little desk and slid open the cabinet door above her to reveal a rectangular wall-mounted safe, three feet wide, with a digital keypad.

She punched in the combination, which only she and Grover knew, and the safe door popped open.

She swung it wide, reached in, and grabbed the shotgun barrel with her left hand and the stock with her right. It was a unique weapon, a single-barrel, twelve-gauge shotgun that could be separated into two parts. The gun had been custom-made for a movie Grover had worked on some years ago, built by an independent gunmaker he had hired. The producers had been so pleased with the results that they had given it to Grover after wrap. He and Lauren kept it in this safe, locked away from the children, except for when they practiced with it at the gun range.

She brought the pieces down, her eyes alternating between the man on the screen and the weapon she was assembling, a semiautomatic with five rounds loaded in the stock. All she had to do was line up the barrel with the stock, slide it home, and twist it closed. The two pieces locked together with a sturdy metallic *click*.

On the screen, she saw the man angle for the back patio. She tapped the "Back" arrow at the upper left corner of the screen, and the image changed to the view of all the smaller windows. She switched to the window for the camera mounted over the patio and saw he was going for the French doors that opened into the TV room.

She slid back the bolt and released it to load the first of its cartridges into the breach. She pointed the barrel at the floor and clicked off the safety.

Before leaving the closet, she reached over to the security keypad on the wall and tapped the badge icon once, sending a silent alarm to the local police. It started to pulse with an amber glow. She tapped it again and it turned red, confirmation that the alarm had been sent. Should only be a matter of minutes before they arrived, but a lot could happen in just a few minutes.

She gripped the stock while extending her trigger finger safely outside of the trigger guard, and left the little room, the gun pointed at the floor next to her feet.

Lauren walked to the TV room. Thursday was book night, so tonight this room was unoccupied and dark. She stepped halfway into the opening onto the hallway that led to the children's rooms, in order to hide the long weapon she held by her side.

With an even, commanding voice, she called out, "Grace! Come here!"

Her oldest child, Grace, fourteen years old, stuck her head out of the room she shared with her younger sister. "Yeah, Mom?"

"Safe room. *Now.* You know what to do."

Grace had been drilled for this moment once per month for the last several years. As the eldest, she was responsible for guiding her younger siblings to the safe room off the master bedroom in case of emergency. She nodded and dipped back into the bedroom, calling her sister's and Amy's names.

With one eye on the French doors and the other down the hallway, Lauren watched as Grace gathered her younger sister and Amy, then her two brothers from their room across the hall, and headed down the hallway to the stairs. The girl paused halfway up the stairwell to let the other kids pass, unlocked her smartphone, and dialed 911.

Lauren could just hear her daughter as she followed the last of her siblings up the stairs. "Hello, I'd like to report a burglary. Yes, he's here now."

The phone call in addition to the silent alarm was deliberate, to convey the urgency to the responding officers.

The children out of sight, Lauren waited until their voices were cut off by the closing of the safe room door. Then she flipped a switch on the wall to turn off the hallway light, raised the barrel of the gun, and stepped into the darkened TV room.

Jordy's running shoes made a slight, rubbery squeak as he stepped off the damp lawn onto the tiles that led to the French doors. He stood next to one of the doors and peered through the glass panes, unobstructed by curtains. The room inside was dark.

He tried the double lever-style door handle, first the left, then the right. Both locked.

First checking that the hammer was down, Jordy gripped the gun's barrel, reversing his grip, and lightly tapped the pane closest to the door handle once for aim. Then he drew back and swung the gun against the glass, shattering it. He reached through the hole, mindful of the leftover shards, unlocked the latch, and opened the door.

After the flash of bright lights outside, his eyes strained to adjust to the gloom.

From the street, the house had seemed small, like the old craftsman cottages built here in the early 1900s. But this room was *big*, which meant the house was bigger than it looked from the street. The flat screen on the wall had to be a seventy-incher, and those tiny satellite speakers must sound super dope when the family was in there, watching a flick. He couldn't make out the details, but he could see there was art everywhere, too—paintings, drawings, sculptures. More toys and a couple of video game consoles were stacked neatly out of the way under the TV. This place was *sweet*.

He swept his hand against the wall, searching for a light switch. As he was fumbling, he thought he saw a tall sculpture across the room move, when a light came on out of nowhere and blinded him . . . *again*. Then he realized the sculpture was actually a woman. The woman who lived here.

He recognized her from yesterday, when he had followed the actor and his cop buddy here. Through squinted eyes, he saw she was holding something in her hands. A shotgun. A serious one. Long, with a wide barrel, held at waist level.

Then he heard her say in a low and even tone, aiming the gun at his midsection while she spoke, "Get out of my house."

It was plain to Jordy from the confident way this woman was holding the weapon that she was prepared to defend the house and the kids inside it against him, no matter what it took. And even though he could see (once his vision cleared . . . again) that the hand cannon she was aiming at him completely outclassed the comparative popgun he held, he felt himself raising his pistol to point it at this woman anyway.

A part of his brain fantasized about getting a round off, maybe a lucky shot to the head, and then grabbing the girl and getting the money, while the rest of his brain knew she had gotten the drop on him, and he should just admit he was beat. But some actions have a momentum of their own, and before he could stop himself, he'd raised the revolver and fired, knowing immediately he had shot wide. In a flash of utter detachment, he saw the plaster explode in the wall behind her, above and to the right.

At the same instant he fired, the woman also pulled the trigger. The blast of the shotgun was so loud, it drowned out the sound of his own weapon, even from across the room. Jordy felt his body blow backward, folded almost in two as the buckshot tore through his abdomen and sent him into the air and through the French doors. He slid across the patio before grinding to a stop on the Spanish tiles.

As Jordy stared into the night sky, he felt the cool dampness the fog had left on the tiles seeping through the thin fabric of his Aloha shirt.

His head was cocked to one side, his cheek against the tile, and he could see he was surrounded by broken wood and glass. He couldn't feel his legs. Couldn't feel anything, really, but that was probably from shock, a sensation he knew well from his tumbles off big waves. So, maybe he wasn't as bad off as he thought. He might have been hallucinating, though, as he could see his legs were where they were supposed to be but were at such an extreme right angle they could have been detached from his body. He thought he could hear the ocean. *Or is that a car passing by a couple streets over?*

His eyesight was fading, so maybe his hearing was off too. He found he could slowly turn his head, and looked up, directly above him. He wished the fog would clear. He wanted to see the stars, all bright and crowded in the sky.

Like they are in Mexico.

60

WRIGHTWOOD

W IN FELT A pang of guilt over the hurt and shock he could see in his friend's eyes.

"The guy was clear," Win said. "I'm supposed to come alone. Listen, if I was pinned down in a foxhole, you're the *only* person I would want with me. But it's my daughter. And I can't take any chances—not with everything you have at stake."

Grover looked down at the table, then out the window. With the darkness outside, Win could see him looking at his own reflection, staring back at him.

"I get it, but . . . I could pick out a spot, hidden. Keep an eye on you."

"You could. But he might see you, and that's a risk I won't take."

Grover's phone rang. He answered, listened, his eyes going wide, and he looked up at Win. He listened some more, then said, "Okay. Yeah, right away." He held out the phone. "She needs to talk to you."

Win grabbed the phone and heard Lauren's voice. "Amy's all right. We made sure of it."

"What? What happened?"

Then Lauren recounted the episode: someone broke into the house, a big guy, blond hair. Winston remembered the man behind the wheel of the SUV yesterday, the one that picked up that skinny prick with the shades.

She told him that the police were at the house now, and the coroner was on the way. The police said it was clear it had been self-defense—the bullet hole from the blond guy's gun in the wall proved it. They were dusting for prints and collecting evidence now. The back doors would need to be replaced, and the blood steamed off the patio . . .

"Jesus, I'm babbling," she said with a nervous laugh. "Anyway, the kids are all upstairs, safe. My sister is coming to take them for the night. She'll get them out through the front door, so they won't see what happened. And once the coroner has removed the body, I'll join them. The police said they would post someone at the house all night in case anyone gets an idea to burgle the place. And Win—" She lowered her voice. "I haven't said anything. As far as the police know, a thief picked the wrong house to break into. End of story."

Win put his hand to his forehead. His face had gone cold. "God, Lauren, I'm so sorry."

"Just get Clare back and we can put all this behind us."

After handing the phone back to Grover, Win sat back in his chair and looked at his friend on the other side of the table as he said his goodbyes and hung up.

Grover said, "Looks like you get your way."

"They were going to take Amy!" Win couldn't help but wonder what that meant for Clare. Why would they do this now?

"We don't know that."

"You think it's a *coincidence?*"

"No, I don't. But I don't *know* that it isn't. Everybody in Venice knows us and our house—it's not the first time we've had a prowler. The main thing is our people are okay."

Win took a deep breath, and some of the color returned to his face. "We both know what this was. But coincidence or not, you gotta go."

"Yeah," said Grover. "I'm sorry."

"Don't be—it's how it had to be."

Winston walked his friend out to his car. Grover paused a moment, then turned to Win, the pain caused by his divided loyalties showing in his face. Win understood. They hugged, no words necessary, and Grover climbed in.

Winston watched as Grover's car disappeared down the dirt drive. Then he went inside the house and turned on the porch light. He hustled across the living room and up the stairs, making a beeline for the bookshelves he'd built in his office. He pushed aside a row of thick, leather-bound classics on the top shelf, revealing a slim hardcover hidden behind them, a spot Amy wouldn't find for years to come.

He opened it to reveal a square hole that he had cut into the pages with an X-Acto knife. Hidden inside was a set of antique-looking keys. He flipped the book upside down, and the keys dropped into his palm.

Win returned the book to the top shelf, then walked to his desk and opened the locked file drawer.

Winston returned to the kitchen and sat down at the dinette table, placing a dark wooden case in front of him.

The burl wood box was sixteen inches long, eleven inches deep, and three inches high. The pattern of brown knots running through the amber-colored grain was so consistent that it could have passed for hand-painted. Win could see his reflection in the highly polished finish. Every time he looked at it, he marveled that something so beautiful could contain something so lethal.

Using another of the keys he'd removed from the book, Win opened the lid and stared into the case. If there had been a faint glow from inside the box, it could have been a scene from *Kiss Me Deadly* or *Pulp Fiction*. But there was no dramatic light emanating from the box. Nor was there much light in Winston's eyes. Instead, he felt he was peering into the abyss.

Nestled in a custom bed lined with crushed gray velvet lay a .45 caliber, Colt Single Action Army Peacemaker revolver, its polished nickel plating gleaming.

It had been a gift from a local chamber of commerce in northern Nevada that had hosted a movie company shooting a western in which he had played the lead. Over four months of prep and principal photography, the production had brought a much-needed boost to the local economy and earned Win the deep appreciation of the town and surrounding area. The Colt had been their way of saying thanks.

In the gray cushion below the barrel were two rows of three holes holding six .45-caliber cartridges. Win took one out and inspected the lead bullet. A hole had been drilled into the tip by the manufacturer. They were hollow points, designed for maximum effect. On impact, one of these bullets would mushroom out like a blooming flower, the lead plowing a ragged hole in the target at least twice the diameter caused by an unaltered round. He turned the cartridge over and got a close look at the firing pin. A tiny "+P" was stamped into the brass rim, which meant there were extra grains of gunpowder packed behind these little missiles, giving them even more power. He pressed the bullet back into its slot.

Win was comfortable with guns and had been practicing with them since he was a kid. It was with this very gun that he had taught Clare how to shoot, up in the hills behind the house. He had waited until she was old enough to hold it steady, but even with the eye and ear protection, she found using it upsetting. He thought she had sensed his disappointment at her reluctance to practice and that she resented him for it. *Another regret.*

He lifted the pistol out of its resting place and flipped it over, feeling its heft against his palm. It weighed a little over two pounds but felt heavier. The grips were ivory and had fine matching carvings on either side, one of a rearing horse and below that, an eagle with its wings spread wide. It felt smooth despite the etchings. Stored in this custom case, the gun's nickel plating had not tarnished over the years. Running the length of the barrel was an inscription:

Presented to Mr. Winston Greene,
in great appreciation for his gracious presence in our town.

At the time he had asked Grover, who had been the stunt coordinator on that shoot, "Am I a gracious person?"

Grover had answered, "You're always good with the fans, man. It's back at the bar with the crew that you can get a little—I don't know . . . rambunctious."

He thought of that kid who took his picture that morning, wondered if it'd show up on InstaTwit or whatever you call it. If it did, he'd never know. He'd avoided social media so far.

Win imagined the kidnappers attacking his home, like the final assault on Dustin Hoffman's house in Peckinpah's *Straw Dogs*. But he knew it wouldn't go down like that, with him mowing down his attackers, one by one. This was not some Grand Guignol celluloid fantasy, shot in slo-mo and edited to perfection. This was just old, over-the-hill Winston Greene, all on his own and out of his depth, trying to get his daughter back without getting killed.

He placed the gun back in the case and closed the lid. Then he went to the living room and took a seat on the sofa that faced the big fireplace, which would normally be crackling away at this time of year. He wrapped both palms around his smartphone and held it between his legs. He stared at it, willing it to send him another message, even as he dreaded what was to come.

There, sitting in the cold, the hazy light bleeding into the living room from the kitchen, he had never felt so alone.

61

ROCKET HAD DECIDED this place was kind of great. Unpretentious little houses nestled among tall oaks, echoed by handmade bird feeders, family names on hanging signs at the ends of the driveways. Fences so low they couldn't keep out a small dog were there for show, not privacy. No place he had seen before, not the locked gates and electrified fences in Pacific Palisades, nor the brick walls of Hollygrove, had ever felt like this. Even in Sylmar you knew that wandering onto someone else's yard could get you shot.

Rocket shook his head to clear it. Fantasizing about an alternate future in a place like this was clouding his focus. Right now, he had a job to do.

He drove up a few more blocks and turned left onto Edna Street, following it until it intersected with Oriole. At the stop sign, something caught his eye: a compound across the street. It was large and dark and looked unoccupied.

The words "Wrightwood Country Club" were carved into a thick wood panel hanging from a wrought-iron signpost. An arrow below the words indicated a turn up the next street, one so indistinct it could have been a fire break. He followed the arrow to the right and saw another wooden sign, also with an arrow: "Parking Entrance." He stopped, glanced around to check for evening strollers, saw none, then rolled into the empty, unpaved lot. He drove slowly through the lot, taking it all in.

Chain-link fencing bordered the street where he turned in, disappearing into the darkness up the hill. It was the first indisputable barrier he'd seen in the town. The moonlight in the clean mountain air lit everything up with a blue glow, and Rocket could see two empty patches of concrete on the other side of the fence: a basketball court, and a tennis court beyond. Farther out was a small lake surrounded by shrubs and trees that had yet to leaf out.

Ahead of him was a building made up of several sections, all with sloping roofs. It looked like a large log home that had been added to over the years.

A door-sized gate was near the end of the lot. As Rocket drove closer, he could see it was padlocked. Next to it, another sign with an arrow pointed the way to the clubhouse and the restaurant. At the far end of the parking lot was a right turn onto a short, single-lane road.

He took it and eased down a gentle slope to another lot below, parallel to the one he had just crossed. Two lots: one above, one below.

He looked up at the higher lot, which was a good six feet above him, held in place by a concrete retaining wall. A three-foot-high hedge ran along the length of the upper lot, creating a nine-foot barrier. He nosed the car right up to the wall and killed the headlights and engine. He looked up through the windshield and saw that, when parked next to the wall, the upper lot was not at all visible from the lower.

He got out and looked down to the street fronting the property. The lower lot was also elevated enough above the street to be hidden from view. Leading out of the lower lot was another short road, sloping down to the street. The sign mounted next to it read "Exit. One Way Only."

He looked at his phone. Four out of five bars. Plenty of good reception out here too.

62

W INSTON'S MIND FILLED the silence with violent scenarios, one after another, each with him and Clare on the losing end. Again and again, he batted them down.

His phone's clock read 7:28 PM. Over an hour had passed, and still no text. No screenshot with a pin. Nothing. Every time he raised his phone, the screen wallpaper glowed with a snapshot he'd taken of Clare and Amy at Magic Mountain last summer. Amy perched on her mother's lap, the two of them giddily sharing a frozen, chocolate-covered banana smothered by a mound of whipped cream and rainbow sprinkles. He was staring at Clare's smiling face when a text popped up.

He unlocked to find another map. This time the sparse white lines on the north side of the highway were centered in the frame. The south side was crisscrossed with the white lines of a grid pattern. The village of Wrightwood. The pin was placed just off the highway, right at the gas station and market, a block down the hill from the Midnight Caller.

He considered the kidnapper's choice. With the ski resort closed, the town wasn't busy, and at an altitude of over a mile, it could go down to freezing tonight, so even fewer people would be out than usual. It hadn't snowed for weeks, and the roads were clear. There were three highways down the mountain, two of which would be pretty empty at this hour. He was organizing it so there would be nobody around, and he would have easy access to an escape route.

Win jumped up from the sofa and went through the kitchen, scooping up the gun case and his denim jacket as he headed to the garage.

He opened the Mustang's driver-side door and tossed in the gun case. It settled on the passenger seat with a heavy bounce. He tossed his jacket over it and got in. He closed the door, killing the dome light, and fired up the engine. It roared to life, its power undiminished by not having been started recently. He carefully backed out to the dirt driveway, pressed the bulky remote mounted on the sun visor to close the garage door, and drove around the old junker that had been left in his driveway yesterday morning.

Before rounding the corner of his driveway and heading to the street, he took one last look at his house. If things didn't go right, this could be the last time he saw it. He hadn't bothered to set the alarm or even lock the big front door. He felt the car idle, the engine's rumble vibrating the vehicle around him. If this exchange went the way he hoped it would, this would be the last time he experienced that sensation as well.

He eased up on the clutch and drove away, the trees along the driveway swallowing the view of the house in the rearview mirror.

CHAPTER

63

As Winston drove toward the gas station just outside town, he thought about the last day and a half, which had been like an out-of-body experience—as if it had all happened to someone else.

There was a dead body in his best friend's backyard. His daughter was being held by kidnappers, and his granddaughter had been ripped away from her routine, only to find herself inches away from a violent home invasion. And now here he was, driving the incredibly rare muscle car he had restored in order to hand it over to the very people who were responsible for creating all this mayhem in his life.

He should be laser focused, but he was distracted, drifting into the oncoming lane and jerking back, the sense of unreality making it impossible to concentrate. If making him wait and wait and wait before reaching out was meant to rattle him, it had worked. He finally found presence of mind to check his rearview mirror. A car with its headlights on was a few hundred yards behind him. It was nearly dark, so that wasn't unusual. *Am I being followed?*

Win's heart rate and breathing increased as soon as the gas station came into view. He turned onto Park Drive and waited for an SUV-driving tourist doing a lookie-loo at the Mustang—*please, God, don't let him recognize me*—to pass before turning across the road and pulling into an empty space next to the business. He shut off the engine, tried to calm himself. He'd been driving all of eight minutes, but it had felt like an eternity.

The kidnappers couldn't know he'd be driving this car. Should he get out, let himself be seen? If they were watching, which Win assumed they were, they would know he'd arrived and was following instructions. They might even get a hard-on for the Mustang, which could make the trade easier.

The sidewalks were nearly deserted, but what would he say if someone he knew happened by? He decided "Just waiting on a friend" was as good as anything. He got out of the car, his phone clutched in his hand.

As soon as he opened the door, he heard laughter and music floating down the hill. The Midnight Caller was doing its usual bang-up business. He pulled on his denim jacket to shield against the evening chill.

How many of Winston Greene's characters had been the target of an assassin? How many trailers for the movies he'd appeared in had included a shot of him in a sniper's crosshairs? When he'd acted those scenes, his character had had no idea he was so close to death. This was completely different.

Win was familiar with vulnerability, the sense of being naked in front of a crowd. But standing here, it felt like being injected with antifreeze, burning as it moved up through his body. If these mystery assholes decided the easiest way out was to just send a high-velocity round into his forehead, he wouldn't even hear the shot.

His face became cold and clammy again, like it had the day before at the phone booth, right before he lost consciousness, and when he'd spoken to Lauren earlier. He took another deep breath and rested his forearm on the Mustang to steady himself. *Don't black out now.*

Ding! Another map arrived. He enlarged it to see where the red pin had dropped. Oriole. *The country club?* Win had never joined, so he had no clue if the place was even open this time of year. It was seven forty-five PM.

Ding! This time it was a text: *Go now*

"Winston Greene, as I live and breathe!"

Win turned to see a middle-aged woman, as wide as she was tall, with a smile to match, standing in the middle of the sidewalk, her hands on her hips. Win mustered a phony grin. He might normally improvise his way out of this one, but his head just wasn't in that space right now.

"Theresa Carpenter!" he replied. "Nice to see you."

He opened the car door to make a quick getaway, but it was never that easy with Theresa. She and her husband, Tom, owned the steak house across the drive from where Win had parked, and she had personally greeted every single customer for the last thirty years. They were lovely people, and Win had a big place in his heart for them, but Theresa was a gossip who loved to give as well as receive. Even a casual sidewalk encounter with her could eat up twenty minutes, easy.

"You can't get away from me that fast, you rascal," she said, shaking a finger at him. "We haven't seen you in months. I started to think you moved away without saying goodbye!"

"Sorry, Theresa," he said. "Another time. Gotta go."

She started walking toward him. "Oh no, you don't. You're going to come in and have a nice little visit with us. I don't think we've even seen you since last Thanksgi—"

"Goddamn it, I can't fucking *talk* right now!" He jumped into the car and fired up the engine.

Theresa stopped in her tracks, her mouth a perfect "O." She had to scurry out of the way as Win backed out and sped down the hill past her, his tires squealing at the stop sign before he roared onto the highway.

64

W IN REACHED THE top of Edna Street. He eased the Mustang onto Oriole, and the car rumbled to the entrance road that angled up to the club grounds. Some years back, he had made an appearance at a fundraiser here for the local kindergarten. Back then, the trees were strung with twinkling white lights, and festive bunting and balloons adorned the big hall where the night's party was held. Tonight, with the moonlight casting sharp, inky shadows on the buildings and asphalt, the deserted compound looked downright menacing.

Ding! He looked at the phone screen: *Hey superstar. parking lot*

Win steered the car up the rise and turned into the lot. When he reached the middle of the open space, he stopped.

Ding! Lower lot

He raised the clutch. The car felt like it was floating across the gravel as he made the turn down to the lower parking area and rolled toward the center.

Ding! Park facing wall stay in car

Win cranked the wheel all the way to the right and eased the car to the concrete retaining wall, pulled the stick shift to neutral, and killed the engine and headlights.

Ding! Turn off phone

He felt that sensation of being in the crosshairs again. He looked at his iPhone, now his only conduit to the world. He debated sending a text or dropping a pin on a map and sending it to someone. Grover. Teddy. Anyone. But he couldn't bring himself to take the chance. He held down the opposing buttons until the "slide to power off" ribbon appeared on the screen, then slid his finger to power the phone down. He took a breath when the screen went black.

He rolled the window down, and the sounds of a lonely evening in the mountains filled his ears. There were no traces of another person's presence.

Then he became aware of the low engine noise of an approaching car, followed by crunching gravel above him as another car entered the upper lot. Win figured they must have watched him arrive from the darkness of an adjacent street and then followed him in. There were no beams of light swinging across the hedges, so the driver must have left his headlights off. Win leaned over the dash and looked up through the windshield, but he was too close to the wall and too far down to see over the hedge.

At the edge of his peripheral vision, he caught a movement to his right, and turned to see the car creeping down the ramp and around the end of the wall separating the two lots. It was too dark for Win to identify the make. The car rolled up perpendicular to his and stopped directly behind him with a soft squeak. The driver left only inches between the two vehicles. Winston was trapped.

He heard the whirr of a power window opening and started to turn in his seat.

"Eyes front," he heard from the car.

Win faced forward.

"That phone off?"

"Yes."

"Throw it out."

Win dropped the phone out the open window and heard it land on the ground with a light crack. He hoped the screen was still in one piece. He tried to grab a furtive glimpse in the rearview mirror but only caught the window closing, its dark tint making visibility beyond the glass impossible in the night light.

The car's door unlatched and opened, followed by feet stepping onto the gravel.

"Nice ride," the man said. Win recognized the voice. It was the man who had called this afternoon. "Go to the wall and put your hands behind your head."

Win pushed open the door and rose from the car. He tried to resist the urge to look at the man, but as he straightened up, his eyes went right to the man's face. Across the car roof he saw a head covered in a dark three-hole balaclava. He also saw the automatic pistol the man was aiming at him.

"Face the wall, goddammit."

"Sorry."

Win closed the door, turned, and stepped forward to the wall. He raised his hands and interlaced his fingers behind his head.

Win heard the man's shoes crunching the gravel behind him, then stop as he picked up the phone from the ground (Win assumed to confirm it was off), then dropped it again.

"Where is it?" the man said.

"On the floor," said Win, turning slightly to speak. "Passenger side."

"Eyes *front*! I'm not gonna say it again!" To Win, the man sounded nervous.

"What about my daughter?"

"When I'm goddamned good and ready! Jesus!" The man opened the Mustang's door. "You fucking twitch, and your brains'll be on that wall. You feel me?"

"I feel you." And his heart pounding so hard in his chest he thought it might break a rib.

Rocket eased into the driver's seat of the Mustang, his eyes and gun trained on Winston through the lopsided V-shape between the open door and the windshield. He glanced at the passenger side and saw a blue and green gym bag in the footwell. He switched the gun from his right hand to his left, fished for the handle strap, found it, and pulled the bag into his lap. He slid the zipper across the bag's length in one motion and spread the opening wide. He pulled out his cell phone and clicked on the flashlight to beam into the bag. Inside were the bundles of cash.

"Not what I expected," Rocket said.

"Yeah, I told you, I just couldn't get any more that fast," Win said. "But you like the car, right? I put the pink slip in there. Take it. It's all yours. Sell it, keep it, I don't care."

Rocket felt around until he found the paper slip, checked it in the phone light.

"It's worth a lot," said Win. "Maybe more than my house."

Rocket eyed Win, then stuffed the slip back into the bag and tossed it to the floor. Then his eyes fell to the box on the passenger seat. "What's this?"

"That's for you too, if you want it."

Rocket turned the lacquered case to face him, struck by the richness of the hand-crafted wood and the heft of the box.

"You now have everything I can get my hands on. I just want my daughter back."

"Yeah, about that . . ." As he spoke, Rocket popped the lid open on the box and inside found a crushed velvet cushion with six small, empty receptacles and a depression in the outline of a Western-style six-shooter. He heard a *click-click* and looked up to find a .45-caliber barrel pointed at his nose.

65

H IS VOICE CRACKING, Win said, "Shoulda frisked me. Now where's my *daughter?*"

The man in the balaclava started to laugh. Winston's eyes narrowed. This was out of a bad movie: the villain gets caught red-handed and then laughs at his own predicament. But this wasn't some movie.

"What's so goddamn funny?"

"You are," said Rocket, his eyes shining through his mask, as if he couldn't believe he had to explain this. "See, you kill me, you'll *never* get your daughter back. I kill you, I still get *all this,* so . . ."

Winston looked hard down the barrel of his six-shooter. "I don't know. Maybe blowing your fucking head off'd be enough for me."

The man's smile disappeared, and his eyes blazed through the ski mask as he cocked the hammer on his weapon. "Then do it . . . *superstar.*"

The quiet night was suddenly broken with the roar of an engine accompanied by the yellow-white blaze of two headlights bouncing through the exit of the lower lot. Grover's two-tone SUV skidded to a stop not thirty feet from them, his headlights shining right at them. Win felt the crushing realization his plan to retrieve his daughter alive, haphazard as it was, was about to go completely to shit.

The kidnapper rose from the Mustang and took a few steps toward the light, then turned to Win, his gun still raised.

Win blurted, "I didn't tell anybody!" The man in the mask said nothing as he squinted into the lights.

As the V8 engine idled with a rumble, the two front wheels turned all the way to the left, the big rubber tires crunching on the gravel, as if the driver intended to make a sharp U-turn.

Then the headlamp high beams flared in a steady rhythm: *Flash-flash-flash.* Then longer. *Flaaash—flaaash—flaaash.* Then short again. *Flash-flash-flash.* Win recognized it: SOS—Morse code for "help." They had used it in a movie years before. It was a signal from the hero's unlikely savior to the hero himself (played by Win), that help had arrived. In the movie, the message was sent right before Grover performed a car stunt called a Rooster.

Grover must have decided the message to Win had been received and understood, because right then, he revved the big engine. *Vroom! Vroooom!* The brakes strained while the engine fed raw horsepower to the rear wheels, and then Winston realized what Grover was about to do. He lunged for cover behind the open door of the Mustang.

When Grover let off the brake pedal, the rear tires spun in place, raising dust and noise as gravel and dirt was sprayed behind the car into the chain link fence and the street below. The SUV obeyed the direction of the front tires and began to spin in a tight circle, the gravel spraying from the revolving rear tires like the flow from twin firehoses.

As the rear of the spinning SUV came around, Rocket was pummeled head to toe with the full force of the flying rocks and dirt. His hands flew to cover his face as he shrieked in pain.

The SUV completed a three-hundred-and-sixty-degree circle and came to a stop, the gravel and dust settling. Inside the car, Grover engaged the high beams, momentarily blinding Rocket.

Win peeked over the car door. He saw Rocket shake the dirt from his face and spit blood from his mouth. Then he saw him raise his gun in Grover's direction.

From behind his mask, the kidnapper screamed, "Mother*fuckerrrrr*!"

Win dropped his pistol and launched himself from where he knelt on the ground and crossed the distance to Rocket in an instant. He was airborne when he tackled him, and the two of them hit the gravel, Rocket face down beneath Winston. When they landed, Rocket lost his grip on his gun and it bounced on the dirt beside them.

Win raised up, grabbed Rocket by the shoulder and turned him over, then dropped his weight on him and punched him in the face through his mask. He could feel the ribs of fabric cut into his knuckles. He grabbed the man by the shoulders and pulled his face toward his.

"Where's my *daughter*?" he screamed.

Red and blue lights flashed across the hedge above them, and the night air was pierced again, this time with the wail of sirens.

Win jerked his head to the road below to see a string of San Bernardino County sheriff's cars screeching up the hill toward them. Two of the cars shot into the lot, maneuvering to each end of Grover's SUV before stopping. A third cruiser stopped on the driver's side of Grover's SUV. More cruisers were lining up on the road outside the compound. He looked down. The man in the mask was also watching the police arrive, his eyes glistening.

The first two officers jumped out and aimed their weapons at Win and the kidnapper. The third was aiming at Grover, who already had his driver's side door open, both of his hands high in the air for the officers to see.

One of the cops yelled toward Win, "Raise your hands! Now!"

Win didn't hesitate. He raised his arms and turned to face the officers. "I'm unarmed!"

Then two palms hit him hard in his midsection. Rocket was forcing him off, and he tumbled sideways to the dirt, the wind knocked out of him.

Rocket jumped to his feet, grabbing his gun as he rose.

"Don't move!" yelled the cop. "Drop that weapon and raise your hands!"

Winston screamed at the cops, *"No! Wait!"* He looked up at Rocket. "Where *is* she?"

The kidnapper looked down, his eyes glaring at Win through his mask. Then he chuckled and shook his head, as if he couldn't believe this turn of events. "A fucking actor," he said, then he turned and started toward the cops.

Rocket had crossed about half the distance to them when he raised his pistol and started firing at the deputies. The officers all dropped behind their vehicles for cover.

The deputy closest to Grover yelled to him, "Get down!" and Grover dropped behind his SUV.

Rocket's bullets punched holes in the police cars and shattered the windows.

Winston fell flat to the ground, the gravel digging into his cheek.

The kidnapper kept firing until the pistol's magazine was empty, and the slide stopped open with a clank. The deputies rose and unloaded a barrage of gunfire, drowning out all other sound.

From his low vantage point, Win saw the man leave the ground as he flew backward with the force of the fusillade. He landed with a hard thump in the gravel next to him.

The man's eyes were open behind his mask, facing directly at Win. The man was dead.

66

"MR. GREENE?" WIN was frozen on the gravel, still fixed on the kidnapper's dull eyes. A dust-covered black leather shoe and olive-green pant cuff stepped into his eyeline. "Mr. Greene? It's over. You can get up."

Win craned his neck to see a young uniformed deputy standing over him. His service pistol was holstered, and he was holding Win's six-shooter in his hand.

"Here," the deputy said, then bent down and took Winston's arm with his free hand, helping him to his feet.

Win stood to see several officers standing over the corpse. A plainclothes detective was there, interviewing Grover, making notes in a small notepad. *Just like Teddy.* He and Grover locked eyes, and Grover gave him a small nod. The detective looked over at Win as another police cruiser arrived behind him, pulling into the lot behind the first three squad cars. The driver jumped out and opened the back door.

Teddy Beauregard rose into view. His left arm was in a sling, and through his open collar Win could make out white gauze circling his chest.

Grover shook hands with the detective, joined Teddy, and they both approached Win.

"You're free to go, Mr. Greene," the officer said. "We'll get a statement from you later."

"But—"

"It's all right, sir. We understand what you were forced to do. But we'll hold on to your weapon for now. Someone will be in touch tomorrow."

The officer, Win's six-shooter in his hand, left him as Grover and Teddy arrived.

Win stared at them both, unable to process what had happened. "I don't . . . what . . ." He shook his head. "What the *hell?*"

CHAPTER

67

SYLMAR
One hour earlier

AS HE STRUGGLED into consciousness, Teddy tasted dirt in his
mouth, could taste it even before he opened his eyes. And
his chest hurt, screamed at him. When he cracked his eyes open,
all he could see was that he was face down on the ground. He
coughed and spat out the dirt.

He had no idea how long he'd been out, but the sun had disappeared below the horizon. The night had arrived, but the glow
from a streetlamp at the sidewalk reached the side of the house,
giving off enough light for him to see.

The last thing he remembered was looking out the open
bedroom window, figuring he'd missed the perp by seconds.
Then a voice behind him caused him to turn, only to see a pistol, pointing at his chest, held by a young man. Then the shot,
and . . . the force must have knocked him right through that
open window.

Judging by the size of the barrel of the gun that had been
pointed at him, he should have a hole in his chest as big as a quarter. And if that was true, it was only a matter of not much time
before he bled out.

Then again, he was awake, conscious.

Why would he wake up after taking a slug in the chest? And he was breathing—not without discomfort, sure, but pretty well, considering. *But man, my chest hurts.*

His left arm was pinned under him, and his right hand was on the ground next to his face. He gingerly spread his fingers and pressed his palm into the ground and pushed to raise himself, going slowly. The pressure of his body against the dirt might be the only thing keeping his blood inside him, where he wanted it to stay.

As he rose, he felt a slight grinding inside his chest. *At least one broken rib.* Once he lifted his head and shoulders, he steeled himself for what might come next. He looked down to see a hole in his jacket, a pretty big one, right over his heart, but no blood.

He pulled his other arm from underneath him and with both hands pushed himself to a sitting position. His left arm hollered in pain but didn't feel broken. Maybe his shoulder had popped out of its socket when he landed.

Teddy lifted his jacket lapel and saw that the bullet had also made a hole in his shirt. He undid a couple buttons to find a massive purple and blue bruise had formed on his chest. But, miraculously, there was no hole in his skin. Then he felt the pull of something stuck in the fabric of his shirt pocket.

He wiggled it a bit to free it and produced his antique business card holder. The bullet had struck the front side and might have gone right through it and into his chest had it not been for the stack of twenty or so extra thick premium cards inside (one of his rare splurges). Traveling at a thousand feet per second, the slug made it through the front, all the way through the cards, and left a deep dent on the back side of the case, which caused the still-expanding hematoma on his chest.

That damn conversation starter saved my life.

He looked up to see two brown-skinned boys under the streetlamp's dome of light, about five or six years old, staring at him from the sidewalk. One of them was holding a soccer ball. The other was standing a little closer, squinting to get a better look at the old man sitting on the ground.

He dug out his cell phone from the bottom of his jacket pocket and dialed Win.

Teddy swallowed with difficulty, cleared his throat. The rings ended with Win's outgoing message. "Win," Teddy said, "don't go to meet 'em. This thing's gone bad. I'm bringin' in the cavalry. Call me back if you can."

He hung up and looked at the boys. "Go find your mother," he said. "I'm calling the police."

Then he dialed a number he had long ago committed to memory.

68

WRIGHTWOOD

"Guess this was my lucky day," said Teddy as he wrapped up his tale.

"But . . ." Winston indicated the cops. "All this. How?" His confused gaze shifted between Teddy and Grover.

"It's not exactly hard to track a cell phone these days, Winston," Teddy said.

Of course it wasn't. In fact, Win had made a movie a few years back, a cop story. He'd had a scene where his character discussed the best way to track someone by their cell phone. One was by cell tower pings and zeroing in on the location closest to one of three towers. But the more accurate method was by using the cell's GPS in conjunction with the number and the carrier. If someone with the right equipment had that information, they could get as close as a few feet.

Teddy shrugged. "Like I said, I still have a few friends in law enforcement. Once they got a bead on ya, they were on the move, but they only had you for a minute or two when your phone went dark." He looked to Grover. "Good thing we traded numbers."

Win looked from Teddy to Grover. His next question didn't have to be asked.

"Okay," Grover admitted, "I hid down the road from your place and followed you here. Teddy called me and I confirmed where you were. I only came in because it looked like you were about to get shot."

Win recalled the distant headlights in his rearview when he drove into town. "I can't believe I didn't see you."

"The way you were driving, I don't think you'da noticed me if I was sitting in the back seat."

Win shook his head in amazement. His circle of friends might be small, but they were mighty.

An unmarked sedan arrived and snaked its way inside the thick boundary of patrol cars.

A middle-aged, plainclothes detective got out of the car and addressed a uniformed officer, who pointed in Winston's direction. The detective nodded, then walked over.

"Mr. Greene? I need to speak to you for a moment."

"Okay," Win said.

A group of onlookers had gathered on the perimeter of the police cruisers, so the detective guided Win away from Grover and Teddy and toward the clubhouse.

The detective informed him that though his daughter was alive, she had suffered a terrible accident, apparently while escaping her kidnappers. The responding ambulance had transported her to the nearest hospital, Providence Holy Cross Medical Center in Mission Hills. She was still in surgery, but the doctors had managed to stabilize her. He said the word they used was "miraculous."

Win listened stoically, then stepped a few paces away. Clare. Amy. Teddy. Grover. All of them could have been killed today. But now . . . they were safe. Winston Greene dropped to his knees on the gravel lot and sobbed.

69

WITH A LIFT from the sheriffs, Teddy headed home for a much-needed rendezvous with his bed and some painkillers. Grover drove Winston and Amy, in the Mustang, straight to the hospital in Mission Hills. They'd already learned that Clare had been moved to the ICU and, with several internal injuries and broken bones, was heavily medicated. Win doubted she would even be aware they'd arrived, but he had to see for himself that she was alive. Not knowing how badly beat up Clare might look, he felt the best thing for Amy at this point was to have her wait in the lobby with Grover.

When he stepped into Clare's room, he had to stop himself from gasping when he saw the bandages nearly covered her entire head. The only openings were thin slits for her eyes to see through and for the breathing and feeding tubes in her mouth and nose. An IV drip was connected to her right arm, and the only sound in the room was the hum emanating from a bank of monitors that kept close watch on all her physical readings. Both her left arm and leg were elevated and in full casts.

He silently brought a chair over, sat, and very carefully slipped his hand into hers. He squeezed it softly, not expecting any response. He just wanted to feel her. To his surprise, her somnolent eyes opened and met his, and she managed just the slightest squeeze in return. He knew that was all she could muster before her eyelids dropped closed again and she fell back into a deep sleep. He decided that was enough for one day, and after a short conference with her surgeon, Win and Grover headed for Venice.

Win sat with Amy in the back seat, where she slept with his arm around her the entire way.

EPILOGUE

"No story ever really ends; you just . . . pick up
where you left off."

—Winston Greene in *Escape from Manzanar* (2020)

70

WRIGHTWOOD

A FULL WEEK WITH the Washingtons had come and gone, Win and Amy camping with them at Lauren's sister's place for a couple of days before heading back to their Venice house. He'd insisted on helping Grover and the workmen repair the French doors, but once that was done Win felt more and more like they'd reached the limits of their welcome. Of course, Lauren protested that they could stay for as long as they liked, but Win decided it was time they left the safety of the Washington home.

They loaded the few things they'd brought with them into the Mustang before hugging their friends goodbye in the driveway, an echo of their hellos from the previous Wednesday. Then Win revved the car's powerful engine to give the Washington kids a thrill, and carefully backed out of the driveway and headed north.

Win decided he wanted to listen to the muscular churn of the Mustang's engine on the drive home, and that was fine with Amy. She wanted to listen to her earbuds, and whenever Win would sneak a look at her in the rearview mirror, swaddled in her booster chair in the back seat, she was lost in whatever she was watching on her iPad.

Win had been finding it difficult to focus all week. *Of course, you are,* everyone told him. *After what you went though, what do you expect?* His thoughts would ricochet from horror to despair, from relief to regret. He wondered about the late Alberto Velez, what kind of a man he had been before the kidnappers had snatched and killed him, and decided he must have been pretty decent if he'd refused to take part in his relative's criminal schemes. Still, he was relieved when he heard from the Sheriff's Office that they had towed Alberto's stolen car to an impound lot until his family was permitted to retrieve it.

He often thought about the night he'd faced the kidnapper, and how he still couldn't recall how he'd managed to tackle the man. Grover told him that from inside his SUV, and with so much dust still hanging in the air, he couldn't be sure either, but he swore he thought he saw Win practically leap right over the Mustang's door. *Oh well, it may come back to me someday.* His heart swelled with gratitude to have a friend like Grover. Like Teddy.

Explaining the truth to Amy, of what had happened to her parents, to Zeke, was something he just couldn't articulate yet. She'd been asking questions over the last few days, and all he could come up with for now was that her daddy had gone to stay with the grandma she never knew, and that her mom would join them in Wrightwood once she was feeling better. He suspected she was aware of a lot more than she was saying, but he wasn't about to probe that. In time, all her questions would have answers.

Now that Clare was conscious, they had gone by for another short visit, but first Win stopped in Santa Monica, at St. Monica Catholic Church. Built in 1925, the baroque edifice was the spiritual home to one of the largest parishes in Los Angeles. Amy had never been inside a church, and it had been a number of years for Win as well—too many for him to recall.

As they climbed the steps to the large double front doors, Amy's hand in his, she looked up at him and asked, "What's this place, Grandpa?"

"We're going to light a candle for your daddy."

"Why?"

"To help him find his way to your grandma, honey. Then we'll go see Mommy."

Once they were home and Amy was settled at the dinette, Win arranged two place settings at the table. He found an unopened package of turkey bacon in the freezer and filled a bowl with hot water and dropped the package in to defrost it. Then he combined flour, milk, and eggs, with a dash of sugar, in a mixing bowl, to make pancake batter. It was dinnertime, but he figured, why not? A little breakfast for dinner never hurt anybody.

Amy was still watching videos, so he turned on the old-school transistor radio he kept tucked against the counter backsplash. He always expected to hear static now that everyone streamed everything and was happily amazed when it worked just as it always had. He kept it tuned to KPCC, the public radio station in Pasadena. Somehow the signal bounced through the canyons and hills into his kitchen. It was just past the top of the hour and a silken-voiced reporter was delivering the headlines.

"In local news," she said, "Winston Greene is rumored to be replacing Kevin Costner in the new *Superman* reboot. Greene, who has yet to speak publicly about—"

Win shut it off, turned to see if Amy had heard, and was relieved to see her earbuds were still in place. The police had yet to return his six-shooter, but amazingly, the press had mostly decided to give them some space; even *Look, Don't Touch* was nowhere to be seen. In the aftermath of the showdown with the kidnapper, Win had learned an *LDT* reporter named Branovich had been found murdered, alongside Zeke, in Clare and Zeke's home. That ended any thought of picking up more toys or clothing for Amy, since the house would be cordoned off as a crime scene for the foreseeable future.

His thoughts wandered yet again: What made people do the things they do? Why do some of us turn out good, some not so good, and some just plain bad? He had portrayed versions of almost every imaginable type of human being throughout his long career, conjuring a history for each character to justify and motivate every given action, identified aspects of his own character that he had in common with those he played. But when it came to actual criminals, and the terrible things that they do, he was completely mystified.

He cut open the turkey bacon. He knew Amy wouldn't touch it, so he only spread out a few strips for himself in a pan.

He thought of their visit to Clare just a couple of hours earlier. He knew the hospital would calibrate her dosage accordingly during her recovery, but he worried how she'd handle coming off the painkillers once she left there. *Jesus, it's always something.*

He thought of Joanie, how she had been his rudder, and how he'd foundered after she died. But as he watched Amy, smiling now at something in her videos, he knew he had a second chance at something, and he intended to make the most of it.

He made a mental note to drop by and thank Theresa Carpenter for the food basket she'd left on his porch. She'd included a nice card expressing her regret for being so pushy the night she'd spotted him outside her restaurant. He figured the embarrassment he felt about how he'd snapped at her that fateful night was nothing compared to the relief she would feel upon his apology.

The first thing he had to do, of course, was get someone out here to look at the foundation and get an estimate on the work of reseating the house. If he and Amy were going to live in it until she went to college, he should probably do what he could to keep it from sliding down the mountain.

And speaking of work, from now on, there would be some new considerations. Was the location shoot out of town or even overseas? He'd only be able to do it if Amy could come along and wouldn't miss any school. Maybe he should think about doing TV. Series work could be steady and stick to one locale. But what if the show was too violent for her to watch until she was older? Then he'd probably give it a pass.

As he whisked the ingredients smooth, something caught his eye, and he turned to look at Amy, still sitting by the window. He did a double take.

The low spring sun had filled the kitchen with radiant light. The mountain air had no filter of city grime to fight through, and it cast his granddaughter in a rich amber glow, a regular reminder of just how beautiful it could be up here. Clare was sitting in the nook next to Amy.

They were both enjoying whatever was on Amy's tablet while they waited for Win to make dinner. Mother and daughter, together again, a vision of how life could soon be. It felt so optimistic, so *tangible*, it was like he could reach out and touch—

"Grandpa?" He heard Amy's voice echo from somewhere, like she was speaking to him from inside a tunnel. *But she's right there . . .*

"Grandpa?" He jerked back to reality. "Are you okay?"

He was staring at her, and his eyes had filled with tears. *Oh, that's all she needs: "Then Grandpa went batshit."* An ache had risen in his chest. But not from the usual sadness or loss he had come to know so well. Instead, it felt like it had in those early days—when he was cold and alone in the dark, with no idea what would come next. And then it hit him.

For the first time in a long time his old friend, hope, had come to visit. And like a good friend, it would be there whenever he needed it. For his daughter, for himself. For his family.

He blinked to clear his vision. "Yes, honey. I'm fine." He shook his head and turned to the stove. Through a grin he said, "They don't call it magic hour for nuthin'."

"What?" said Amy, her earbuds still in place.

Win cleared his throat. "I said . . . you want syrup or jam on your pancakes?"

She shrugged. "Jam." And went back to her screen.

"Jam it is," he said, and began ladling batter onto the hot griddle.

ACKNOWLEDGMENTS

As a debut novelist, I can freely admit that not that long ago I knew next to nothing about publishing. So, to be here today, to be writing these words, I can tell you I had help. A lot of it. It's still a criminal understatement to say I could not have done this without the aid of too many people to list here. But there have been contributions by certain friends and family that have been so immeasurably invaluable that they require specific mention.

First, the extraordinary people at Crooked Lane Books. Jess Verdi and her team, Rebecca Nelson, Madeline Rathle, Stephanie Manova, and Dulce Botello, treated me from day one as if I were the world's bestselling author. I am in awe of your kindness, flexibility, and support of my creative journey. To have CLB as my publisher is a dream come true. I am also blessed with perhaps the best literary agent in the business, the wonderful, resourceful Liza Fleissig, whom I immediately liked (and somehow trusted) from the moment I met her. But I can't overlook Ginger Harris-Dontzin and the entire Liza Royce Agency for inviting me into your exceptional family. It is indeed very warm and cozy in your house, and yes, I am that guy who won't leave your holiday party. Thanks to Nathaniel Marunas, the man who helped me edit this book to the point where it was not only readable, but submissible. Your great knowledge, expertise and gentle guidance is gold to any author. To my LA managers, Gordon Gilbertson and Michael Borden of Gilbertson Entertainment: you always have my back and manage to keep the trolls on the other side of the moat while answering my every crazy request or idea with "Sounds great! Send it over!" My talent agents at BRS/Gage and KMR Talent, who graciously accept my need to take time to write, not only represent to me the pinnacle of professionalism, but I also count them as friends. I am blessed to have them in my life.

Thanks to those early readers who suffered through embarrassingly overwritten drafts, but never made me feel inept: Paula and James O'Byrne, the original readers, who helped trim off that baby fat and then urged me to keep going. My gratitude also goes to Castle Freeman Jr., who, in my mind, is among our best American novelists, for your friendship, honest critique, and encouragement; to Davyne Verstandig, a lifelong educator who somehow instilled in me a career's worth of advice in a single Zoom call; to Dan Musselman, who invited me into the world of audiobook narration, which then led me to begin writing this book; to Paul Agwu, who provided some true inspiration here (I'll let the readers guess what), and for being the best godson I could hope for; and to my family of friends who generously gave their time and thoughts to those early drafts: Doane Perry, Tom Schanley, Michael Easton, and Lynn Marie Latham (who also reminded me that every chapter could use a cliff-hanger).

Thanks as well to these great and generous authors, whose gifts go far beyond their superlative writing skills and who have made my road so much easier: Alex Finlay, without your input, advice, and friendship, I never would have even found the road, let alone be on it. I owe you more than I could ever repay, but would a beer do in the meantime? Thanks to that irrepressible, unstoppable cheerleader, Yasmin Angoe. And Samantha Bailey, a class act and a selfless giver. If you haven't read these people's books, you should. And I have to give props to Kimberly Howe and the International Thriller Writers (ITW), without whom so many of us would be aimless and unsuccessful. And let's not forget those who kept me honest, and technically correct, like master stuntman Manny Perry, my friend Vivian Gundaker, and Dr. Rico Simonini. As I mentioned above, there are many more who will have to be left off this list, but I hope you know who you are. I am deeply and forever grateful to you all.

And, of course, Cady McClain (aka, the Dynamo Genius), whose endless patience, love, and support helped me keep going when I often felt I couldn't. You are a living reminder to us all to keep our standards high.

Lastly, to "Hollywood," for giving me a career . . . and a truck-load of memories.